I0550529

WHISPERING

In 1921 America's victory celebration is in full swing. The Flapper
Era has begun. Cleo Snow is poised between her Victorian raising
and post-war liberal ideas. Women got the vote in 1920. They
work – Cleo's a nurse. Hemlines are rising. Jargon is spicier.
Songs are racier. The fox trot is the cat's meow. Everyone smokes
coffin nails. The great experiment, Prohibition, has ushered in an
era of fascinating gangsters and illegal speakeasies. Drinking and
dancing go together like bathtub gin and painted dolls.

On Sago Island Cleo meets fly-boy hero Graham Henry, the
dazzling son of a steel magnate. They fall in love dancing to
"Whispering", the rage song of the year. Complicating their love-
at-first-sight is Shafer and Josie Drake. Shafer is Graham's cousin.
He lost his liquor business and is about to lose his money-loving
wife, Josie.

The morning after the dance, Josie is missing. A note she
purportedly wrote says she's leaving the island to get a divorce
and marry Graham. Graham swears the note's a lie and that he
and Josie were nothing more than friends.

Where did Josie go and when? Did she return to New York where
she danced in the Ziegfeld Follies? No one saw her leave the
island. But Cleo knows Graham had nothing to do with her
disappearance because Cleo was with him in the lighthouse the
night Josie vanished. Cleo vows she will never confess to making
love with a man she's known only two days. But Will Graham
compromise Cleo to clear himself?

Island resident, the enigmatic Doc Holliday, who claims to be
related to the infamous gunslinger, is a veterinarian and a
falconer. His falcon, Billy, captures Cleo's severely crushed heart.
Cleo captures Doc's heart, but she's reeling over her gullibility and
her body's occasional betrayal of her resolve. Will he win her with
his darkly sensuous charm?

Everyone on Sago, it seems, has something to hide, even villagers
who distill homemade hooch - and it all pivots around Josie and
Graham. With her spirit firmed by deceit, Cleo vows to uncover
the truth and keep her own secret.

Also by GERRIE FERRIS FINGER

The Ghost Ship

The End Game

The Last Temptation (2012)

Look Away From Evil

As GERRIE FERRIS

When Serpents Die

Honored Daughters

Wagon Dogs

NON-FICTION (as editor)

The Last Bus to Albuquerque

Southern by the Grace of God

WHISPERING

Copyright © 2011 by Gerrie Ferris Finger

www.GerrieFerrisFinger.com
gfinger@mindspring.com
Published in the United States of America
Crystal Skull Publishing
Atlanta, GA.
All rights reserved

No portion of this book may be reproduced or transmitted in any form
or by any electronic or mechanical means, including photocopying,
recording or by any information retrieval and storage system without
permission of the publisher. Ebooks are not transferrable, either in
whole or in part. As the purchaser or otherwise lawful recipient of this
ebook, you have the right to enjoy the novel on your own computer or
other device. Further distribution, copying, sharing, gifting or
uploading is illegal and violates United States Copyright laws.
Pirating of ebooks is illegal. Criminal Copyright Infringement,
including infringement without monetary gain, may be investigated
by the Federal Bureau of Investigation and is punishable by up to five
years in federal prison and a fine of up to $250,000.

This book is a work of fiction and any names, characters, places and
incidents are products of the author's imagination and are not to be
construed as real.

Cover Photographer: Victoria "Tori" Ferris
Crystal Skull Publishing © 2011

GERRIE FERRIS FINGER

WHISPERING

Crystal Skull Publishing

Atlanta, GA

This book is dedicated to my late mother, Genevieve, a romantic and flapper extraordinaire in the 1920s. She wasn't much for singing, but she loved it when I played songs like *Whispering* on the piano.

CHAPTER ONE

SAGO ISLAND, GA.
1921

The unpaved road was dreadful enough, but it was the colossal trees casting sinister shadows that portended an ill-omened holiday. Cleo thought. Twisted low branches almost as big around as she extended nearly to the ground. High branches arched over the road with their flickering leaves blocking the sun. Curious gray strands hung from them like unkempt beards. She glanced at her cousin. "Are these the trees you bragged about?"

"I am rather keen on them," Neill said, his red hair fanning his forehead.

Neill's rakish roadster had a fabric top that lay folded over the boot. When he'd driven off the steamboat ferry, he tossed his straw skimmer at Cleo. "Free as the breeze," he'd said. Riding in the breeze now, her fingers went to the brim of her cloche. The fitted hat secured her black hair very well, thank you.

Neill glanced at her. "High time you saw more than Philly streets and mown grass."

"To say nothing of seeing an armadillo at the dock." She wrinkled her nose at him and looked up at the ancient trees, at how their tops embraced to form a canopy over the road, and how they bobbed and swayed to the rhythm of the wind. "They're like giant bearded ogres whispering secrets to each other. About me."

"Whispering about you? That's good, Bearcat. Why are they whispering about you?"

"They wonder why I'm here."

"Tsk. You're here to have a jolly good time." He looked ready for a jolly good time, the way he drove with his right arm resting on the polished wooden rail of his English car, his fingers tapping to a beat only he heard. She wished she could feel so at ease and wriggled her back into the curve of the leather bench. He said, "Here's one for your noodle. Those ogres are live oak trees that have been warped by the sea and the wind."

"Live oaks as opposed to dead oaks?"

"Live oaks, cousin, are called that because they're oak trees that don't drop their leaves in winter like our Pennsylvania oaks do."

"Is it ever winter here?"

"Nope."

Sun rays lit a pocket of shadows, revealing a gathering of animals in a narrow meadow. She laughed. "Neill, look at the oodles of tiny horses over there."

"They're wild."

"You sure have the lowdown on this place," she said, intrigued by the small, stumpy horses with their tails swishing across their rumps. "How many times did you say you've been here?"

"A few times before the war when Graham and I were in college. Several, since we got back from Limeyland."

In early 1919, Neill came home from England, the same year she'd been shattered by the news that William was missing in action and likely buried in some French village. Six months ago, the Red Cross located him and brought him home. She drew in a deep breath and told herself to stop remembering. *You're here to forget.*

Neill was saying, "Sorry you couldn't come to Pittsburgh for the bash the Henrys blew for Graham, the Hun killer."

"I wasn't in a bashing mood," she said, then regretted chastising him. He'd never been engaged, nor, as far as she knew, had a steady girl, so how could he comprehend hideous pain of losing someone so beloved?

"You'll have a grand time," Neill said. "Graham is a good fellow. His family are not high hats."

"You've said." It was virtually all Neill talked about on the two-day trip – in the car, at breakfast, at dinner, before they retired to their hotel suites. She was on the very verge of reminding him that he'd made the sale on his fifth long distance call to her in Philadelphia. She was here, riding over a sandy lane, under grotesque trees, on an exotic island, to have a grand time with strangers, with her nerves quivering like an over-strung violin. Crossing her legs, which were hot in the silk stockings, she fussed with her dress so the hem hung straight across her right calf. Tasting the salty drops of perspiration on her upper lip, she patted her mouth with a handkerchief. "I feel like I'm in a Finnish sauna."

Neill reached over and placed a gentle hand on her knee. "It'll be copacetic, you'll see."

She looked straight ahead, out the wind screen. The Silver Ghost had cleared the live oak canopy, and, oh, it took all her composure to keep her mouth from falling open at seeing the massive building coming into view. Buckingham Palace couldn't have been grander. She turned to Neill. "You said a *place* by the sea, not a castle."

Neill laughed. "Nice joint, eh?"

She pointed a finger ahead. "One, two, three, four stories high."

"And a bell tower on top of the heap."

"Can I be the princess in this drama?"

"Southerness is only one of the Henry family sheds."

She laughed. "Sheds?"

"Graham's words."

"Is Graham always so understated?"

"Graham is Graham, you'll see."

Reaching to lay a hand on her cousin's arm, she squeezed through the sleeve of his hand-tailored suit. "I'm so glad you made it home safe and sound."

"Why Graham and I made it and not others, like William, is a baffle."

"Mother would say it's God's will. I don't believe in a God that would take someone as kind as William." She'd blasphemed the Lord, but William had been young and ambitious and her mother approved of him. "But I'll have you know, my dear cousin, I've thanked Him many times for saving you."

"And Graham, my best buddy. You said you prayed for him in your letters to me."

"I did pray for him since he means so much to you."

Graham Henry. She was finally to meet the fabled one. Neill had gone to school with and served in the Great War with the son of a Pittsburgh steel tycoon. That tycoon's palace glistened ahead, brash and bright in the sunshine – just what a flamboyant big cheese would build. "What's the shed made with?" she asked.

"Tabby, with marble and stone trim."

"What's tabby when it's at home?"

"Concrete made of seashells, lime and sand. Took a few simoleons to pile it up."

"Hmmm. Ostentatious wouldn't you say?"

"Having second thoughts?"

"Third and fourth, too."

Neill had made it sound so romantic – a cottage by the sea. Rest, relaxation after the hospital slog. Would the wounded from the war ever stop coming through the portals of City Hospital? Or the cases of influenza? Or polio?

Waving an arm over the panorama of palace, blue sea and tittering palm trees, Neill said, "Look around you, exotica everywhere you peep."

"Now I know I don't have the right clothes."

"Graham is a very informal sort of guy."

"What about his mother, sister and brother?"

"His mother's a corker; his sister is fourteen and his brother is eleven."

"Oh, swell. I have so much in common with corkers and children."

More than a couple of times Neill had nattered on about the late Edgar Henry's family. Graham's grandfather immigrated to Pittsburgh from Scotland and founded Henry Steel Works. The Henrys were those nouveau riche that her mother said were turning Palm Beach into a Coney Island. Cleo thought of her snooty mother, a mainline Philadelphian, who, before the war, had sunk into genteel poverty to the point she was forced to discreetly sew for some of those disdained nouveau riche.

The Rolls had cleared the giant oaks. Ahead, where a road intersected, going north and south, a man riding a black horse emerged from a forest of pine trees. The horse danced to a stop. "Someone has come to welcome us," she said.

Neill slowed and thrust his face forward to look around her. "Not Graham. The vet."

"Vet?"

"Veterinarian – nurse and doctor to animals."

"I knew that."

It appeared for a moment like the horse and rider had turned to stone. The man was hatless and his hair was black and full, a perfect match with his horse. A curious expression charmed the man's face, although it wasn't classically handsome. His beige Bedford cord breeches, brown field boots and brown hacking jacket looked comfortably worn. "What a beauty he is," she said.

"The vet or the horse?" Neill asked, pressing the gas to cross the intersecting road. A crude wooden sign called it Oystercatcher Trail.

"Both," she said, lifting a hand to wave. He nodded and tugged the horse's reins. She looked over her shoulder to see him disappear into the short pointed plants and tall skinny pines.

"Neill, what are those spiky plants called?"

"Palmettos."

"Little palms," she murmured, letting the man's crooked face linger in her mind. With his simple nod, he'd made her feel easier, and she found herself bouncing to the jaunty rhythm of the Rolls on the uneven road. As Neill would say, using his familiar slang, everything was going to be jake.

*****

Neill piloted the car through the pillars and gates of Southerness, around a floral circle where the stars and stripes flew on a pole in the circle's center. A second flag with stripes and an emblem waved beneath it. "Georgia's flag," Neill said, braking alongside a row of manicured shrubs bearing white fragrant blossoms.

"What heavenly flowers," she said, laying her head back and breathing in their perfume.

"Gardenias," Neill said. "We can't grow them in Pittsburgh or Philly. Too far north."

She stepped out of the silver automobile, feeling the crunch of shell and sand beneath her shoes. Bending, she lifted a small seashell and held it for Neill to see, "I'm calling this good luck."

"Still nervous?"

"It's been eons since I've been around the rich and famous, except for you. You won't find any swells in City Hospital."

"You really should take your place in the Daughters of the American Revolution," Neill said. "Get back to your roots."

"I don't speak the Daughters' language any longer." Her female ancestors had been proud members of DAR because a male ancestor was one of the first settlers of William Penn's city. He established a shipyard, became rich and went into politics. Several generations later, the business foundered and the fortune dwindled, but the name of Jernigan was still on the social register.

"Too modest," Neill said, shaking his had.

"Easy for you to say, rich boy."

She heard a noise and turned toward the mansion. Shading her eyes at the brim of her cloche, she thought there must be at least twenty steps ascending to the massive double doors. One opened and a man dashed out.

Her cousin rushed up the steps, calling "Grammy, old sport."
"Neill," the man cried, skipping down the steps.

Half way up, Neill met Graham on a wide landing. The two clutched at each other, jerking each other's shoulders. She watched, fascinated by their exhilaration and the difference between them. While Neill had bright red hair, sunburned skin and freckles, Graham was blond and richly tanned. To her, they were the epitome of sophisticated young men – Neill in his gray sacque suit, peach shirt, gray-and-peach silk tie that was pinned neatly in the middle of a peach stripe. His black and white shoes with fringed tongues must have cost him a hundred dollars, even at cost at Connolly's Department Store. Graham wore tan knickerbockers, a pale blue shirt and requisite silk tie. His brown oxfords were impeccable. Neill had turned twenty-four in August, and since he had gone through prep school and Yale with Graham, they were the same age, a year older than she.

Neill looked over his shoulder at her and pulled Graham down the steps. He shouted loud enough for her to hear, "Come, meet Cousin Cleo."

Neill and Graham came down, side-by-side, with a grace so easy they appeared to float, their toes lightly tapping the stone. When they'd reached the last step, and when she looked into Graham Henry's sapphire blue eyes, a flash burst through her chest like heat lightning, taking her breath. All of a sudden, her dress seemed sizes too small.

Neill's arm circled her waist. "Graham, my cousin, Cleo Jernigan Snow."

Graham bowed as if he'd just met Princess Elizabeth. "My pleasure, Miss Cleo Jernigan Snow."

Neill completed the introduction. "Bearcat, this is Graham Henry."

She wished the butterflies in her tummy would fold their wings, but she managed a smile. "I think I've heard your name a couple of times."

"Your humble servant," he said with a bow. He, like Neill, mimicked English mannerisms. He reached up and ran his fingers through his hair, and said, "Now the formalities are over, shall we go wash the dust down with some giggle water?"

Neill looked back, toward his car. "My Roller?"

"Fredik will see to it." He clamped his hand on Neill's arm. "That's quite a breezer you're driving."

Neill looked at Cleo. "Nothing but the best to carry this bearcat through the mountains and over the seas."

Pride filled her, and she smiled at her cousin.

"I'd desperately love a 40/50 like that," Graham said, "but Teddy won't have a foreign car. Fords for us." He waved his hand in silent invitation to climb the steps. "Have a good ride on our airy ferry?"

"No beef here," Neill said.

"You, Miss Snow?" he said, falling in step with her.

She raised her face to his. "A little choppy maybe." Gee whiz, she'd sounded so breathy.

"The Sound gets that way this time of year." His baritone voice was like mellow music. "I say, Miss Snow ..." He paused.

His smile warmed her cheeks. "Call me Cleo."

"Short for Cleopatra?" he asked.

Neill groaned.

Graham slapped his forehead. "Guess you get asked that every time you meet a numbskull like me?"

"Every time," she said.

His embarrassment rode well on his face. "Well, I'm absolutely head-overs to meet you."

She bobbed her head. She didn't trust her vocal chords, thinking no one had ever taken her breath away like this. Not even William. Her mind spooled back to William's way of wooing, which was turning up wherever she went until she noticed him. Falling in love had been slow and rather sweet. When he was gone forever, she knew she'd never love anyone again.

Graham placed his fingers at the back of her elbow. She smiled up at him. If she stood on tiptoes, her forehead could touch his strong chin and first-rate mouth. His eyes fixed on her, like he was studying the colors of her face. Her thoughts tumbled over themselves. Was her skin white enough, her lips red enough, her rouge deep enough?

He grinned, tightening his fingers in comfortable intimacy.

The butler, an imposing colored man with gray hair, stood in the open door. "Mitty," Graham said, "have Fredik see to Mister Connolly's automobile."

"It is being effected," Mitty, said.

Effected. She glanced at her cousin and both grinned, not that she and Neill didn't reel off some pretty fancy words and phrases themselves. Before the war, they had taken to the new crossword puzzle game published on the Fun Page of *The New York World.*

Graham urged her through the door of the grand house. Lord, the Taj Mahal couldn't have been more splendid. She'd grown up in a handsome house in Philly, but it wasn't palatial to begin with, and the expense of keeping it up was too much for her father after he'd sickened with consumption. When the war came, her mother got a job at City Hospital, first sewing gowns, and then nursing wounded soldiers. All the while, the house faded with the passing years.

In the time it took to think this, she'd gone dry-mouthed. It had something to do with the man standing so close his hip brushed hers. Pressing her lips, she met Graham's gaze. His eyelids flickered merrily. "Shall we meet the chatelaine then?"

"Um-hum."

He guided her through the rotunda, his fingers light as fairies dancing on her skin. Her feet skimmed across black and white marble tiles and around white columns rising to the gold ceiling. Between twin marble staircases, a fountain had been constructed. In the center of the pool, a statue … Goodness, was that Eros relieving himself? From behind, she heard Neill's devilish chuckle.

Graham opened the door into an incredibly blue drawing room – blue velvet sofas and paisley chaises, blue patterned rugs, blue silk lamp shades, draperies. Even Chinese lacquered tables sported bowls of periwinkle and hyacinth. "I prefer the morning room," Graham said, "but Teddy insists we use one of the drawing rooms in the afternoon."

"*One* of the drawing rooms?" she said.

"Our cottage by the sea has wings," he said, his lips curving into an ironic twist. "Withdrawing rooms in every one."

"How many rooms in this …?" Should she call it a castle or a mansion?

He filled in the word. "Abomination? Beats the band for Victorian grandeur, eh?"

She remembered something Neill had said about Graham. "I hear you sing to beat the band."

He laughed. "Neill lies, Neill dies. Anyway, the fools' paradise has four wings, but we use one at a time to save on generators. No electricity on the island so we must make our own.

Each spring Teddy switches wings. This year it's the Blue Wing, so if you should get lost, check the upholstery and draperies. Excessive blue means you're right at home."

Cleo heard a new sound and turned her head. A tall woman came toward them, saying, "I think we'll keep the Blue for next year, too. The sun in the morning glows over the sea."

What darkly tanned skin she had, Cleo thought. And what brilliant blue eyes. She walked stick straight and wore her dark, graying hair in a bun that couldn't contain the mass of curls. She had on a flowered cotton frock with a solid blue jacket that belted at the waist. Her shoes were sensible T-strapped brogues. The whole unpretentious ensemble cost half the earth.

"Teddy," Graham said and went to kiss her cheek.

Teddy, apparently Graham's mother, glanced at her and at her cousin. Teddy stretched her arms. "Neill, how wonderful." Neill walked into them. How introverted Neill looked, but Teddy hugged tight, giving his back a hearty slap. He stepped back and Teddy grabbed his hands. "Always happy to see the boy who had my son's back against those despicable Huns." She dropped Neill's hands and looked at Cleo. "And you must be …"

Graham blurted, "Cleo. No patra." He crossed his elegant arms. "And … ah … Jernigan and Snow."

Teddy asked, "Is Jernigan your mother's name?"

"Yes, ma'am."

"The Philadelphia Jernigans?"

"Yes, ma'am." Obviously, Neill had related her biography.

"I like a woman who uses her maternal name."

Graham clapped his mother's shoulder. "Teddy here's thinking of joining the suffragettes."

Teddy waved away the idea. "I'm too old to go on a hunger strike, and I don't like to smoke that much."

"Not more than half a deck in a day," Graham said. "To say nothing of the little torpedos." He looked at Cleo. "Cigars. And once Mother Dear wore father's bags to work in the garden, totally upsetting the villagers."

Teddy held out her hand to Cleo. Her grip was firm and smooth. "Theodora to strangers, Teddy to family and friends. First name basis here. We're not in Pittsburgh, thankfully."

"When you are returning?" Graham asked his mother.

"I sail in two weeks."

"I better get a crew together."

"The waters will be calm. Fredik, you and another strong back should do."

Graham turned to Cleo. "We travel down here by *Monongahela*, Teddy's two gaffer. Neill's been on her."

"Lovely ship," Neill said.

Graham said, "We'll do some sailing while you're here. Great time of year."

Teddy said, "For sailing, it's always a great time of year."

Graham laid his hand on Cleo's shoulder, and she understood what ecstatic meant. "Teddy crews," he said. "She races ol' Hela on The Point and swears like a sailor." He looked at Teddy. "Which makes me wonder, why are you returning to Pittsburgh so early? You usually wait until the dragon flies are biting."

"The bridal season is upon us," Teddy said. She regarded her son with a narrow gaze. "Lila's getting married in case you forgot."

Graham sucked though his teeth. "I did forget."

"Go find Mitty," Teddy said. "We need a drink to celebrate our guests."

As if on cue, the mandatory stately butler entered, pushing a cart over the marble threshold onto a blue and gold oriental rug.

"Ah, the giggle juice arrives," Graham said.

"Mitty will serve old-fashioneds and champagne," Teddy said, pushing back an unruly strand that escaped her bun. Her handsomeness bewitched Cleo, and, seeing her son, standing next to her – they could have modeled for Renoir. Thank God the Great War hadn't claimed such handsome skin and bone. But in the next instant, she felt shame – my poor William. Oh, it was all so beastly, a mistake coming here, around these extraordinarily beautiful people. She didn't deny she was pretty, but her set in Philadelphia didn't entertain in ritzy drawing rooms wearing casual clothes that made up their combined dress budgets for the entire year. No matter, she told herself, she was proud of her accomplishments. Her mother had scraped enough money for her to enroll in The Women's College, and, after graduation, she took up nursing in the same hospital. When the war ended, she and her mother had the house debt-free and a small savings banked for her trousseau. That money was now invested in the stock market, safer than in a bank, everyone said.

Graham seemed to sense she had interior thoughts and waited for her to break with them before he touched her back, urging her toward a velvet sofa. Its upholstery matched the color of the delphiniums on the tea table. While she arranged her dress folds, he slid down beside her and held up his glass. "To Cleo, the bearcat. Where'd you get the moniker?"

She leaned her head toward Neill. "He used to call me Cat's Meow. In case you haven't noticed, Neill makes use of every new word or phrase his crowd invents. This month it's Bearcat." Her glass met Graham's, and his smile broadened. "To Graham," she said, and, feeling awkward, turned toward Teddy, standing at the fireplace, sipping champagne, listening to Neill as if his words were the most charming she'd ever heard.

Cleo spoke loud enough to interrupt him. "And here's to Mrs. Henry, our hostess."

Teddy looked over, smiled and waved a hand. "Teddy, please. We're informal. I don't play hostess on the island." She came across the room. "You young things are on your own to roam the place. If what you want isn't in plain sight, check in the cupboards or closets. Don't be bashful, and you can always ask Mitty. He runs the place. Or Fredik, who, as we joke, is our footman, but don't say that to his ugly face."

"Which means," said Graham, "he takes care of the cars. If we want to drive one, we don't have to check them out or anything like that – although he wishes we had to. Woe unto anyone who returns one dirty or smashed. Except, of course, Teddy."

"Fredik is an interesting name," Cleo said.

"Fredik is from Romania of Hungarian extraction," Graham said. "Greek Orthodox, he says, but I think he's a plain old gypsy. He's imposing, that's for sure. If you ran across him in the dark, you'd scream bloody murder."

"I'll watch out for him and armadillos."

"Ah ha, you've spied our armor-plated rats."

"Ugly creatures," she said with an exaggerated shiver.

"Like Fredik."

Teddy said, "Stop picking on Fredik. He's a godsend for lifting cars with his bare hands and hoisting main sails." She looked at Cleo. "Now as to our routine, I may sometimes only see you at dinner. I adhere to a strict schedule of swimming, riding, squash and gardening, but not necessarily in that order. Do you play golf?"

Working in the hospital didn't allow much leisure time, especially for a sport such as golf. "I don't, no."

"Graham, take Cleo to the links. She has marvelously broad shoulders holding up that skinny frame, and I detect a strong mind. Perhaps we have a natural in our midst."

"Swell idea," he said, making an energetic move, touching his knee to hers.

Cleo hated to admit she didn't have sporting clothes. "Well …"

Graham anticipated her dilemma. "Take heart, Teddy has plus-fours in all sizes."

Teddy laughed from her lower reaches, which was as flat as her chest. She said to Cleo, "You'd look good in Edgar's old knickers, but I do have golf suits for guests. I'll have several sent to your rooms to try on. Also, at Southerness, bathing pajamas are fine. Men and women take the baths separately, unless…" She flashed her eyes at her son. "They want to mount a game of water polo, or something …"

Cleo felt Graham's closeness and dry-swallowed. When she looked at Neill, she saw him roll his lips inward as if containing a grin.

*****

Her trunks had been unstrapped from the back of the Rolls, taken to her rooms and unpacked. Her clothes hung in a rosewood chifforobe, her under garments placed in drawers. What had the maids thought of her wardrobe? She'd brought eight day dresses. Three, including the one she wore, were the latest in fashion. Waistlines were coming down, and she wished she could have afforded more than the three she bought at Connolly's, at cost, thanks to Cousin Neill. His great-grandparents had come from Ireland – half-starved on a coffin ship – in the 1850s and worked as servants. The family's fortune changed when Neill's handsome father married Cleo's free-spirited aunt. The poor Irishman with the gift of blarney worked all day and night to save and open his Pittsburgh department store. In ten short years, they were rolling in dough, enough for Neill to go to private schools where he met Graham Henry.

Graham Henry. The way he'd looked at her several times started a delicious flowering in certain places. "Don't be a dumb Dora," she said aloud. He probably has hundreds of girls at his beck and call.

Looking over the other five dresses, she regretted they were dated, even if of fine quality. Worse was coming to the sea without bathing pajamas, something her mother stoutly condemned. She'd already raised her mother's disapproval quotient by abandoning the cotton bands with which she'd bound her bubs, in favor of sidelacers to flatten her chest.

A cheval mirror stood in the corner of the elegant room. She angled it to fit her stature and swished herself left, then right. Yes, this cream Dotted Swiss had been perfect for today's activities, but she must change for dinner. Her dinner dresses, though of the finest silk, were pre-War, and she couldn't wear a head band with them. Head bands were for the latest dress and coat fashions, as were cloches. Marcel waves were all the rage and looked glamorous without hats or headbands, but she must tone down her rouge and lipstick.

She thought about Teddy; Teddy with the tan of a man; Teddy, who wore trousers to garden and plus-fours to golf. She smiled at her mirrored self, and thought, I'm not a half-bad grown-up bearcat, if I do say so myself. She pinched her cheeks, and said, "So to hell with fashion."

*****

Graham had said there would be cocktails before dinner. "A quick gin martini to sharpen the appetite." When she came into the drawing room, she drew everyone's attention. Although self-conscious, she relished the look in Graham's eyes.

Teddy, she was happy to see, wore a turn-of-the-century frock. Her hair was rolled in Gibson girl style.

"My dear," Teddy said, coming toward her, "your hair is divinely lovely. The color of coal. It highlights your beautiful fair skin." She turned to Graham. "Don't you think so, Graham?"

Graham, who had been staring, suddenly seemed to see something over Cleo's left shoulder. "Yes, indeed," he said to that something.

Cleo couldn't help a secret grin at his bashful moment, an atypical bashful moment she was sure.

At dinner, Graham sat at the head of the table and Teddy at the foot. Cleo sat at Graham's left and Neill sat at Teddy's right. Graham's brother, Eagan, and his sister, Linith, sat on either side of the table. They were inclined to bicker, but cut it out when Teddy said, "Children listen until invited to speak." The Henry children had refined manners, Graham especially, with his elegant way of eating the anchovy canapés. Odd though, while Neill and Teddy chatted and laughed, Graham remained silent, often glancing at her before his face would go through peculiar twitches that made her as nervous as he seemed.

During the crab soup (with corn in it, how interesting), Teddy and Neill talked of sailing up the coast. Graham leaned close to her. "There's so much I want to talk about, to ask, I don't know where to start."

Fearing her voice would warble, she pitched it low and said quickly, "My life is dull. You're the war hero."

"Only because I didn't get zotzed."

Those six words spoken in his firm self-deprecating voice eased her tension. Still, when he held her eyes with his, it was an effort to not lick her lips. She said, "Neill was lucky to have you."

"And I him."

She thought of William and lowered her lashes.

Graham's words rushed out, "Sorry about your fiancé." This was the second time Graham seemed to have read her thoughts.

She couldn't look at him. "Neill told you?"

"Yes, Uncle was glad to put the screws to the Army to find where he was buried and expedite his return."

In her mind she saw the coffin as it was lowered into the Arlington grave. "I didn't know."

His self-possession seemed to give way to nerves, but, at that moment, a godsend came in the form of a manservant with a tray of fish. Teddy said, "Amberjack with capers. Freshly caught this morning." The manservant held the tray while a serving maid filled their plates. Teddy went on, "Old Jack here weighed about sixty pounds. I was at the wharf when they brought him in. They say old jack was a fighter. Went straight down, heading for cover. Unlucky for him, no reefs for him to snap the fishing line."

Cleo's hand went to her tummy. Hearing one's meal had the intelligence to fight for his life didn't boost the appetite.

Graham cleared his throat, a non-verbal signal to his mother. Teddy twisted her mouth as though unsympathetic with such weakness.

When the manservant left, Graham spoke softly to her. "Perhaps I shouldn't have said anything about your fiancé. I apologize if I've upset you."

"I thought it was the Red Cross …"

"With a little help from the military."

She looked at Graham, her thoughts tumbling over each other. "It just that I'd begun to imagine William in the Tomb of the Unknown Soldier, representing all those needlessly killed over some Archduke getting himself assassinated."

Neill's voice broke in, "Hey, you ducks down there, why the long mouths?"

Cleo clutched her wine stem and raised it. "A little tribute to our fallen in The War to End all Wars. To those we loved and lost."

"Here, here," Teddy called and drank off her wine. Mitty was there to refill her glass. Taking a healthy swallow, Teddy put her glass on the table, and, folding her hands behind her plate, leaned forward. "Chickadees, the Great War has changed us."

Cleo looked from Neill to Graham. Neill had put his hands on his lap as had Graham. Eagan and Linith folded their hands to imitate their mother. It was apparent, Teddy was going to speechify. Graham asked, as if wary of the answer. "In what way has the Great War changed us, Mother?"

"Hardships give us more appreciation of life and its pleasures," Teddy said. "It shows in our clothing. Philadelphia is more fashion conscious than Pittsburgh. Don't you agree, Cleo?"

Cleo hadn't thought about the change in fashion and how it could have been influenced by the Great War, but it made sense. "I've never been to Pittsburgh, but my mother abhors the new fashions. She would have us going back to skirts brushing the floor."

Teddy picked at her sleeve. "This old thing is passé. I enjoy wearing it because next year I will look like my own grandmother in it. Hemlines are coming up, waistlines are coming down. Hats are small and cheeky. Cleo looked the picture of modernity this afternoon."

Cleo felt Graham's eyes on her as she tried to think of something cheeky to say. She looked at him. He said, "A beautiful picture of modernity, if I might say."

The manservant came in with potatoes Hollandaise and medallions of lamb.

"Spring lamb," Teddy said. "Fat and happy little things …"

"Teddy," Graham said. "Not everyone at the table was farm-raised." Graham knifed into his lamb. "I think Prohibition has something to do with the square heads becoming rounder."

Neill laughed. "And women getting the vote."

Teddy cut Neill a sharp glance. "Mister Connolly, would you care to further speak your mind on that?"

"I shouldn't, perhaps, but I believe it is an honorable experiment." He looked at Cleo. "I trust my cousin," – he turned back to Teddy – "and you to vote rationally, but women on the whole tend to speak with their hearts. Voting that way could promote more liberal thinking."

"Nothing wrong with liberal thinking," Teddy shot back.

"I don't agree," Graham broke in. "Liberal thinking got us into Prohibition."

"Bah," Teddy said. "Prohibition is taking us back to caveman days. Soon the Prohibitionists will see the evil in their grand experiment. It will be repealed by right-thinking men *and women.*"

"Boozehounds united," Graham said.

"Mother was against the temperance movement," Cleo said. "She predicted people wanting to swill will find a way."

Graham said, "In Pittsburgh there are two speakeasies selling Tiger milk on every corner. Clip joints fobbing bathtub hooch in between."

Teddy looked at Cleo. "In case you're wondering, our whiskeys and wines are genuine. We import."

"Import!" Graham laughed. "All your fine words will not make bootlegging legal."

"It should never have been made illegal, and that's all I have to say about it."

"Graham turned to Cleo. "Our islanders make themselves enough rice hooch to stay sogged-out for days on end."

After a disquieting moment, Teddy addressed Eagan and Linith. "What did you two do this afternoon at the beach?"

Cleo listened to their tale of stealing turtles' eggs, making her feel sorry for turtle mothers. Before the children's eager chatter grew out of proportion, Teddy put up a hand. "Enough. Leave some to hatch so we'll see babies crawling down to the sea."

"And to make turtle soup," Eagan said.

Ugh, Cleo thought.

The meal was finished, blissfully, with petit fours and cream, and nothing having been deprived of its life.

*****

After cognac had been served and Neill and Teddy yawned themselves to their feet pleading exhaustion, she found herself next to

Graham, walking down the hall to the bottom of the staircase. She swallowed the knot at the back of her throat.

"Would you like a moonlight walk on the beach?" he asked.

She stood with her hand on the banister, unable to meet his eyes. "I need sleep."

"I bet. Traveling can give one the screaming meemies."

She grinned at him. "More like swooning."

He covered her hand with his. "No swooning, it's out of fashion."

"I see you're a slave to fashion."

"Absolutely. My own idea of fashion."

"You dress very smart." *What a dumb thing to say.*

"That's because a smartly-dressed man can hide a multitude of idiocies."

"What idiocies?"

"Ummm, I don't confess everything to a woman I've just met, no matter how gorgeous. Wait until tomorrow."

"I shall." She placed a foot on the first step. "Time …"

"Teddy has taken to you, too, you know."

"Teddy is fun."

"If fun's not included, Teddy doesn't do it."

"Like you?"

"I look for a little fun in my life."

"I guess so, after that beastly war."

"It was beastly, but there were happy times."

"You can say that now you're safe at home."

"I say, Cleo, I am sorry about …"

She bobbed her head trying to see William in her mind, but his image didn't come. How could it, she thought, with all the unfocused emotions swirling there?

He drew in a breath. "I want to see happiness in those marvelous green eyes."

How could she forget the sharp pain of those unhappy days? "I am happy."

"But sometimes a little melancholy?"

"What's wrong with melancholy?"

"We at Southerness do not tolerate melancholy." He lifted her chin with a finger. "Got that, little Bearcat?"

She was not sure if she could get the words out of her mouth to say that her mood was beyond categorizing. She drew away from his finger. "Good night, Graham."

"Can I ask you something?"

She held her breath for a second. "Yes."

"Promise a walk on the beach tomorrow night? The lighthouse shows best by moonlight." He sensed her hesitation because he squeezed her arm. "I'm harmless."

She gave him her best I-don't-believe-that-for-a-minute smirk. "What if it rains?"

"It wouldn't dare. What say?"

"Let's see about tomorrow."

"That's not a no."

"No, it's not a no."

"I'm a happy fella then."

"Good night."

"Golf after breakfast?"

"I shall give it my best," she said.

He went off singing, "*Nothing could be finer than to be in Carolina in the morning*

Finally – she could take a deep breath.

CHAPTER TWO

"Cleo?"

She opened her eyes to the now familiar voice across the room. She hadn't slept well. It was as if a part of her she didn't recognize had awakened and refused to go back to sleep. She tossed restlessly and blamed it on the mattress. It was so very hard while hers at home was slung in like a hammock. But she knew the mattress wasn't the cause of her mind's stirrings. Damn him, he had robbed her of sleep, singing *Carolina in the morning* before she went to bed. His voice echoed through her skull, a voice full of humor and flirtation disguised by elegance and vitality. She had longed to get up and prowl the halls, halls that were mile-long mazes, to walk off the tension, but she couldn't risk getting lost in this vast place and asking the servants for directions while in her night-dress or, Heaven forbid, running into *him*.

Then Teddy opened the door.

"Morning," Cleo said, rising to sit.

As Teddy walked across the room, Cleo thought how, despite her beauty, like a man she was. Her stride was strong in the plus-fours, her eyes a confident blue, like Graham's.

Teddy sat on the foot of the high poster bed. "You up for golf? I usually don't pester guests this early. Just say no if you don't want to. Won't hurt my feelings."

So Teddy would be there, too. "Swell by me," she said and threw off the light cover.

"We tee off early so we don't swelter in the afternoon. Swimming's good in the pee-m. Sailing, too, although I don't know if *Hela* will be re-gaffed today. Maybe tomorrow."

"Everything sounds lovely," Cleo said, standing and letting the hem of her night chemise fall to the floor.

Teddy's eyes appraised her candidly. Then, as though feeling her discomfort, Teddy got up quickly and strode across the room. She turned the door knob and looked back. "Eurella will bring in golf suits shortly."

"Thank you, I appreciate all you've done for me."

"Some might be a little baggy, but Graham won't mind."

Graham, mind?

"Throw on your bloomers and camisole. No corsets allowed here. Eurella will be along. Whichever you choose to wear, it's yours absolutely. A gift, and I hope you enjoy the game. We're a pretty competitive bunch, but we go easy on first-timers."

*****

She adored Eurella the moment the small, wiry black woman walked into the room. She couldn't weigh more than a hundred pounds and the mass of clothes she carried weighed about as much. "Mornin', Miss Snow. I'm Eurella." Her voice was soft as it drew out her words like honey dripping on a buttermilk biscuit.

"Morning. And you must call me Cleo."

Eurella nodded and dropped the bundle in her arms on the dressing chest. An iron and pin cushion emerged from a bag she carried.

The golf suits were works of art in fabric and design. She chose the foulard print kimono style pullover blouse with a modified hobble skirt that came to her midcalf, the most daring length she'd worn. A smashing belt fitted her waist perfectly. She fastened her silk stockings to her knicker suspenders and laced the white flat-heeled sports shoes she'd brought, glad to be wearing something on the outside that belonged to her. She whirled before the mirror, satisfied. Eurella had crossed her arms and was nodding approval.

Before they left the room, Eurella showed her a gold braided rope hanging from the ceiling. "Pull anytime, miss, when you be needing something."

She remembered a time when she was a little girl, when they had servants who came running to the pull of the bell rope. It was nice being waited on again, but only here. At home, she was very happy to see to herself, thank you.

In the breakfast room, Teddy chewed a cinnamon pastry and spoke around it. "Graham and Neill will meet us at the tee. They'll start on one, but we can meet up with them wherever they are."

"Good." Graham's name, his image, made the hot cakes stick in her throat.

Teddy finished her coffee and stood. "Graham has a driver, mashie and putter for you. We can start with those clubs and see if you've got game."

"I'm … um … looking forward to it." She pushed her plate back.

Teddy stared at her plate. Was there nothing this woman didn't notice? "You finished? Don't let me rush you."

Cleo dropped her napkin on the table and stood. Eurella was beside her, handing her a duck cloche to match the golf dress. Teddy watched as she put it on. "You're charming in that hat, although you don't have to hide your forehead. It's quite nice."

They hiked to the golf links, Teddy carrying a leather bag full of clubs. "I enjoy being around you , Cleo. When Linith grows into womanhood, I hope she's like you. Of course we have to toughen you up a bit."

"I don't know what to say, except that's kind of you." *I think.*

"Kind I am not. Wait until we play golf."

At a rise in the ground, where grass looked impossibly green, Teddy said, "Graham and Neill have left this teeing ground. They'll be on two or three hole by now."

Cleo caught movement ahead and saw Graham hurrying toward them, a golf bag swinging from his shoulder. He looked like Apollo wearing plus fours and a paddy cap, the same kind Teddy wore. He doffed the cap. "Good morning, Bearcat."

"Good morning," she said. "What's your nickname?"

"How'd you know I had one?"

"Neill had one. It was Yank. I figure you did, too."

Graham laughed and her heart ballooned. "Mine was Cracker."

Graham Cracker. She glanced at Teddy. Cleo knew the story of the Graham Cracker.

"Old Sylvester Graham was a nut," Teddy said. "He thought his flour would cure all manner of ills from alcohol to lust, from which springs blindness, insanity, epilepsy, promiscuity and a host of other societal ills."

"He was a vegetarian," Cleo said. She looked at Graham. "Did you eat beans and Graham flour? Is that why they called you Cracker?"

"No," Graham laughed. "I slept on a hard mattress and opened my bedroom windows, another Graham nutism that was supposed to build character."

"Okay, Cracker, let's play golf," Teddy said.

Graham said to Teddy, "Go ahead and meet up with Neill. I'll give a few pointers to Cleo, get her acquainted."

"Don't tarry. I don't play slow."

Graham winked. "Bet this bearcat's a fast learner."

"Don't wear her out," Teddy said, trudging away.

"Well," he puffed out, looking at her a beat too long. "Now for a lesson." He pulled out a golf club and a ball. At least, she was acquainted with what they looked like. "This here's a mashie." He handed the club to her, bent to put a peg in the ground, and placed a golf ball on top of it.

She turned the head of her club up and read the writing on it. "Hand forged steel, number five, mashie. One-twenty-five slash one-forty. What's that mean?"

"It means I should be able to hit that club one-hundred-forty yards. You should be able to hit it, oh, I'd say a hundred. Give it a try?"

"Why not?"

He took another club from the bag and sat another ball on a wooden peg. "Place your club on the ground behind the ball, like this," he said, demonstrating. She mimicked him. "Good. Now put your hands like this." His hands folded around the handle and extended down the club. "Point your thumbs down the shaft."

She mirrored his hands. "Like this?"

"That's it, my girl. Loosen your grip just a little, like your holding a bird in your hand."

She lifted her fingers off the club shaft. "How can I swing it?"

He laughed. "Not that loose."

She repositioned her hands lightly.

"Perfect. Now do what I do." He swung the club back and so did she. "Hold it right there." She paused with her club back. He looked at her. "Lower your head and look at the ball." Which she did. "Now bring your left shoulder under your chin. That's my girl! Perfect form. Now, without moving your head, swing the club to the ball as hard as you can."

She swung the club and the ball spit off the club into the ground.

He said, "Raised your head, which you can't do and hit the ball, and you must follow through." He leaned his club on the bag. "Here let me show you." He walked behind her. "Okay, take the position with the club head behind the ball, your head down and …"

His arms wrapped her forearms, and she felt a stir in her hind region where he was touching her. She tried to ignore the sensation, but she'd already flinched.

"I'm not being fresh," he said in her ear. "Not now anyway. I'm your teacher, and I'm going to swing the club along with you."

It went quite well, and, after three together-swings, he backed off and she swung. The ball went flying off the club. "Excellent," he said. "Once more."

She put the ball on the peg and swung back and forward, remembering to keep her head still. The ball fizzled on the ground. He laughed. "Tell you what. Hit at the ball as if it's a snake about to strike. You want to fling it as far away as possible."

The next swing sent the ball sailing into the sky.

He clutched her waist. "You're a doll."

His blue-eyed smile threatened to paralyze her.

"I say," he said, his tone serious, "you might make me lose my concentration. Teddy hasn't beaten me in a long time."

"Let's catch up to Teddy," she said, walking away from him in quick strides.

Graham walked jauntily alongside her. Everything he did had a jauntiness about it. She told her heart to stop humming like bees around a hive.

She heard Teddy's voice. "Over here!"

Neill and Teddy stood beneath a large oak. Graham said, "Crikey. Old sport's hit into the trees. He's stymied."

Neill swung at the small white ball lodged in the roots of a big oak tree. "That's five," Teddy said, laughing. "You can pick up, I'm laying two."

Neill took another mighty swing and the ball jumped the root and landed a foot away. "Six!" Teddy crowed.

"Your hole," Neill said, picking up his ball. His face was red from exertion. Neill looked at Graham. "How'd my bearcat do?"

"Hit a screamer a hundred yards," Graham said.

"Really, Cleo? A hundred yards?"

"I don't know yards, but it did go far, didn't it, Graham?"

She felt as proud as Graham looked. "Very far, my girl. Now let's join the old sports and cheaters. I'll teach you scoring, but you don't have to play our game. You wouldn't want to lose hundreds now would you?"

"Hundreds?" She only made a few in a year's time.

"You lose, you pay," Graham said. "Teddy is a gambling addict – something not eating Graham Crackers will turn you into."

Teddy cawed. "I do like taking the boys' money."

To Cleo's dismay, she didn't hit the ball quite as well as she had with that last swing.

"It's called golf," Graham said. "Spelled backwards, it's flog. We might as well be on a chain gang."

Graham did not flog the ball, and she got a thrill out of watching him. He would twitch until he got set good and proper, and then he'd swing the club back impossibly far and smoothly swing it at the ball, sending it sailing above the trees.

Poor old Neill, though, he hit as many grounders as she did. And his red face matched his hair.

At the end of the game, Neill said, "I'm down fifteen. Oh boy."

Teddy counted Neill's money. "A fiver from you, Graham. May be the start of a losing streak, old son."

"A mere distraction," Graham said, smiling at Cleo, then putting his clubs in his bag.

Teddy pocketed her money and said, "Now for lunch, my dearies."

Graham clasped his hand in Cleo's, and Teddy led them a fast pace back to the palace. It seemed harmless, like she held hands with Neill sometimes when they walked down the street in Philadelphia. But in her knickers, she knew it wasn't harmless.

Her eye picked up movement from the grove across the road. She looked over to see the dark-haired man coming from beneath the fruit trees, riding the same beautiful horse. "I see your vet," she said. "What's his name?"

Graham looked toward the orange trees. "Sam Holliday. How'd you know he was a vet?"

"We saw him yesterday when Neill drove us here."

Teddy had slowed to join the conversation. "We call him Doc."

Neill laughed. "You just made me think of Doc Holliday. Last month there was a piece in the Pittsburgh paper about him. Somebody in that gunfight died, or something."

Graham said, "It was a feud. Our Doc's a relative twice removed or something like that."

"I've heard of Doc Holliday," Cleo said, glad to add her knowledge of historical figures to the conversation.

"Doc was born in Georgia," Teddy said. "Boths Docs. Sam's famous relative was a dentist as well as a gunfighter and gambler."

Cleo laughed. "What'd he fill teeth with? Gunpowder?"

Teddy grinned. "I guess Sam decided dentistry wasn't the best practice for a Holliday so he confined himself to animals. They don't gamble, as far as we know."

Graham said, "Sam says Doc Holliday's exploits are mostly myth."

"Our Doc's something of an adventurer himself," Teddy said.

Neill asked, "Why here, though? Last time I heard, the West was still pretty wild. Just the place for adventurers."

Graham said, "You don't think our glorious island is a draw to adventurers?"

"What's he adventuring about?" Cleo asked.

"Who knows? Damn good man with the horses and dogs, though." Graham lifted Cleo's hand. "Speaking of hay burners, would you like to ride this afternoon?"

"Too hot," Teddy answered for her.

Graham didn't give in. "Late this afternoon, on the beach?"

Cleo shrugged, wanting to go with him, but skittish about riding a horse without a cart in front of it. "I've nothing to wear."

Teddy waved a hand. "I've got just the thing."

Graham asked, "You ever wear breeches and riding boots?"

"Everyday on the Main Street with a jacket and a man's tie," Cleo said.

Graham laughed heartily. "That's the ticket."

Damn the man, if he didn't stop taking her breath away, she'd die of suffocation.

*****

She looked quite comely in the French riding breeches, even if she thought so herself. She could visualize the expression on her mother's face – the open-mouth shock. Giggling, she tied a red head band at the back of her hair and let the ends slip to her shoulders.

Graham met her at a back door, one that opened onto the balustrade. He whistled and said, "Hi, gorgeous."

Walking down the long flight of steps beside him, she asked, "Is Teddy coming?"

"Teddy rides at dawn. She's swimming now. Does hundreds of laps."

"That's why she stays so slim."

"We're a wiry bunch to begin with."

"Where's Neill?" she asked, following him along a path that lead to the side of the house.

"He swore off. He found Dreiser's book, *Sister Carrie,* in the library."

"Mother will be scandalized when I tell her."

"After the war, it's quite tame, you know."

"Neill's a great reader, especially of Shakespeare. Are you?"

"Not the bard for me. Too dense. I pick up a dimer now and then, but I'm a man of action."

"I can tell."

They crossed a lane, and he glanced at her. "What else can you tell about me?"

"You're gay and sophisticated."

"That all?"

"You're rich."

"Nothing owing to my skills. Born that way."

"Do you work?"

"As in?"

"Do you go to an office?"

"Only when they miss me and send out the posse."

"Really? I thought you might be a big cheese on Wall Street with all the other sons of swells."

"I am a committed man of leisure, but unfortunately, Uncle, who runs the joint since Father died, doesn't see it that way. I'm all too familiar with the open hearth process, the Bessemer, too."

"What would you rather be doing?"

"Don't go thinking I'm a loafer. I want to fly planes, but Uncle threatens to write me out of the will. I can't build a plane with sticks and rubber bands."

"You'll never be poor."

"Perhaps not, but I intend to fly the Atlantic solo one day and that takes moola."

"Where to?"

"I think Paris. That's my plan. What do you think?" His face lit up. "Would you like to come along?"

"Then it wouldn't be solo."

"We could stow you away." He grabbed her hand. "Heck, I'd be proud to tell the world you were with me. What say, my girl?"

There was so much coming at her now, she tried to make sense of it. She shook her head. "You say the silliest things."

"Not so," he said, swinging her hand as they walked in step down the rocky lane.

"You ever ride horses before?"

"Not on their backs. Just in carriages behind their tails."

"You'll get the hang of it."

At the stable, a colored man stood between two horses that were tethered to a hitching post. He led Graham and her inside the tack room and handed her a pair of riding boots. "Miz Henry says you be about a size seven, jes like she be."

"Six-and-a-half, but seven will be fine."

Outside, near the horses, Graham said, "Let me introduce you to your steed. You get to ride Linith's pony. She's a grand little mare, but mind her mouth. It's sensitive. If you feel you need to hang on, grab the mane."

"Is this easier than golf?"

He laughed. "Much. You don't have to do any work. Let Mutt do it."

"Mutt?"

"The horse's name. After Mutt and Jeff."

"Mutt's a boy."

"Mutt's little, like Linith's horse. Linith wouldn't settle on any other name."

When he put his hands together to give her a leg up, she lifted her foot and stepped into his cupped hands. She wobbled, her foot slipped, and she slid down the side of the horse, her heels coming to rest near his toes. She could feel his warmth against her back, hear his breath in her ear. She daren't turn to look at him, but she knew he was grinning. "Here we go again, my girl." He cupped his hands. This time, she planted her shoe firmly, and he helped her settle into the saddle by positioning the top of her hips just so. She looked back at him. He smiled and patted the horse's rump.

A lane lined with old gnarled oaks led to the beach. She couldn't see the sea, but she could smell the brine, like the nickel oysters served with fifteen cent beer at the Oyster Market off Main Street. Graham's horse trotted next to hers. Through trees on the right, she saw a group of small horses, like the ones she and Neill had seen. Was it just yesterday? The horses nudged their noses into the tall grass. "Do you ride those horses, too?" she asked.

"Nope. They're feral."

"Meaning?"

"Wild. Once upon a time the Spanish brought ponies and abandoned them here."

"How long ago was that?" Mutt slipped and she grabbed her mane.

"Oh about five hundred years ago," Graham said. "Then hundreds of years later – don't hold me to these centuries – when the island was discovered as a place for rich northern people to winter, the swells brought their own steeds. Over time, they mixed with the wild horses and you see the result. Those guys are rough and rugged and don't take to training. Easier on the bum to bring your own. We won't get too close, those stallions are territorial with their mares and their colts, and this is the breeding season." He pointed at the horses. "That group you see is a family." His hand swept left. "Across that marsh over there, you'll see another family."

"I don't know much about horses."

"When the old stallion decides to kick his kid colts out of the harem, they have to go find dames of their own. So they raid the neighbor's fillies. You should hear the screams. They fight almost to the death sometimes over … over…" His face actually colored a little. "What comes naturally."

She felt her face warm, too, although as a nurse she was aware of mating behaviors, having learned in biology class and seen physical evidence in the wards, much to her mother's chagrin.

They came to a creek and sloshed through it. "This is called Blackbeard's Stream," he said.

"The pirate?"

"Right-o. Natives around here say they're related to the old pillager. If so, you wouldn't be able to tell. Everyone's pretty dark."

"Where is the village?"

"North end. I'll take you there. It's rather picturesque. Great food."

She had doubts about the food. She'd heard Negroes ate possum and pig's feet – another Philadelphia delicacy sold in Irish beer halls, or what used to be beer halls. Now they called them buttermilk parlors, which was a joke.

The horses climbed down the last dune to the shore, and beached waves made up a welcoming committee. The afternoon sun lit the sea with rays like sparklers and a fresh breeze blew in her face.

Graham positioned his horse next to hers. "What do you think about our paradise here?"

"It's quite lovely." She saw birds with pouchy bills skimming the water, their wings combing the white caps. "What are those birds?"

"Pelicans. First time you've been to the sea?"

She looked at him and smiled at how his squinting eyes reflected the sparkling water. "I have cousins on Rhode Island, but I've never ridden a horse along the beach." A sea gull flew close to her head. She waved at it, and, offended, it squawked away. "The seagulls on Rhode Island aren't so tame."

"Teddy brings bread to feed the gulls, and every tern and plover she can entice."

"I'm fond of birds. I don't know sea birds, only city birds."

He looked at her. "You're rather a little city bird yourself."

If she said anything, she feared it would come out in a chirp. She looked out to the sea. The waves scalloped together right before they came rushing onto the beach, and then ran away like a little boy kissing his first girl and fleeing to hide his bashful face. That imagery made her grin.

They rode on, the horses stepping high in the sand. The leather of the saddle creaked and rubbed against her legs. In the distance, she saw a hut – a straw roof held up by stilts. When they drew closer, she saw the rattan furniture inside.

"Cabanas," Graham said. "We built several up and down this beach. Let's give our mounts a rest."

She gave a shrug to say, why not? He got off his horse and held his hands for her to slide straight into them, but she determined she would get off her horse the same way he did. She shifted her weight to her left foot as she took her right shoe out of the right stirrup. She raised her body and slung her right foot over the back of the saddle and slid down, landing both feet on the sand.

"That's my girl," Graham said, grabbing her for a congratulatory hug.

Inside the cabana, the breeze tumbled through the canvas like it did through Philadelphia's blustery streets. Graham whisked sand off a glider and waved for her to sit. Feeling uneasy, she watched him brush sand off the other chairs. "Nice to get out of the sun for a while," she said. Was her hair mussed? She pressed a finger against her cheek. Had the sun blotched her skin?

He brushed his hands together, his eyes wandering over her face. "The sun hasn't burned you. It would take a lot to get it like Teddy's."

"It seems right for her, but it isn't fashionable."

He grinned. "You tell her that."

He sat next to her, rocking the creaking swing. She wished she could think of something clever to say. He took her hand and turned it over in his. He seemed quite fascinated by the lines. "A long lifeline. I'm glad."

She looked at the lines. "Me, too."

"What say we get out of this rusty old thing?" He rose, took her hand and beckoned her up with his chin. She had to admit, it didn't take a lot of beckoning. He nimbly tugged her to the double chaise where he sat and patted the adjoining straw cushion. "Much more comfortable."

He beamed with such allure, she felt as if she hovered on a cliff, deciding whether or not to dive. Leaning back, he reached for her hand. She looked into his eyes and her mind misted with the memory of her fiancé and how he would get that craving look that made her blush and squirm. William would grab her and kiss her and pinch her nipples until she pushed his hands away. He would laugh. "One day, sweetheart, I will have you."

She shook her head to clear the memory. She must look like a silly goose, not knowing what to do now with Graham holding her hand and stroking her arm. Turning her head so he wouldn't see her creeping hysteria, her throat made a sound like, "Ummmm…"

He took her by the upper arms and moved her so she faced him. Joy and trepidation battled inside her. "Ummm, what?" he said.

She looked up the beach as if the sand or the sea or the sky would supply the answer. "Just ummmm."

"Will you kiss me?"

She fought to breathe normally.

"What say, my girl?"

"A brief one, maybe."

"You'll have to bridge the great divide between us."

She swayed closer, and he slipped his hands into the notches of her armpits. He tugged her toward him until her nose met his chin. His lips lightly touched hers and drew away. He did it again, and again, fleeting baby kisses, sweet and soft. The next kiss lasted longer and began to stir the hollows of her body. A sudden, unbidden thought made her flinch and pull away. She looked at his lips and then into his eyes. He looked mystified, as if unable to understand. The unbidden thought had her marveling at how different Graham's lips were than William's. William's had been eager, his puckered mouth pressing too hard.

"Are you okay?" Graham whispered. "I want everything to be right for you."

She smiled, joy overcoming trepidation. "Ummm-hummm." She laid her lips back on his, caressing them lightly before settling in for a long, gentle kiss. His submissive lips floated over hers as if oiled, spreading the heat of his desire. She knew she should control their rising passion, but she couldn't break from his embrace. As if he'd sensed her hesitancy, he drew away and kissed her mouth three short times before he moved his lips to the tip of her nose, to the side of it, to her cheek, to her ear where he sucked delicately. She closed her eyes when his lips brushed her eyelids and felt the coils in her private places winding tighter. His lips moved to her mouth and urged her into a long, gentle exploring rhythm. For the longest time, he seemed content to kiss her and hold her in his strong arms, concentrating on the feel of her mouth, creating an awareness of their rising intensity. His mouth parted slightly and his tongue touched the rim of her lips, circling lightly, slowly. She touched the tip of his tongue with hers, and he drew it inside his mouth, probing with care as if he'd just discovered there was something wonderful beyond her lips.

His body seemed to demand more, his subtle movements starting a surge in her like an orchestra's crescendo. Against his need, his unexpected pressure, she pressed harder, becoming as greedy as he. Lord, he was spiraling down into forbidden places, tightening tendons, moistening tissues. She sucked his lips and heard herself groan. Her hip felt his pleasure and pushed against it.

As if he became aware of her touch there, he pulled back and kissed her throat, burying his head in her neck, laying a hand on her bub. Then his mouth was back on hers, his desire stoking hers, long and hard, into a wonderful frenzy in which she thought there was no turning back, no wanting to turn back.

Wait.

Suddenly, as if her mind and his conceived the same thought, she felt his hand release the pressure on her bub. His head moved up, away from her lips, leaving her to surface like a diver with a frantic need to breathe. Their eyes met, and she saw him blinking the daze away. Watching him for a moment, thinking what a wonderful lover he was, she rose quickly to sit and look toward the sea and sky. A seagull flew straight over the cabana. She studied it like she'd never seen one before, wondering what would have happened if their unfettered hunger had burgeoned, and it became too late.

He touched her shoulder until she looked at him. He grinned. "I was damn near a goner." He sat up and raised a knee to hide the rise in the front of his trousers. It was something she was familiar with. Her fiancé often shifted his perpetual bulge. She'd never been eager to explore the bulge and that was why she hadn't agreed to marry William before he went to war. It had weighed on her when he was killed, but now seemed far away, inconsequential.

"Are you okay?" he asked, smoothing his sleek hair.

She closed her eyes and raised her chin. "I don't think so." Her voice had quivered.

"Me, neither." He took her hand. She looked at him. "You overwhelm me, my girl. I hope that's okay with you."

Shaking her head, she touched his chin and felt a shock. "I never thought …" It took her breath, how different two men could be.

She stood and so did he. He pulled her face to his chest. "What?" he asked.

He smelled of warm sand and a mysterious substance she could only identify as sweetly masculine. Her fingers clawed lightly at his chest. "That I would ever feel so – that I would enjoy kissing another man."

He clutched her forearms. She looked into his curious eyes. "It's been two years, Cleo. Time for a wonderful little bearcat to get on with life."

"He's only been home six months."

"I know, and I know you loved him, but he's never coming back. Let yourself heal. Let me be your salve."

She put her finger on his lips. "You have good bandages."

He twined his fingers in her hers and kissed her temple. "All yours, my adorable delight." His arm circled her waist, and they walked to the horses.

When he put his hands together to give her a leg up, he said, "I hope those kisses won't be the last."

"I should say absolutely yes. No more," she said, putting a foot into his hand block. Once in the saddle, she looked down at him. "I should have slapped your face for being so fresh."

He held her arm and pulled her down, to his face. He kissed once, twice, three times, quickly and eagerly. "It's madness," he said and laughed. "The heat."

"Spring fever."

She'd almost slipped and said: The breeding season.

CHAPTER THREE

At dinner she sat in a dream state next to the man she'd made love to on the beach. Not that they'd gone all the way. She shivered at remembering how the nerves in her intimate places sang out for more of him. She'd never before looked forward to going all the way with a man. She'd listened to the other nurses when they spoke of the horrors of the *initial invasion*.

Riding home this afternoon, the horses moving leisurely toward the stable, he'd asked her questions. "Did you make love with your fiancé?"

"Silly, yes."

"All the way?"

She'd gasped. "Of course not."

"I'm glad."

"He wanted us to. I wish I had, now he's gone." Knowing she'd fibbed coquettishly, she glanced at Graham to see his reaction.

He'd looked somber. "You know, I wouldn't blame you if you had, I'm not that kind of beggar. It was the war."

And she'd asked him questions. "Were you ever in love?"

"A gentleman doesn't kiss and tell."

"I think you just said yes."

"No."

"Engaged?"

"No."

"Got a girl now?"

He looked at her. "I hope so."

"Before the war?"

"Too busy learning to fly."

"During the war?"

"Too busy flying. I don't consider myself a man of the world, like some. That's why me and Neill got along so well."

"Neill's reserved around girls."

"Like I said, we were alike. When we brought our show boats home from a raid, we palled around while others headed for easy street."

She believed him. Like Neill, Graham, for all his charm, projected an aura of incorruptible virtue.

From the head of the table, Teddy broke into her reverie. "Hey, kiddies, at that end, why so quiet?"

Cleo twitched her shoulders and Graham grinned. "The chops are too delicious to talk around. Besides it's rude to speak with a mouth full."

Cleo felt Teddy's eyes roam from her to Graham and back. Cleo said, "I've attempted two new things today, so I'm a bit tired."

"Not too tired to fox trot tonight, I hope," Teddy said.

Dancing. Dancing with Graham. She recalled his desire and her own longing. "Not too, I think." She avoided his glance.

"I'm up to shaking a leg," Graham said.

Teddy picked up the bell. "Good. We'll have dessert now. The Thompsons are coming over and so are the Drakes. I had to invite Mr. Swinnerton. He's dining with the Thompsons."

"Good ol' Swinny," Graham said. "Teddy'd be better strutting her stuff with herself."

*****

Albert Swinnerton and the Thompsons arrived on the dot. Swinny turned out to be a funny old bird. Cleo knew he wouldn't be a good dancer the moment she laid eyes on him. He was a throwback to what Mark Twain satirically dubbed the Gilded Age because of its excesses. About sixty or so, red-faced, over-weight, he wore mutton-chop side whiskers that met up with a moustache. Instead of a tie, he wore an ascot under a velvet smoking jacket. His shirt featured ruffles on each side of the fastenings. She thought his get-up was none too clean.

"No laughing," Graham whispered.

The Thompsons were Teddy's age, mid-forties, dressed in simple expensive clothes. Lillian was plump, with a pretty, sweet face. She held her beaded pocket book next to her abdomen as if the thief amongst them would snatch it. Cleo had been told beforehand that Forest Thompson was an enormously rich planter, originally from South Carolina. He looked like he should be wearing plowboy trousers and thick boots. He was bigness itself – bones, ears, nose.

Gin rickeys were served in the ball room while everyone awaited the arrival of the last guests. Soon, Mitty ushered into the room a man of about thirty and a younger woman. The tall thin woman rushed to where Cleo stood with Graham and Teddy. "So sorry," she gushed at Graham, "Shafer just can't get himself ready to leave on time."

"No go," Shafer said, coming up behind her. He was almost bald on top and a bit lumpy in the middle. Cleo had never seen narrower shoulders on a man. He said, "It takes her an hour to pick out her pearls."

Cleo eyed the string of pearls circling the woman's neck and swinging across her bosom. Quite the fashion, as was her drop-waist, sleeveless silk dress.

"Nice that Prohibition hasn't affected your budget when it comes to pearls, Josie," Teddy said.

Josie pressed her lips and blinked once at Teddy. Cleo wondered what that meant.

Teddy continued with the introductions. "You know Neill, of course." She flashed a ringed hand toward Neill.

"Oh yes," Josie said, batting her eyelashes like a Kewpie Doll. Shafer and Neill shook hands.

Turning toward Cleo, Teddy said, "This is his cousin, Cleo Jernigan Snow."

Josie curtsied. Her eyes shone with a mischievous hazel hue. Wide smile, flashing white teeth, Cleo thought this is someone who got by on glitz and glitz alone.

Shafer put out his hand. "Shafer here. Glad to meet you, Miss Jernigan Snow."

"Cleo," she said to both of them.

No one spoke. After an awkward interval, Neill walked away. The uncomfortable interlude lasted but a few more seconds before Graham said, "Let's shake a leg."

"Let's do," Josie said, looking at Graham.

Graham circled Cleo's arm around his and led her to the Victrola where Mitty stood. "Request, sir?"

"*Whispering*," Graham said. "The Paul Whiteman version."

"As you say, sir." Mitty selected the record, blew on the black circle and placed it on the turn table.

Graham took Cleo's hands, and they faced each other. Their arms locked in position, and, before she knew it, he was sweeping her across the floor. When she could speak, she would ask him if he took lessons from The Three Graces. For all of his jauntiness, his fox trot steps where smooth, none of William's herky-jerky that she'd found so exhilarating before it became exhausting. They glided in rhythm, and then she found herself moving gamely with his quick side-steps. He began to sing softly, "*Whispering while you cuddle near me, whispering so no one can hear me, each little whisper seems to cheer me, I know it's true dear, no one but you, dear....*

His voice spun in her head as he danced her across the floor with effortless poise, her chiffon gown whirling just above her ankles.

"*Whispering so no one else can hear me...*"

There was no one else in the room, no one but she and Graham, close together, floating as one to the mesmerizing strains of Paul Whiteman's latest musical sensation. Too soon, the music stopped.

Next came *My Wonderful One.*

While they did a rhumba-like fox trot to *My Cuban Pearl,* she caught a glimpse of Neill dancing with Josie. Josie was leading. Having the legs of a dancer, she was one of those natural leaders, but Neill didn't seem to mind. The look on his face said he was in a faraway place. Cleo smiled and thought Neill needed to find a girl.

Three O'Clock in the Morning came next. Graham led her expertly through the intricate dance steps before they were almost side-swiped by Lillian and Neill. Cleo giggled and noticed Josie taking a turn with Forest. Cleo whispered in Graham's ear, "Forest dances like he's got a bum leg, and he's two beats behind Josie. She's quick."

"Indeed," he murmured, "In more ways than one."

Just as she was wondering what that meant, the song ended.

Trying not to heave indelicately, she said, "I must rest, Graham."

"I could hold you in my arms all night," he said. "You're a feather."

"And you're smooth," she said.

Swinny walked up. "You're monopolizing this beautiful girl, old boy. Let me have a go."

She'd seen Swinny plod around the floor despite Teddy's efforts to lead him into some kind of form. "Just one," Cleo said. "I'm nearly done in."

"Young thing like you," he said, jerking her away like she was a skipping stone. "Bet you could dance all night in the arms of that young swain." *Swain* was just the kind of word Swinny would use.

As they got set to fox trot, she saw Josie make a run for Graham.

Swinny hobbled and tugged her through *I'm Forever Blowing Bubbles.* When the record ended, she glanced over to see Graham propped against the wall, watching her, smoking. He'd apparently finished dancing with Josie before the record stopped playing. Neill was standing a little apart from Graham, looking odd. Suddenly Shafer was making a beeline to his wife. Cleo's eyes caught Teddy's profile. She looked pale and as if she'd been slapped.

Graham hurried forward. "Come, Bearcat, let's scram to the balcony for some air."

"Suits me," she said. "What's up with Teddy?"

"You'd look grumpy if Swinny trod on your toes all night."

"One dance, and it feels like it."

"Let me get my fags and get you a gin rickey."

"I'll walk with you," she said. "I don't want Forest claiming a tango."

"He's a real heeler, too."

Mitty must have given the Victrola a rest, because music didn't start up and the dancers stood on the floor, in graceless attitudes, like they didn't know whether to bolt for the bar or start a conversation.

Outside, Graham touched her arm. "Cash or credit?"

She grinned. "Now or never?"

"Better not be never," he said, and leaned over to kiss her.

When their lips touched, a fragile pleasure built like a low-lit flame. She broke the kiss. "What am I doing?"

He slipped his hand to the small of her back and pressed. "Getting goofy, like me."

"Graham ..."

"You don't want me carrying the torch alone, do you?"

She thought she saw a shadow linger at the French doors. "Someone's watching." She stepped back from him.

"Let's see who the peepers belong to." He walked toward the doors, peered inside and looked back at her. "Don't see anyone."

"Edgy, I guess."

He was beside her. "Me, too."

"Graham."

"Yes, my lovely."

She hated to say it. "I'll be gone from here next week."

"So will I. Pittsburgh isn't a world away from Philly. I got a nice breezer, even if it isn't a Roller."

To give her heart a chance to settle, she walked to the marble balustrade and placed her palms on the ledge. He came to stand next to her, placing his elbow on the ledge. She faced him, noticing how the stars and moon shimmered on his hair. He held out his arms and hummed *Whispering*. She was the moth drawn to his flame. He kissed her lips lightly, but she could feel his body's tightness when he pulled away. "*... cuddle near me... Whispering so no one can hear me ... .*" He kissed her nose and caressed her cheek. He backed away and breathed a deep sigh. "Wow."

"Wow," she echoed.

"Let's relax now, okay? Cigarette?"

Reaching into her bag, she took out a small holder. She seldom smoked, but she needed a cigarette to calm her emotions.

He took the holder, inserted a cigarette and lit it. Handing it to her, he lit one for himself. "I try not to inhale too many coffin nails, but one does get a bad habit during a war."

"I know," she said, exhaling the satisfying smoke. "The last year of the war, I began working in the hospital. It was a gas house on the ward floors."

"How about that walk on the beach?"

"You promised to show me the lighthouse." *What am I saying?*

"So I did, my sweet."

Something inside the house must have caught Graham's attention, because he whirled toward the door.

"I haven't heard the music lately," she said, putting her hand on his arm. "Is something wrong?"

"Teddy's dances end at ten o'clock. She's a disciple of Ben Franklin's – early to bed, early to rise."

The balcony doors opened. "There you are, Graham," Teddy said, sounding short-tempered. "Everyone's leaving now. Come, say goodbye."

"Certainly." Graham escorted her and his mother into the ball room. "Did our departure for a smoke cause everyone to go into the doldrums?" he asked.

"In the a. m. the Thompsons are leaving on an early steamboat to go to Charleston. The Drakes, well, who knows with them?"

"How'd you get rid of Swinny so early?"

"He rode with the Thompsons."

"Lucky you."

"My feet are killing me. Let's go say goodbye."

*****

He held her hand, and they walked the tabby footpath, winding through lush tropical gardens where, beneath her feet, the moon washed the slope silver. She stepped onto the boardwalk. He walked beside her, his hand caressing the small of her waist. He paused and looked at the sky. "Waxing gibbous."

"Have you taken to speaking French?" she said.

He grinned and draped his arm over her shoulders. "When the moon is getting full, but not quite, it's called a waxing gibbous moon. After it begins losing its fullness, it becomes a waning gibbous, eventually becoming a crescent moon."

"Is this written in your flyer's handbook?"

"In fact, my girl, it is."

"Did you fly at night?"

"Once. I can tell you I got spooked. It's not something we practice. Mostly, Neill and I were air-to-air fighters. The Brits, God love their souls, considered it ungentlemanly to raid at night."

"I think I agree, unless someone I love … loved got killed in a night raid."

He hugged her tighter. "Those damn cowards, the Germans, used to fly their Zeppelins over London and bomb during the darkest phases of the moon."

"The moon was their friend then."

"Not for long. A few Brits took to their Camels and blew the gas bags up. But mostly, Zeps were ineffective because they blew off course crossing the English Channel. Our guys gunned down many and a lot of Huns blew themselves up. Hydrogen is a very explosive gas."

She found walking next to him the easiest thing in the world. "How did you and Neill wind up at Dunkirk at the same time?"

"Signed up together."

"You said you always wanted to fly. When did you begin?"

"Me and Neill joined the flying club at Yale, which became part of the Naval Reserve."

"I remember. Neill's daddy wasn't happy. His son and heir flying sent him into furies." She actually giggled. "The second richest man in Pittsburgh wouldn't buy his only son an airplane."

"I took care of Neill."

"You always did."

"He took care of me, too."

At the end of the boardwalk, up the beach, stood the pristine white lighthouse. Her foot was poised to step down when Graham held her back. "I'd take my shoes and stockings off if I were you. I'm going to."

She drew her skirt around her bottom and sat on the boardwalk step. She unbuckled her Mary Janes while Graham removed his brogues. She stood. "Look the other way."

"Why?"

"I'm going to raise my dress and unhook my stockings."

Grinning, he turned toward the sea.

They walked, she carrying her shoes and stockings while the sand and sea oats tickled her tender soles. He took hold of her hand, she wove her fingers into his, and they strode to the shore. Neither spoke, but their intimacy had become a comfortable companion. Gazing at the stars in the clear night sky, she welcomed his arms when they wrapped her shoulders. She breathed deeply of the sea air – tangy, luscious, sensuous. While the warm sea foam lapped her ankles, he kissed the back of her hair.

Curiously, she thought of her cousin and what he might think of her spooning with his friend. She said, "Neill loved his plane, his Sopwith Camel. He's got a photograph of himself with it. What about you?"

"We got caught by the same shutterbug." He spun her around and walked her to where the sand was dry. Sitting, he urged her down next to him. He put an arm around her waist and she snuggled into the crook between his arm and shoulder. "It would mean a lot to me if you would accept my photograph."

"Oh I couldn't, but I'd like to see it. I know what it means to you, because I know how much the photograph means to Neill. He said the Camel's flimsy canvas and wood saved both your lives."

"Sure did." He hugged her closer, his muscles taut with excitement. "We flew regular patrols with the Brits – good lads one and all, but when it came to combat, we wanted to fight those bastards, just us, me and Neill, like in our fantasy play when we were kids."

"The Brits let you go out by yourselves?"

"We were a team within a larger squadron. Heck, the Brits would let you do whatever you wanted if it included shooting down Huns. Once, we flew into a bunch of Fokkers. We took lead until the Huns ran out of ammo. Sitting ducks they were; we picked them off one at a time. Seven-to-two. We came in on threads and splinters."

"Once your planes were destroyed, what then?"

He leaned to kiss her nose. "We got new Camels. Why not? We were fearless. Next time out, Neill shot down a gas bag and a two-seater."

It was hard to visualize her studious, freckle-faced cousin a hellion against the Huns. "That how you got your distinguished medals?"

"That's how, my girl."

Several moments slid by, astonishing moments filled with thoughts that clashed in a battle of eager anticipation against quiet misgiving.

"Care to walk?" he asked.

She shook her head yes.

"You sure?"

"I'm sure."

She rose and he led her up the dune, toward the lighthouse. The whitewashed round tower had two sets of windows – the first set built about fifteen feet above the ground, and, the other set, ten feet above that. The slick sides tapered to a black rim. Atop that, a faint light shone from a lens that turned at intervals. Three stone steps led to wooden double doors.

"Shall we scrape the sand from our toes before we climb the steps?"

"Let's."

*****

Turning the key, he pushed the door. In one sweeping motion, he scooped her up. She laughed nervously, never dreaming a man would really do this. She put her arms around his neck, and he carried her inside, up the spiral iron steps. He never faltered. She put her mouth against his ear. "Your poor back."

"From hefting all eighty pounds of you?"

"Ninty-seven."

He let her slide gracefully to the floor and hurried to light the lanterns. The place was fragrant of salty sea and old wax like the maritime museums she'd visited. The oil lamps cast shadows over the single round room with long rectangular windows. Under one, an old roll top desk sat with a roller chair tucked under the front. An easel stood next to the other long window, and, at hand, a palette and tubes of paint lay on a table. Here and there were bookshelves filled with leather bound volumes. An iron bed had been made up with clean white sheets and a counterpane turned down. Two pillows were fluffed like the place had been prepared for them. He stood behind her, and she glanced back at him.

"Just to let you know, this room is always kept like this," he said, palms raised against the skepticism that had come into her expression. "I have a secret life. I paint."

She walked over to view the canvases of men and planes mounted on the walls. They were good, and she felt proud of him.

"This is *my* place," he said. "I wanted you to see it."

Air cavorted through the open windows. "This room is perfect," she said, moving to look outside a window. "Look at your gibbous moon hanging like a big fat pearl over the sea. And the sea twinkling from star dust." Her voice sounded small, but she wasn't nervous now. "Stars like jewels. If only I could reach out and touch them and bring them in and ask a million questions."

He stood behind her. "Best we can do is take pleasure in them, my bearcat."

Heat rose from the base of her spine. He folded his arms around her and kissed her ear.

Her smile began in her heart and blossomed to her face.

He said, "Let me make love to you."

The words, so bold, so romantic, yet so scary. "It's so, so ..."

"Nothing is too soon, my darling. Yesterday, seeing you for the first time, I knew ..." He turned her around. She looked into his passionate eyes. He said, "I thought maybe ... maybe you felt ... well ..." He shrugged and blinked – his lashes battling uncertainty. "I hoped anyway."

"Yes," she said, remembering that first sight of him. "It's just ..."

He placed his finger beneath her chin and raised her face. His lips brushed hers lightly. He broke away and stared into her eyes. "Just what?"

"Do that again."

While he kissed her, he pressed his full body into her as if sharing a new dimension of himself, powerful yet tender enough to caress her heart. Her blood began to hammer through her veins overwhelming any lingering scruples. His touch eased, and he drew away, as if knowing she needed a release from the pressure mounting inside. She opened her eyes. His, just inches away, were full of love and inquisitiveness. Something inside of her let go, and she touched his chin and raised her face for his kiss. Savoring the pleasurable strumming in her body, she opened her mouth to let his tongue touch hers.

Lightheaded with ecstasy, she felt him reach to unbutton one of the gold buttons that marched across her shoulder. He drew his face back an inch. "Is this all right?"

He'd wreaked havoc on her ability to think and speak. "I ..."

He laid his hands at each side of her face. "We can enjoy a few more moments kissing, and depart this place, or ... I leave it to you, my love."

She was at the top of the slope, ready to plunge with no brakes. "Do you want me?" she whispered.

"Silly girl. I ache for you." His hands slipped to the sides of her bosom, and, moving his lips to her ear, he nuzzled it and said, "We're going to Paris, don't forget."

"Sounds lovely," she said.

He looked into her eyes. "It is lovely there. It will be unbearably lovely with you there with me."

He reached to unbutton another pearl. He paused as if asking permission to proceed. She ran her tongue around her lips which were dry as cotton strips. "Please, yes," she said. He unbuttoned another. And another, until the flap crossed downward onto her chest. He tugged the sleeves down her arms and pulled the bodice to her waist. She looked down to see her camisole exposed and his hands moving across her bubs light as a bird in flight.

He paused and laid a palm at the bottom of her throat. "All right?"

She bobbed her head, and, seized with a sense of certainty, wiggled the dress past her hips and let it drop to the floor. He removed his tie and unbuttoned his shirt. Reaching for her, and, covering her with his golden arms, lifted her and laid her on the counterpane. Guiding his fingers to the laces of her camisole, she heard her own purrs of need, feeling the want sucking at her bones. Her eyes never left his face as he tugged out of his trousers and removed her bloomers. He observed her nakedness with a tender smile, but she was nonetheless embarrassed to be in a room, naked, with a man. All her shyness fled, all her thoughts took flight, too, when his arms wrapped around her. His lips met hers, and, all of a sudden, she was moving to their mutual passion, uninhibited, wild with joy, with not a hint of reserve.

CHAPTER FOUR

She awoke, her mind plucking at an alien memory. Her elbow touched something solid. She heard the sound of breathing. Turning her head, she saw that he lay on his back. A rush of carnal knowledge had her scrambling to sit. Graham awoke and his glazed eyes met hers.

"Lordamighty," she cried.

He grunted a laugh, yawned sleep from his relaxed muscles and rose to an elbow. He gazed at her, his fine light hair arching over his brow. His smile scraped the tender edges of her heart, but she couldn't let him get to her just now. She jumped from the bed and quickly felt the breeze sweep across her nudity. She dove back into bed and grabbed the cover. Laughing, he reached for her. One hand clasped her lips to his and the other clutched her body. Before he let her loose, her body began to respond, but she wouldn't, couldn't, and squirmed free of him. She stared at him and he at her, his eyes blurred from the sting of denial. She couldn't hurt him and reached out. With their arms entwined, he kissed her like he'd never let go and soon he had her treading near frenzy again. She drew back and managed to find her voice. "Graham, we must go."

"Hmmmmm." His purr pushed against her longing. "We have not had enough of each other."

She closed her eyes to savor his lovemaking – but no, her eyes flashed open to see daylight seep into the black sky outside the window.

"Your mother," she said. "Neill."

"It's not five o'clock," he said, his voice hoarse. "Teddy won't be up for another hour."

"The maids, the butler."

"They hear nothing, nor do they see, or speak."

Her heart beat unsteadily. His mouth was on hers, and she felt the moist, tense impulsive stroke of his tongue. Again, she pulled away from his face. "It's late. Light is …"

He drew back. "My sweet, gorgeous Cleo. Time means nothing. Don't you know? I'm yours, forever." Smiling, he brushed her hair off her face and gently urged her head back to the pillow. He kissed her until time was out of mind, and primal hunger forgot the break of day.

*****

Graham was wrong. It was five-thirty in the morning when she found herself on the path to the mansion. Graham had gone ahead to scout for Teddy or whoever may be out so early – although he was certain the entire household would be fast asleep. When he showed himself in the fourth floor window of the mansion, where she could see him from the lighthouse, it was safe to make a dash for the house.

The heck with wearing stockings and shoes. She tucked the stockings into her bloomers, and, carrying her shoes, ran up the beach, over dunes to the boardwalk. She reached the tabby garden paths, ouching to the prickle of shells on her bare feet.

She came around a gardenia hedge and almost smacked into Neill carrying a book. Shakespeare's Comedies. He looked at her strangely, then laughed. He pointed to the shoes in her hand. "So you found out it's not good to walk on the beach in those. I thought you brought beach shoes."

Her face felt warm. She pushed a stray strand of hair off her forehead. "I didn't … I hadn't unpacked them."

"I didn't unpack my trunks, either," he said, frowning. "The servants did that. I didn't know you liked early walks on the beach, and in your evening dress."

She reached down and picked at the chiffon skirt. "I soiled it last night so I thought I might as well walk in it. It's quite nice and airy. I'll ask Eurella to launder it, and it will be fine."

"Indeed," he said.

She walked beside him toward the house. "What brings you out so early? I've never known you to be an early riser."

"The entire house is in a tizzy," he said. "You must not have heard. Josie Drake is missing."

"Josie? Missing?"

"Her husband came banging on the door before five. She left a note that she was going to get a divorce to marry Graham."

Funny how a single sentence could paralyze. "Marry Graham?" Neill frowned slightly, most likely at the tightness in her voice. She swallowed. "How very odd."

Neill waved his book. "Heck, Shafer said he knew they were playing around, but he didn't think it would come to this. No one did."

Funny how another sentence could send life whirling out of its orbit. She couldn't speak or swallow.

Neill was saying, "Teddy's in a state. She can't believe he would promise to marry a married woman."

She could not believe it. Her Graham. Her, "*I'm yours, forever,*" Graham.

Neill continued, "There was that stink on the dance floor …"

"What stink?"

"It happened when you were button shining with that oaf, Swinny, when Graham danced with Josie. It was quite embarrassing, actually, the way she rubbed him with her bubs." He swiped his hand across his upper chest as if to define bubs. "I heard her say, 'I'm leaving him.' I think Teddy heard it, too."

She felt raw throughout, like a fish filleted. "What did Graham do?"

"Oh Graham, that suave campaigner, laughed it off. Said something like, 'Don't make a scene, girl,' and made a dash for you. Josie called you a bitch and Teddy looked daggers. Everybody made haste for the door. Quite something. Now Graham and Josie are missing."

"Are you looking for Graham, is that why you're out so early?"

"What's to look for? He's no where to be found. Still, dammit, I can't believe he'd run off with Josie. He might have his fun with her, but, well, let's face it. It's Josie."

"Is that what Graham's like? Has fun with girls?"

Neill's shoulders jerked at the shrill sound of her words. He studied her and laughed it off. "He's a gay old sport, my cousin. I can tell you, he's a real cuddler. But who would have thought he'd cuckold a cousin?"

"Well, if he was – cuddling with Josie – that's what he was doing."

"Still can't quite believe Graham's a double-crosser."

Yes, the gay old sport was a double-crosser. She looked up at the mansion, its polished whiteness luminous in the face of the rising sun, suddenly dissolving like a sandcastle in the miasma of her broken dreams.

Neill stood looking at her, and she must say something. "You two were buddies. I hope Neill …" What could she say? I hope you're not like him. She shook her head remembering Graham's words: *When we brought our show boats home, we palled around while others headed for easy street.*

"Don't worry," Neill said, "I'm not one for the skirts. To quote the master, Graham has a profound respect for chastity – in other people." Neill also read the complete works of Mark Twain.

"I misjudged him," she said.

"If you happen to see old smoothie in this maze of a garden, tell him to hitch with Teddy. I'm going to the sea to read."

If she saw Graham, she would tell him a lot more. She dashed away. There would be no tears today. Her anger was as profound as it had ever been, and she felt an unrestrained revulsion for Graham – and herself.

*****

"Teddy," Graham exclaimed. "What brings you out so early? It's barely six."

Teddy had come into the summerhouse, where he smoked while he waited for Josie. Things had to be straightened out with her. Mitty said that his short note to Josie had been delivered straight into her hands. Graham had dashed it off before going to the lighthouse with that darling, wonderful woman of his dreams. The note asked Josie to meet him at six in the Southerness summerhouse, which was down the beach from the Drake's Bellflower estate. It was Josie's habit to ride out on her horse, Jumper, at six.

This morning Teddy's eyes were round blue stones, and Graham knew trouble brewed.

"Where have you been?" she demanded.

"Whoa. Why the high dudgeon?"

"Where's Josie?"

He took a deep drag on his cigarette and exhaled a stream of smoke toward the octagonal ceiling. "All right, so you know. I asked her to come here to get things straightened out. After last night ..."

"What happened last night?"

"You were there. She acted like a jealous fool."

"You acted like a heartless cad."

"Mother, she's married."

"That didn't keep you from playing around with her."

"It was harmless."

"Don't kid me."

He began to pace. "I am most certainly not."

"Where is she?"

"I don't know. Last night I asked Mitty to have a note delivered to her. He said it was delivered personally. She should be here by now." He looked at his watch. It was fifteen past six.

"She's missing."

He stopped pacing. "Missing?"

"The whole island is buzzing. Where the heck have you been?"

"In my room."

"Mitty says not. Not at five."

"As you are aware, I often sleep in my room in the lighthouse."

"With Josie?"

"No. Josie has never been up there, unless she stole up there unbeknownst to me." He made a complete turn and fingered hair off his forehead. "Josie is an unstable woman. She was mad last night. She'll turn up."

"Do you swear you slept in the lighthouse by yourself?"

"Yes," he said, without hesitating. At times he had outright lied to his mother, but not often because she could tell he was lying. Now he would lie until he was blue in the face to protect Cleo.

"Josie left a note. It said she was divorcing Shafer to marry you."

The magnitude of the statement appalled to the point of ridiculousness. "What?" With a half laugh, he flipped his cigarette on the floor. He glanced at Teddy. The look on her face told him she wasn't joking. "It's a damn lie, Mother."

"Shafer showed it to me."

"It's a damn lie," he repeated, and stomped the cigarette. "Is this lie spreading across the island?"

"I imagine there are few who haven't heard."

"My God!" He whirled, and sped for the screen door.

He heard Teddy on his heels and jumped down the steps. *Must see her. Oh God. Cleo.*

From the porch, Teddy yelled, "Graham. Wait." He heard her clop down the steps. "Graham, you'd better stop this minute."

He halted and turned. "What?"

She ran up and caught his arm. "Where are you going?" Her eyes searched his. "Do you know where she is?"

"I don't give a damn where she is."

"I asked, where are you going?"

"I must get to … Never mind."

A knowing smile parted her lips, and she relaxed her grip. "Ah, Cleo Snow."

"Don't think too far ahead, Mother. I must get to her before she hears ..."

"She knows," Teddy said.

"What?"

"I saw Neill talking to her in the garden. I thought it interesting that she wore her dancing dress, apparently for a dawn walk on the beach."

He mouth was dry, his palms damp, his mind hurtling around the sharp curves of his emotions. "I can't stand here ..."

He turned and ran.

*****

Teddy stood still, looking after him, nodding. Graham was being called to account. He'd braved the war and many amorous women, but you don't get out unscathed as easily as Graham had up to now and not run up against life's big book of reckoning.

At least this time his lie was understandable.

CHAPTER FIVE

"Miss," a man's voice called. She looked to her left. He drew his horse to a prancing halt. It was the man they called Doc.

"Hello," she said, forcing a smile. To ease the devil of a headache, she rubbed a temple that was covered by a headband.

"You shouldn't be walking in this palmetto."

After her encounter with Neill when he'd imparted the news of Graham's terrible betrayal, she'd run to her rooms and spent eons trying to wash him off her body. When that didn't work, she put on a sport dress to walk off the feel of him. Better if he had actually run off with Josie, although she knew that he hadn't. Hearing his calls for her in the great house's halls and in the garden, she'd left the house by the servant door and dodged him by hiding amongst the shrubs and trees until she crossed Oystercatcher Trail.

She moved closer to the man and the horse. "Why not this palmetto?"

"This or any palmetto. Snakes."

She jumped and looked at the ground. Her t-strap brogues stood on rotting leaves and bent wire grass. "Snakes?" She crossed her hands across her scoop-necked bodice. "I've never seen a snake except in a zoo."

"You'll see many on this island if you tromp through the forest and marshes."

"What will they do?"

"Strike and bite. Or just bite."

"Then I'll watch where I tread."

He got off the horse. As he came closer, she felt his eyes trying to soothe her feelings like he knew she'd been swept off her feet by a silver-tongued lothario so fast she didn't have time to consider what kind of man he really was. She pressed her lips. Doc shook his head, and she was struck by his face. Hard-muscled and tanned, it looked stitched together unevenly, robbing him of good looks. His hair was wildly jet black as were his eyes, which were too close to the bridge of his straight nose. The combination of his color and his strength was striking, but the best of him lay in the sultry mobility of his mouth.

"Come on," he said, "I'll show you how closely you've come upon a snake."

He sought out a tree limb and stripped leaves from it, revealing a small fork at the end. He plunged it into the ground and brought it back out. She gasped. A large reptile emerged, wrapped around the limb, flailing its tail.

She hopped away, ramming her rump against a tree trunk. The snake writhed and rattled. "Its tail's like a baby's toy," she said.

"He's not having fun with it," Doc said and wagged the snake off the tree branch into the grass. Before it could uncoil, the man caught its head in the branch fork and held it to the ground.

She asked, "What will happen when you let it go?"

"Get away."

"Let him." Suddenly the rattling stopped. "What's it called?"

"A canebrake rattle snake. It's a viper, poisonous."

"I've heard of rattle snakes."

"Now you've seen one."

She had always wondered something. "What do they feel like? Slimy?"

One half of the man's mouth twisted into an inviting grin. "Would you like to touch it?"

Raising her chin to the challenge, she said, "I think I would."

He shifted his weight, and she stepped closer to the reptile. The rings on the tail of the snake vibrated. "Why's he doing that?"

"He's warning you off."

"He doesn't want me to touch him?"

"He is frightened of you."

She rubbed her fingers together like they itched. "I'd like to touch him."

"You need to get behind me, but move slowly."

Stepping around to approach the man and the serpent from the rear, she flexed her fingers. She contemplated what she was about to do, and, at the same time, the snake went still. She bent and touched the widest part of its back, stroking it with her index finger. "I do believe he likes me."

"Maybe he does. But he doesn't much like me."

"Can they like and dislike?" she asked, flowing her finger over the dry skin.

"I believe they have instincts like that, yes. Every living thing on this planet has intelligence. Why should we humans be the only ones?"

She rose and cocked her head at him. "Nature isn't ignorant."

He lifted the fork off the snake's neck. It stayed motionless for several seconds, flicked its tongue, then glided into the palmettos.

Doc faced her and held out his hand. "I'm Sam."

"Cleo." She brushed her fingers on the palm of his hand. His skin was rough, unlike Graham's silken tan.

She thought about what she'd overheard in the hospital while she bandaged a soldier's arm wounds. The soldier listened to a friend in a wheelchair parked by his bed. The wheelchair soldier said, *"She was just another easy quiff. Criminy, you can't find a good girl with a flashlight and a magnifying glass."* He'd chuckled. *"But that's the way we like 'em, right old sport? All silk and skin and no brains."* She'd taken pains to not look at the speaker, but she knew he watched to see if he'd offended her.

She said to Sam, "I heard they call you Doc."

"Sometimes."

"After Doc Holliday."

"We share a name."

"You're a veterinarian."

"That I am. You're well-versed on the help."

The uncomfortable feeling that he knew a lot about her crept in. "I must get on, I suppose. I'm taking the fresh air."

"Why don't I ride you for a while?"

She looked at the horse with his nose to the ground, biting at the sparse grass. "Together, won't we be heavy on his back?"

His mouth slipped into a smile. "Little girl like you? No ma'am."

He hoisted her onto the back end of the horse. There would be no straddling in her sport chemise, so she sat sidesaddle on the horse's rear end. Doc slipped his left foot into the stirrup, hoisted his body upward and swung his right leg straight across the saddle. He landed softly in the leather seat.

She didn't know where to grab hold. He said, "Tuck those arms around me, and we'll be off." She pushed her arms around his waist just above the belt. "You got to hold tighter than that," he said.

She tucked her elbows into her sides because she didn't want to touch near those sensitive spots so capable of treachery. Although she couldn't see his face, she sensed this amused Doc. *What's the matter with me? My senses are filled with deceit, so maybe I'm imagining Doc's reaction like I imagined Graham being in love with me. Everything I held dear has been peeled back, my protective shell stripped from me. Everybody knows.*

"Relax," Doc said. "Move to the horse's rhythm. It'll be easier on you."

It was sure easier to straddle a horse like a man. She sagged her shoulders in an attitude of relaxation. Two clops later, she slipped backward. The stallion swished his tail and caught her on the chest.

Doc reached back with one hand and pushed her to the middle of the horse's rump. "Not that relaxed," he said over his shoulder, a wry grin playing on his supple mouth. "Try breathing easier and holding onto me tighter."

After a while, her muscles and bones rose and fell with the horse's hind quarters. They reached the oak-canopied lane, and she said, "That gray stuff hanging from the branches look like old men's beards."

"They would be Spanish then," he said. "Spanish moss."

The hundred-year-old oaks made her wish she could reverse time, back before she became a fly boy's quiff. Disconsolate, her head fell forward, and her cheek came to rest against Doc's back. The sweet odor of honest sweat curled into her senses. She thought this is a good man, not a louse like Graham. At the thought of his name, her tendons tightened. She jerked back. The horse mis-stepped. *My fault.*

"Whoa," Doc said, turning a cheek and saying out of the side of his mouth, "You okay?"

"Bad thoughts make bad reflexes," she said.

"I won't bruise, so hold tight."

*****

She asked him to let her down at the edge of the sea, below Southerness.

"I can do that."

He dismounted and held a hand up. She slid easily from the horse's rump.

She smiled up at him. "Thanks, Doc."

"You sit a horse well." The look in his eyes, so close to his straight nose, implied something she didn't quite get.

"I just learned how."

"I saw you riding yesterday."

With Graham. Suddenly her nerves were like a flock of birds twittering on the air. "It was my first time, on a horse."

He smiled like he knew all the mysteries of life. "You got natural balance."

She looked to the sea and breathed in and out twice. For all his spying, how much did Doc see? The hut? The chaise?

"You're troubled," he said.

Was he out last night? The lighthouse?

He repeated, "You're troubled."

"Uh, no ..." Lord in Heaven, don't let him say anything. He's all over this island. I don't want to know what he knows. She raised a hand to ward off her fears and tugged at her headband.

"It's a small island," he said, as if to salve her spirit. "I fly my falcon from Petrel's Bluff. It's up the beach a ways, but you get a good bird's eye view of what's below. That's when I saw you on the little mare."

"And Graham on his horse."

"Graham cuts a fine figure on a horse, too."

She glanced away, at the sand, at the shells embedded in it. She knelt and picked up a round one. "Pretty."

"A perfect sand dollar," he said.

"Is it good luck to find one, like picking up a penny when it's heads up?"

"If you want it to be, then it is."

"I want it to be."

She stood next to him, and they both stared into the deep gray waters of the Atlantic for a disquieting time. He said, "Well, then, I'll be seeing you."

"Wait. I want to ask you something."

The skin around his eyes crinkled. "Sure."

"What's it like to fly a falcon?"

"It's like different things."

"What things?"

"There's a bond between the bird and the falconer. It's as individual as the personalities of both."

"I see."

"If you'd like, and you have time, you can come along when I take Billy out."

She twitched her nose. "A falcon named Billy. I'd like that, but I don't know how long I'll be here."

"I recall Graham saying that you would be staying for ten days."

"My plans have changed."

"Well, if you'd like, look me up."

"Where do you live?"

"Up Plover, a hunting lodge by the stable."

"Okay."

"Can you drive?"

"I know how."

"Miss Teddy is generous with the cars. Borrow one."

"I wouldn't ask. I like to walk."

"I take Billy out around eight in the morning."

"I'll try to make it."

"Fine."

*****

Walking up the dune, to the boardwalk, she didn't look in the direction of the lighthouse. When she got to the garden she wondered if he was still looking for her. Surely he'd stopped the desperate calling. One good thing about the enormous mansion, she could avoid Graham until they left. She would talk to Neill about ending this visit as soon as possible. She'd have to think of a good reason. *Sick, I'll be sick. Hell, I am sick. Doesn't heartsick count?*

She couldn't tell Neill about – oh God – she couldn't bear to think about it. How had she not have seen what Graham was like? So urbane, yet naively persuasive. She massaged the line between her eyes and realized she was crying. Damn my eyes. Damn his treacherous eyes and his treacherous words. For how long would his lying words echo in her mind? She hung her head and cried like a baby. For everything that was and never would be again.

*****

She steeled herself to enter the grand foyer. It was a room seldom used, but she would get to her rooms by the servants' staircase because she didn't want an embarrassing encounter until she prepared herself. At the back of the house were many doors. She'd need to put her ear against the wood to hear if anyone was on the other side. After peering into three closets filled with dishes and linens, she found the narrow staircase. Halfway up, she heard footsteps coming down. Please don't let it be …

Eurella emerged from the second landing. "Why Miss Cleo, you shouldn't be using the servant's stairs. Three's no carpet and you could slip …"

She touched her headband. "I'm a mess." She brushed her dress sleeves. A leaf had been in a fold and floated onto a step.

"Miss Cleo, ever body be looking for you."

"I'm here."

"We got to let Miss Teddy know. She's running aroun' worried."

"I like to walk in the fresh air."

"Walkin's fine, miss."

"Eurella?"

"Yes, miss?"

"Have they found Mrs. Drake?"

"Not that I'm knowin', miss."

A fearful instinct sunk into her bone marrow and turned her blood cold.

*****

She rapped on Neill's door, just two away from hers. She turned away just as the door opened.

"Bearcat, where in criminy have you been?"

"Walking."

"Everyone's in a tizzy," he said, standing back and opening the door wider. "Do Teddy and Graham know you're back from your walk?"

"No, I haven't seen anyone but Eurella. She'll tell them. We need to talk."

His mouth puckered as if in wonder. "Okay. Come in, sit, we'll palaver."

Neill's suite was masculine, while hers was frilly, pinkish and nearly childish. She envied the library shelves in here, the brown leather chairs and ottomans, cigarette stands and brass lamps. "Got a cigarette?" she asked.

"I'll have a butt with you. My nerves are all in. Everyone's beating their gums about Graham and Josie."

"That's what I wanted to talk to you about." She took the proffered cigarette and let him light it. "I think we should leave."

"Leave?" He lit his own and sat. "What's eating you?"

"Besides the scandal, I'm getting ill. It's the bugs, and I saw a snake today. This place stinks."

"Well, Bearcat, I can't think what I'd say to Graham and his mother."

"That I'm ill."

"This thing with Josie ..." He flicked the ash from his cigarette into an ashtray. "Graham bawled me out for telling you more than I should have. Anyone can tell he thinks you're a doll."

She swallowed; he'd stirred up the hurt, the treachery. "I was somewhat shocked – Graham and a married woman ..."

"Graham says it's all balled up and he doesn't know from nothing. She was a pushover, but not for him."

A pushover, like me. "Anybody have any notion where she could be?"

"She hasn't left the island that anyone saw. Not by the ferry anyway. They're searching high and low."

Not everyone. Not Doc. Why hadn't she and Doc talked about Josephine Drake?

Neill was saying, "There's a reward. That's got the villagers high-stepping through the forest."

"I was thinking she could have gone on the steamboat to Port Maria." She said this for something to say. She had no idea where she could have gone or on what.

"The steamboat left late this morning with the Thompsons on it. People at the dock are certain only the Thompsons boarded."

"Other boats?"

"Accounted for. Shrimpers were out early. Josie wouldn't be on a shrimper. A supply boat came in with ice and perishables. It unloaded and left at noon. The coal and kerosene boat came in after that. I say, Bearcat, you look absolutely grummy."

"Why should I be depressed?"

"I think this is upsetting you more than you let on. I'm your cousin, don't you know, and I know you can keep your feelings tight."

She put her finger and her thumb together in a circle, something she'd seen Neill do often. "I'm a-OK."

"I noticed you and Graham got on rather well at dinner and on the dance floor."

She waved a hand, affecting boredom by glancing at the book shelves. "He's amusing, that's all."

He didn't speak until she looked at him again. He said, "Graham dashed like a greyhound all over the place looking for you."

"He needs to be looking for Mrs. Drake."

"Well, he is, but he's rather nervy about finding you."

"I'm not lost."

He rose. "We're meeting in the Blue drawing room for tea." He looked her over. "Once you shake the leaves from your hair and your get-up, you'll look like the cat's meow."

"I won't be taking tea," she said, standing and picking at her hair. "I'm ill. Impart my concern about Mrs. Drake's disappearance and sincere hope that she returns soon." She gathered her skirt like a heroine in a hurry. "Now, I shall take to my bed."

"Oh glory, Cleo, so positively melodramatic."

She put the back of her hand to her headband and raised her chin. "Melodrama suits me now."

"That's baloney, Bearcat, not like you." He picked up his cigarettes and matches.

Bearcat. A split second of outrage flamed through her. *What kind of a bearcat are you, anyway? A sniveling one?*

"Wait a minute," she said, hurrying for the door.

"What's up?" Neill asked, turning off a lamp.

"I've changed my mind."

"Ducky."

"I don't feel well, but I can't bear the thought of being cooped up in a room, even if it is quite nice."

"Now you're on the trolley. I'll hang around until you change."

"Back in a jiffy."

The burgundy satin that buttoned at the neck with a paler satin tie would do nicely. It was a good color with her black mesh bag. She finger-waved her hair until it was Marcel perfect. Lining her eyes, she blurred the margins over her eyelids. She powdered her face ivory, and then colored her lips burgundy. When finished, she'd created a perfect Cupid's bow.

She returned to Neill's rooms.

"You're the elephant's eyebrows," Neill said, giving her his arm.

"Just because I don't feel good, doesn't mean I can't look good."

"Attagirl."

CHAPTER SIX

She entered the drawing room head elevated as if the gathering waited for her entrance with tingling anticipation. The shock on Graham's face gave her a mean measure of satisfaction, but it evidently made Neill uneasy. His arm twitched as they stepped to the mantle where Graham stood, hands jammed into his pockets. His mouth moved without sound, like a fish caught in a net.

Teddy came up. "My dear girl, we've been apprehensive."

She smiled at Teddy. "Terribly sorry. I didn't mean to worry you."

"With one woman missing, the thought of another was terrifying."

Cleo laughed, sounding to herself like paper being wadded up. "Neill must not have heard me say I was going for a walk and would be on the lookout for Mrs. Drake." She hoped Neill wouldn't speak up against the lie, and, mercifully, he shook his head.

She looked at Graham. "Any idea where Mrs. Drake might be?"

She heard Teddy catch a quick breath. Graham's Adam's apple bobbed when he swallowed. "No."

Teddy said, "Shafer's gone home to check if she's come back." She moved to a blue flowered arm chair. "Let's sit. Mitty's bringing in tea."

Cleo walked with Neill to the sofa. Graham tried to cut between them, and she elbowed him aside. "The sofa clashes with my dress. I'll sit in the cream chair."

Teddy poured tea into cups. "Where did you walk, Cleo?"

Cleo took the cup and saucer, firming her hands so the china wouldn't rattle. "The forest."

"She saw a snake," Neill said.

"To be expected," Teddy said. "We're quite used to them. Mostly they slither away, but you have to be careful in the roses, too."

From the corner of her eye, she noticed Graham's crossed leg. It moved erratically, first jiggling, then swinging in nervous rhythm.

"When does the ferry leave in the morning?" Cleo asked.

Graham shot up on the sofa seat. "Why?"

"I think … Neill and I have talked, and I believe we should cut our visit short."

Graham and Teddy protested at once. Teddy's voice overpowered his. "No need because of this. We quite enjoy you two. Don't change your plans. We've waited for months." She set her tea cup on the saucer and addressed Cleo, "Later, we'll talk."

"Yes," Graham said, his eyes darting to her face. "You have to know, there's no truth …"

Teddy interrupted. "Graham, we'll let the matter lie for now."

In the tense interval, Mitty appeared with Shafer, who came into the room staggering. "Nothing yet." He leaned against a chest and flapped his arms. "Damn woman."

Graham stood. "Think man, where would she go off to?"

Cleo knew he was asking this for her benefit. Surely they'd been over this time and again.

Shafer's gaze had trouble finding a target. "Don't know, I tell you."

"Could she be hiding to get even?" Teddy asked.

"Why?" Shafer said, waving his arms.

"You two were angry last night."

He took a handkerchief from his pants pocket and blew his red nose. He looked at Graham. "She left that damnable note."

Graham's eyes shifted, filling with guilt or fear or something equally appalling. He shook his head. Despite her resolve, the memories flooded in, his flesh on hers.

Graham said, "You know that would never happen. You're just saying that, Shay. She made things up."

Shafer moved to a paisley chair and fell backward on the cushions. His shoes smacked on the floor. "She liked to flirt, make me jealous."

Graham looked at Cleo like that explained everything.

Shafer shook his head. "She didn't mean things most times. But you, Graham, oh cousin, she had a thing for you." His glance had trouble finding Teddy. "You saw it, didn't you, Aunt Teddy?"

Teddy twitched her lips like she could say a lot, but just said, "Josie was Josie."

"But by God," Shafer said, thudding his fist on the arm of the chair, "I didn't think my own cousin would mousetrap her."

"I did no such thing," Graham snapped.

"Shafer," Teddy said, her voice hard as marbles, "we've had this out this morning."

Shafer pushed himself forward and tried to stand. "I got something to do."

Teddy said, "You go on home." She turned to Mitty at the door. "Get Barnabas here to take …"

"Too depressing," Shafer said. "Going to the bluff. Maybe she fell over …"

"You said she packed clothes," Teddy said.

"I said that?"

"What was Mrs. Drake wearing?" Cleo asked.

Everyone in the room looked at her.

"Wearing?" Shafer said.

"When you last saw her."

"Her fancy gown, she wore last night, here."

"What time?"

He flipped a hand. "Ten?"

"What did you do when you got home?"

"A drink … gin rickeys …"

"Only one?"

"Two, three?" He shrugged.

"And then?"

Shafer said, "Up to my eyeballs … so turned in."

"And Mrs. Drake?"

"Headache. Always headaches."

"She go upstairs with you?"

Graham made an impatient sound, and she flashed a hard look his way.

"Never does go up when I do. She's … night owl."

"Were the servants asleep?"

"My man Barnabas saw me up. Prepped me … hic … rolled me in the hay."

"Did Josie have a personal maid?"

"Off yesterday."

"What does the maid do when she's off?"

"Village." He flung his arms up. "This gets nowhere."

"Perhaps the authorities should be called in," Cleo said.

Graham's mouth opened and his eyes looked like he couldn't believe what she said.

She looked at Graham, "That's normally what happens when someone goes missing. Maybe Shafer's right and Josie's lying at the bottom of a bluff."

Teddy, her lips pressed tight, stood. "Too early for the authorities. Josie may have gone somewhere to cool off. She was pretty hot last night."

"Not with me," Shafer said. "Sweet. Ask Barnabas."

Teddy sighed. "She's excitable."

Shafer's head bobbed up and down. "Be just like her, stay away, make sure people worry."

Cleo said, "Yet she wrote a note."

The silence in the room was as loud as if everyone started shouting.

"Nonsense," Shafer said. "Graham," – his hand wavered in Graham's direction – "my favorite cousin wouldn't inveigle my wife away from me, now would you, old bean?"

Cleo itched to see the note, but asking to would be more out of bounds than she'd gone already.

"I say, where's the hooch?" Shafer said, stumbling to his feet. "Nerves shot."

Graham went to a cabinet in the corner and took out a bottle of whiskey. He opened another cabinet and turned to the group. "Anyone else want a snort?"

"I'll have one," Neill said, and addressed her. "Bearcat?"

"A small one," she said.

Teddy said, "Put the bottle and glasses on the marble table. We can pour for ourselves."

She moved toward the table where Shafer was trying to stay on his feet. Neill went to look out the window.

Graham closed in on her. "Cleo?" His voice broke like it must have when he turned thirteen.

Her gaze skimmed his face, and then looked casually at her painted fingernails like they were of overriding interest.

"We have to talk," he said.

Fragments of her emotions spun like they'd dropped on a roulette wheel. They clicked on pride and she stared at him. "Whatever for?" She walked toward the marble table.

"Listen, everyone," Teddy said. "Here's what I propose."

Graham's forearm touched hers, a tender brushing movement. "We're all ears," he said.

"I've asked Mitty to prepare a buffet supper of soups and sandwiches. We should mount another search before we lose the light.

Half of us will go to the south end of the island, and the other to the north end."

"Wonderful idea," Graham said. "Neill, Cleo and I will take the south end. The docks."

"I wasn't including Cleo," Teddy said.

Resentment flashed through Cleo, and she said, "Why not? You wanted us to stay."

Teddy's eyebrows went up. "Okay. Shafer and I will take the north end – the village."

*****

Fredik was the largest mass of human muscle she'd ever encountered. Muscle and hair. It was thick on his arms, at the throat of his open shirt.

Teddy said, "This is Cleo. She's one of us."

"Pleased, Miss Cleo," he said, looking at his knees, his accent thick and guttural.

"Pleased, too, Mr. Fredik."

His lip twitched a fraction. He wore a tan shirt and dark brown trousers that were impeccably pressed. His shoes were stout but shone like obsidian. Dark of skin, hair and wiry goatee, he looked like a villain in the films. She looked for scars where his skin had to be stitched to keep his face in place. His eyes, which dodged hers, refracted light as if he didn't want her to see beyond the lashes.

"We'll tour the garages, Fredik," Teddy said. "Get Miss Cleo acquainted." She set the pace to the long, low building. Neill walked with Teddy, and Graham fell in step with Cleo. Fredik and Shafer brought up the rear. She felt Graham studying her profile, but he didn't speak. Inside the converted stable, there were six, seven, eight different vehicles, not including Neill's Rolls, which was parked on the far side, in a wider spot.

Teddy said, "All Fords down here. We keep Henry and his family in skivvies. Truth is, Fords are tough. In our terrain, we need tough cars and trucks. Cleo, you see that little pick-up over there?" Cleo nodded. It looked like a two-seater with an open cargo area instead of a trunk. "We have several on the place."

Cleo was intrigued by two vehicles, identical except one was black and the other had a wooden case. "What are those that look like boxes on wheels?"

"Hucksters. Workhorses," Teddy said. "I'll take Woody, Fredik."

"Yes, ma'am," he said, and got into the wooden Huckster and turned the engine.

Cleo spied a long vehicle with three rows of benches behind the driver's seat. "Is it a bus?"

It's called a Depot Hack," Teddy said. "Edgar's favorite. In case you don't know, he's my late husband. The Hack doesn't get used much. Sentimental." She looked at Fredik, who sat behind the wheel of the idling Woody. "You might take the Hack for a spin. See the tires are proper."

"Yes, ma'am," Fredek said. He drove the Huckster out of the garage and got out. Shafer got into the passenger side.

Teddy scooted under the wheel. "Well, I'm off, kiddle-dee-dees." She toodled her fingers.

Cleo hoped they'd take the Touring Car. William had one, and he'd taught her to drive it. But Graham looked at Fredik, "We'll take the Single Door."

"Fine, Mr. Graham."

Although it was a cute car, with its oval window in the back, it was an odd duck. The single door was centered between the front compartment and the back. Graham had to enter the car in the rear passenger compartment and cram himself into the front seat. Neill occupied the passenger front seat and Cleo sat in the back, directly behind Neill. It wasn't the way Graham wanted it, but she had insisted on the back seat.

At Oystercatcher Trail, Teddy turned the Huckster north. Graham turned south. He said, "Teddy gets along with the natives quite well, and she'll keep Shafer quiet. Lord, the man's about to jump out of his bags."

"Can't blame the ol' blighter," Neill said. "Quite a thing."

Graham angled the side of his head toward Cleo. "I've known Josie as long as Shafer has. Always was a scatterbrain. She'll turn up in her own time, but Teddy has the right idea. Can't sit around and wait to go nuts."

They rode in silence, past a sprawling stone lodge, through pines and live oaks and came to a marsh, which cut nearly to the sea. The crisp scent of brine reminded her of the night at the lighthouse, the big pearl moon and the stardust on the sea. *Stop it.* "How big is this island?" she asked.

"Thirteen long, four wide," Graham said.

"A lot of hiding places," Neill said.

"Half the island is marsh, the Sago Sound side," Graham said. "The Sago River cuts through the Great Marsh on the village end of the island, which is where she'd be hiding. There's some empty stone cottages and God knows how many old barns and sheds."

"If she's hiding," Cleo said.

"Of course, she's hiding," Neill said, turning to look at her.

"I didn't know you knew her so well," Cleo said.

"What else could have happened?" Neill asked.

"I hate to think," Cleo said.

"Of what?"

"Human nature."

Graham's laughter rang hollow. "Meaning?"

"Jealousy and rage. Retribution and silencing."

"You've seen too many Elsie Ferguson movies," Neill said.

"I'm not thinking of a movie."

"But you did see *The Avalanche*, you told me so."

"And *Counterfeit*, but so what?"

"Drama, my dear Bearcat. Real people are boring."

"I don't think Josie was boring, do you Graham?"

Graham braked the car. They had arrived at the docks. He turned in his seat. "No, Josie wasn't boring. She was a nice girl who liked to flirt. She married my cousin. The end. Movie over." He stared like he was trying to drill that into her thick skull.

She tossed her head, tossing him off. He climbed between the seats and sat beside her. "Wave a white flag?"

"Wave whatever you want. Let's get out of here."

CHAPTER SEVEN

"Mr. Graham," the colored man said, shaking his head, "we ain't seen nothing of Miss Josie."

"What boats have left here?" Graham asked.

"Jes the steamboat ferry this'er mornin'. Shrimpers in the sound."

"Have you asked around? Anyone know of any boats leaving in the night?"

"Naw, sir. Nobody credits it."

Cleo surveyed the boats bobbing in their slips. One was a handsome wood boat with two cockpits, one in back of the other, covered with canvas. *Steeler* was pained on the side. "Whose boat is that?"

"The family's," Graham said. "Our runabout, but anyone on the island who wants to borrow it can. She's a rip-roarer on the sound and in the river running through Great Marsh."

"She's fast." Neill assured her. "More than twenty-five mph."

"How far across the sound to Port Maria?" she asked.

"The direct way, which you wouldn't do if you're in your right mind, is three miles straight across," Graham said. "But if you don't want to snag your boat on a sand bar and keep in the channel, you have to travel at an angle northward, and that's seven miles."

She looked south, mindful of the wind ruffling the waves in her hair. "It wouldn't take long."

Graham let a beat or two go by before he said, "No one would take out across the sound at night but an expert."

"Like you?"

"What does that mean?" His voice went flat, a balloon deflating.

"Could Josie pilot a boat?"

He pushed his hair back. "Sure. We all can. You can. Learn the channel markers and it's a snap."

"What are you thinking, Bearcat?" Neill asked.

"Somebody could have taken Josie across in the night."

"Why would they?"

She looked at Graham. "To get rid of her."

Graham's face lost color.

Neill said, "Cleo, you're daft."

Graham grabbed her arm and pulled her away. "It didn't happen, and you know it!"

"I didn't say you did that," she said, jerking her arm back. "Shafer could have."

"Why?"

"She made a fool of him."

"He was used to it, dammit, Cleo. She always tried to make him jealous."

"She succeeded – maybe too well."

He scowled. "Shafer's easy going. Let's move along and talk to people. If anyone was out last night, somebody saw them."

She looked over the sound, at a curve near the shore that made an inlet. A boat bobbed in the water. It had two masts. "Who's sailboat?" she asked.

Graham ruffled his hand through his hair, maybe in an effort to cool down. "That's *Monongahela*."

The long, low boat pitched merrily in the dark waves. "How do you get to it?"

"The skiff," he said and walked ten yards down the wood dock. He stopped short. "What the …?" He looked around. "Where the hell is it?" He spun around and took off in an all-out run toward the colored man. She and Neill hurried after him.

Halting, Graham asked the man, "Where's the skiff?"

The man shrugged. "She be here this morning early."

"She's not now."

Graham and the colored man loped to the end of the boardwalk, she and Neill hurrying along, too. Graham stopped so suddenly she almost bumped him. He clamped his hands on his hips. "Damn, would you look at that?"

A small empty boat rocked sideways toward a rock outcropping on the shore.

Graham turned to the colored man. "Was she tied good and proper?"

"I didn't see she wasn't."

Cleo asked, "Has anyone checked the sailboat for Josie?"

Graham rounded on her. "She's not on the damn sloop, for the love of Mike."

"How do you know?"

"I …" He tossed his hands up and muttered something not meant to be heard.

"Do the Drakes have a boat?" she asked.

Graham pointed to a row of docks, farther over, extending into the sound. "Shafer slips it over there. Doesn't go out much. Can't afford the gas."

"Can't afford gas?" she said. "I thought everybody here was rich as Croesus."

"The Drakes were in liquor. Prohibition wiped them out." Graham rubbed his forehead like a troubled man. "I got to get a motor boat after that skiff before it rams the rocks and gets Teddy's pantaloons in a wad." He looked at Cleo. "You coming?"

"I think I'll stay on dry land."

"I'm coming," Neill said.

The two men struck off leaving her to wander the boardwalk. There were two small sloops in slips: the Clementine and the Georgian. Tied alongside the dock were fishing boats of differing shapes and sizes, most needing paint. She looked over to see Graham and Neill get into a motor launch. Graham pulled away from the dock. Why wouldn't Graham think Josie was on the sloop? She studied the superstructures on the sailboat's deck. She made out the windows of the long cabin.

A loud yell brought her mind back to the dock. Another yell echoed across the water. She saw a young boy on the boardwalk pulling a fish out of the water. Walking toward him, she watched as he took the fish off the hook. "That's a big one," she said.

"Pompano," the colored boy said, holding the fish for her inspection.

"You catch a lot here?"

"And o're there," he said, pointing toward the end of the dock where they'd spied the skiff.

"A skiff got loose," she said.

"Heared," he said.

"Must not have been tied good," she said.

"Weren't."

"How do you know."

He gave a short shrug. "Saw."

"It was loose in its slip?"

"Yes um."

"Somebody's going to get in trouble. Whoever used it last."

"Miss Teddy."

"Well, since the boat belongs to Miss Teddy, she won't be getting herself in trouble, now will she?"

"Guessin' not."

"Lucky the skiff didn't get loose last night."

"Weren't loose las night."

"Miss Teddy went to the sailboat this morning?"

"Yes um."

"Early?"

"Yes um."

"You fish early, don't you?"

"'Fore dawn."

"You ever ride on that sailboat?"

"When Miss Teddy asks. I helps."

"Miss Teddy is getting ready to go north. Guess she's taking stuff to the boat."

"Trunks."

"Trunks?"

"She be needin' my Daddy's help."

"Where is your daddy?"

"Shrimpin'."

"Shafer could help her."

"Yes um."

"Did he?"

"No um. Mr. Fredik."

*****

As far as she could see, the tabby, three-story inn was the largest building on this end of the island. A billboard stretched across to the ends of the pitch roof. On the sign, a gray dolphin splashed in painted droplets of water. Beneath the mammal was the name of the place: The Dolphin Inn

Inside, the innkeeper greeted and ushered her into the lounge. He offered and served lemonade. "Don't have much custom this time of year," he said. His thin mustache curled toward his cheeks and his hair was slicked and parted in the middle. "The season's ending, but it being Prohibition don't use this room much."

"Miss Teddy's preparing to leave," she said, and sipped from the straw. She picked a vanilla shortbread from a plate and bit into it.

"Yes ma'am. She don't mind the bugs and the heat so much. Only goes north for sailboat races and weddings, if she can't help it."

"Seems like Graham would go, too," she said, popping the last of the cookie into her mouth and realizing how hungry she'd become.

He laughed. "Not likely. The girl getting married, she had her heart set on Graham, said they had an understanding, but Graham, well, he's a strapping young man. Got a good many days ahead of him afore he needs to be thinking of settling down."

The cookie stuck in her throat. How much more was she going to have to swallow? "Did he stand her up at the altar?"

"Nothing like that," he said, refilling her glass and adding another shortbread to the plate. "The girl, name of Lila, was down here twice with her mama. Nice looking thing, but I could see it was no-go with him. You can tell, these young men, what catches their fancy."

She leaned forward. "I may be out of line here, but I heard Mrs. Drake caught his fancy."

Cautious lines creased his brow, and he methodically swiped a towel over the mahogany bar. "Makes you wonder, doesn't it? A man like that, girls going crazy over him. Some others, nobody pays attention to."

"Where do you think Mrs. Drake went?"

"No telling. Not here, although twice she came here to stay a few days." He raised his head, his expressing telling.

"She and Mr. Drake have a fight?"

"Didn't ask, but she was crying mighty hard both times."

"Could she have come here and gone up to a room without you knowing?"

"No." He waved a hand at the dogs near her stool. "The dogs, you see. But I checked everywhere when I got word this morning. She's not on this end of the island, you can be sure of that."

"We passed by a lodge about a mile back. I was wondering …"

"No cause to wonder about hunting lodges. Miss Josie won't be staying rustic, if you get what I mean."

"I hardly know her."

"She's a fancy lady."

"One that likes nice things like pearls and fashionable dresses."

"Har, har. None of those fancies at that lodge."

*****

On the ride back to Southerness, Graham drove past the sprawling stone lodge. "Who owns the lodge?" Cleo asked.

"It's Swinny's lodge," Graham said.

"It's quite imposing," she said.

"Swinny invites his pals to come here in the winter to shoot duck and quail and deer, anything that roams this island, actually. The great white hunter."

"Anybody check the lodge?"

"What? For Josie?"

"Isn't that our quest?"

"She wouldn't set foot in a lodge where animal heads hang on the walls," Graham said.

"Squeamish, is she?"

He didn't answer that. He knew a lot about Josie. He said, "Old Swinny, he stays longer and longer each year. Be here year round soon."

*****

The buffet was elaborate with chowders and sandwiches and cakes and cobblers. Linith and Eagan were served in a playroom that existed somewhere in the interior. Cleo put roast beef on a slice of bread and took the plate to the verandah. A mosquito tent had been erected and five places were set at a round table. She sat between Teddy and Neill, across from Shafer and Graham. Shafer was what she came to know as "his usual self" – that being drunk.

They ate in silence until Shafer said, "She's not here. She's gone off island."

"Perhaps," Teddy said. "But how?"

Shafer stared at Graham.

Graham looked at Cleo, his eyes dull and miserable. "Maybe in the morning at high tide we should go for the sheriff. Things are getting sticky-wicket, and I don't much like it."

"I didn't say it's all your fault," Shafer whined. "Josie's culpable … hic."

"You didn't have to," Graham snarled. His good nature gone, he looked haggard.

"Gentlemen," Teddy said.

Graham said, "Cleo, Neill and I will take the runabout. While we're there, we'll lunch at the King's Inn. So far, our guests have been shortchanged."

"There's room in the damn boat for me," Shafer said.

"No there's not," Teddy said. "I'm going. I need some things from Seymour's Grocery."

Shafer huffed, "If I'm right, she could be staying at the goddamn King's Inn."

"If she wants to be found, she goddamn well might be," Graham said.

"Gentlemen, your language, at the table," Teddy said.

CHAPTER EIGHT

Cleo didn't know when high tide was and cared less. Dressed in riding clothes, she slipped from the house and walked the mile to the stable. It was not quite eight, and she didn't see Doc. When she entered the barn, horses whinnied softly. She stuck her head in the tack room. Empty. Outside again, she walked past the barn to a road that led to a lodge half the size of Swinney's, but as handsome. She knocked on the door.

"Minute," she heard him say.

When he opened the door, she noticed his guardedness, which probably was as much a part of him as his crooked smile and lean body.

"I said I'd try to come," she said. "I tried, and I'm here."

"Come on in," he said.

She looked around the low-ceiling room that smelled of sweet musk and wood smoke. A man's home. A walk-in stone fireplace took up most of the back wall. A kettle hung from an iron arm above dead coals. Doc went to an oak table in the center of the room. He said, "I'm just finishing my coffee."

She saw a clean cup sitting by a chair and biscuits, butter and jam in the center of the round table. "You knew I'd come."

"I knew you wanted to," he said, and picked up his white cup. His hand and fingers were fine-boned, like a doctor's. He went to a wooden counter by the wash sink and lifted the nickel percolator. "I believe you do what you want."

"Mother always called me stubborn," she said, thinking it was a dumb thing to say. She arranged herself in the chair and folded her hands on the table.

"Sugar, cream?"

"Both, if you have them." *Nut*, he wouldn't offer if he didn't.

He poured coffee and brought a small cream jug and a matching sugar bowl with a little spoon in it to the table. "I usually take Billy out for as long as he wants, but this morning I got a sick calf, so we'll let him show off for a bit. Then I have to come back and tend to her." He sat and stirred cream into his coffee.

"That's fine," she said, spooning sugar. "I was going to tell you that I can't stay long because we're supposed to go to Port Maria." His eyebrows rose in a question. "It's about Josie."

The up-and-down motion of his head was so slight she wondered what it meant. She said, "You know she's missing."

"I'd have to be deaf, dumb and blind not to."

She sipped the strong brew and considered his seeming unconcern. "I guess the family has asked you the usual questions like …"

"Where she is?"

"Un-huh."

"Miss Teddy came and told me about it."

"Do you have any ideas?"

"Not a one."

"Well …"

"So, let's finish up here and go meet Billy."

"Can't wait." She couldn't feel more excited if she were meeting a movie star.

They walked to the stable. He said, "Birds, same as you and me, have personalities, but peregrines are higher strung. I have to say Billy might take a dislike to you. Don't think he will, but he doesn't like everybody."

Why did the image of Josie come into her head? "What would he do?"

"Well, he'll tell me – and you – by making a particular sound like kek-kek-kek. That's the sound peregrine parents make when someone threatens their nest. They kek when they're nervous, and they give you a short kek as a greeting. Be around long enough and you can tell the difference in their keks." He grinned slightly.

She smiled and looked up at him. Such a tall man. "What should I do?"

"If he's nervous and carries on, we'll give him a second chance. We'll go outside and come back in."

"Is he inside?"

"Yes. He has his own house, called a mews. Here we are."

A square wood-slatted house the size of a room had been built three feet from the barn. Doc led her around to the east side of the house, which had solid walls and a door with a lock. Doc explained, "Billy is shielded from the sunrise by this wall and the sunset by the barn. He likes light, but not sunshine."

He fiddled with the padlock, which came loose, then led her inside. There were shelves and rings and lines where a lot of leather appliances rested. On one shelf was a row of peculiar looking leather bulges with knots and one had a plume on top.

He'd obviously noticed her noticing, and said, "Hoods. Part of the bird's furniture. Goes over the eyes."

"What if a bird's claustrophobic? I never could use sleeping masks over my eyes."

"It soothes the bird. Everything is visual to him, so hood him, and he isn't scared anymore."

"Oh …"

"I usually free-loft Billy because he's a naturally calm raptor, but this morning, seeing he's having a visitor, I tethered and hooded him."

"What's free-loft?"

"Let him fly free in his mews. You'll see the perches."

"I'd rather free-loft than be tethered."

He pointed to large gloves and leather straps. "These are gauntlets and jesses." He took up a gauntlet and a strap and opened the door. He called in, "Billy boy, I'm bringing a pretty lady to see you."

She saw the falcon and drew in a soundless breath. He was perched on a round beautiful exotic drum, the kind she'd seen in rumba bands. "He's gorgeous," she whispered.

"He is that," Doc said.

She giggled. "Looks like he's wearing pantaloons."

"That's what his leg feathers are called."

"If he didn't have that thing on his head, what would he be doing?"

"Sizing you up with his considerable vision."

"Can I see his eyes?" She looked up at Doc. "He hasn't made any sounds so far."

"We'll see." He went to the block and unhooked the leash. He touched the glove to Billy's talons, and Billy stepped onto his fist. He raised up, and Billy spread his wings and danced from talons to talons before settling on the gauntlet. Doc said, "Billy's real good about riding my gauntlet without a jess, but things are a little different this morning, so we'll keep him hooded and jessed. He won't mind." He turned to her and in that instant she felt like bowing down to this tall lanky man with the crooked smile, wearing a beautiful creature on his arm. He could be a pagan god, the kind she'd seen in magazines about Egypt.

He asked, "You feel like walking a little bit, or we can get in the Huckster. Billy likes to ride."

"Me, too, after the walk here." She stuck out a shoe. "Not exactly for hiking."

"Okay, then, we'll ride."

In the back of the Huckster, another drum sat, and Doc tethered Billy to it with a very short leash. He said, "When I ride Billy, I always hood and tie him up short because he gets excited to be on the hunt."

He started the truck and turned on Plover's Lane. She asked, "Would Billy fly away?"

"He's been gone longer than he should sometimes, but he comes back. Some day if some girl falcon catches his fancy, he might not."

He turned onto Oystercatcher. "How old is Billy?"

"Almost two. Time for mating."

Breeding season, time for mating. Guess when you're in the wild, you think of those things. She said, "Maybe he'll bring his girlfriend home?"

"No, she'll pick some nice nest on a cliff and lure him into it."

She studied his profile to see if he was joking. "Would that really happen?"

"He's got an independent spirit, but I'd guess not. What I'd like to do is find a female before her first moult, which means she's just started hunting, which is how I found Billy, and train her, then let them form a breeding pair. Falcons mate for life, but you see, around here, they require a lot of territory so there aren't a lot of females flying around out there just waiting to capture ol' Billy's heart."

Capturing a heart was one thing. After it's broken, how do you heal it?

They rode without speaking until they reached the cliffs. He braked and said, "On down the road, couple of miles, at the point, is the village. Visit it before you leave. The women make seashell jewelry and the men weave baskets that are so tight they can carry water."

"If I can," she said. "Because of Josie, I might not stay as long as planned."

He hunched his shoulders up and down. "No need to rush off."

He got Billy out of the truck and jessed him by braiding leather straps onto two round bands on Billy's legs. Billy perched like he was on King Tut's arm, and they walked up the cliff path. Doc stopped on the promontory. "Now what we're going to do is take off Billy's hood."

She held up both hands, with crossed index fingers, and he reached around the back of Billy's neck to loosen the leather straps. He grasped the knot on top of the hooded eyeholes and pulled. Billy jerked his head back and spread his wings, fanning them. His round black eyes bore into hers. Her fingers moved tighter, but she found herself grinning at one of the most magnificent creatures she'd ever beheld. Billy's head cocked and he looked at Doc.

"What's he saying?" she whispered.

"I think he's fine by you."

Billy began to dance on Doc's arm. "He's ready to fly."

He pulled the knots on the jesses, tossed his fist and Billy took to the sky. He circled above them, came low over her, and then shot away into a flock of birds skimming over the sea.

"Watch this," Doc said.

Billy emerged from the flock, shooting straight upward until she thought she would lose sight of him. He looped in the air and then folded his wings and dove toward the flock of birds. "He's going for a young noddy," Doc said.

"Noddy?" she said, watching the spectacular speed Billy gained as he bammed into the squawking flock. Feathers scattered from a burst body. Billy turned and swooped to catch the plunging, mortally wounded bird.

Doc explained, "Noddy's are terns, seabirds. He's partial to noddy's and pigeons."

All of a sudden, Billy flew at eye level and dropped his prey on the ground. He landed and stuck his beak in the bird's neck. "Going for the kill," Doc said.

She shuddered.

"It's their instinct to bite the neck until it's dead."

Billy flew up to the gauntlet. "Now here's where it gets interesting," Doc said. "He's asking me what he should do with the kill. Of course, he wants to pluck it and eat it, but he hunts for me, too. I'm going to tell him he can eat it. Like I said, I got to tend a sick calf. This afternoon, we'll go out and he'll get ten, twelve doves for my supper."

"Can I come, too?"

"I think Billy likes showing off for you, so I may get fifteen doves," he said, grinning.

Doc made a series of low whistles, Billy dropped to the ground and ripped into the dead bird that had been out for a morning's fly, when swoop, comes a cold killer out of the sky.

Doc walked away, to a stone that looked like it had been molded to a human's backside and motioned for her to sit. "He'll be about ten minutes." He reached into his pocket and removed a pack of cigarettes. "Have one?" he asked.

"Think I will," she said. "You two have taken my breath away."

He held up a cigarette. "This won't get it back for you."

"I don't smoke a lot. Mother doesn't approve."

"I try not to."

"Didn't Doc Holliday die from smoking?"

"Consumption."

"Doesn't that come from smoking?"

"No, cancer does."

"I thought …"

"Tuberculosis is caused by bacterial spread. His mama had it, too."

"You won't get it?"

"It's not hereditary."

"Is there a cure?"

"Doc went out west to a dry climate for the cure. He didn't take to his bed like he should have. He wasn't going to die lying down. It's pretty much a death sentence when you get it."

"Your family tell stories about Doc?"

"Not so much anymore."

"What was he really like?"

He looked over at Billy holding down his prey's wing while he ripped at its innards. "He was a gentleman and a scholar. What happened out west? No one really knows. We were, are, a political family, and politics doesn't keep one gentle."

"What did your father do?"

"He owned a farm, he was a mayor, he ran for the state senate and lost, he had a general store, he was a hell-fire preacher and could handle a gun. Like Doc, my daddy had a temper." He snorted. "We all do, but it takes a mite of stringing on our nerves to get it up."

"Why did you come here?"

"Why?"

"Yeah, to this island?"

"To work."

"Do you have a home back on the mainland?"

"My family has a place in Valdosta and in Griffin."

"Isn't life here lonely?"

He looked out to the sea, then back at her and smiled that crooked smile. "It's peaceful, and busy." He stood and whistled. Billy looked up from his meal, a mean expression on his face. "C'mon boy, you've had enough. You got to watch your figure, too." He held out his fist, and the bird rose and flew forward, making a perfect six talon landing.

When they were back on Oystercatcher, she asked, "Where do you suppose Josie is?"

He looked over at her and didn't say anything for a bit. "I don't know. But I think you're going to need to find out."

"I think you're right."

*****

Standing on the marble balcony, she looked out to sea. The door behind her opened, but she didn't turn. Hearing her cousin's voice relaxed her shoulders. "Cleo, you keep disappearing."

She faced him. "Woke early and got about."

"Our host and hostess are nervy about you."

"They shouldn't be."

"Where'd you hot foot it to? You didn't take a car?"

"To the stable. I met the vet. He had his bird out, and I watched it hunt."

"Huh! A nice thing for a girl like you."

"Ever see a falcon hunt?"

"Can't say I have."

"They fly upward, way above a flock of birds, and then they dive bomb into the one they want. They make a turn in the air and grab their kill."

"Grab their kill? Bearcat, what kind of palaver is that?"

"Since I've been on this island, I've heard a lot of earthy terminology I don't even hear at the hospital." Breeding season, mating time.

"From now on, knuckle my door. Tell me where you're going."

"Not if I want to go by myself." He frowned. "Don't mean to hurt your feelings, but you'd want to come with me."

"You got a torch for Doc?"

"He's an interesting man – polite and easy to be around."

"I'm not?"

"I'm not saying that, silly. I think you would like him." Neill's frown lines and downturned mouth said otherwise. "You'd get a kick out of the falcon. I thought about how maybe you flew your plane like Billy flew."

"Billy?"

"The bird's name."

"That's right. We did a little dive bombing, I have to say."

The door opened and Teddy came out. She smiled, sort of. "There you are. Did you have an interesting outing?"

"I did," Cleo said.

"Fine." She looked at Neill. "Tide's right. Are we ready to board the runabout?"

"We are," Neill said.

"Graham's gone to get the automobile. We four can fit. Shafer's beside himself that he can't come." She looked at Cleo, perhaps to invite her to stay behind so that Shafer could come.

Cleo pulled her hat lower on her forehead. "I'm ready."

"Good." Teddy went inside. Cleo walked alongside Neill through the halls of the great house, through the French doors that came out on the lane side. Graham sat behind the wheel of the Ford.

They boarded, Teddy and Cleo in the back, Neill beside Graham. Graham turned his cheek to her. "Almost left you behind, Cleo."

"Glad you didn't."

She found that whenever thoughts of Graham snuck in, she could replace his face with Doc's. It was one way to get her heart back together, and she very much liked Doc.

"Shafer isn't glad," Teddy said. "He's absolutely steamed."

"In more ways than one," Graham said.

"It's none of my business," Cleo said, more snidely than she intended, "but Shafer should be at home in case his wife returns."

"Shafer counts on the servants," Teddy said.

"Only two servants," Graham said, turning onto Oystercatcher. "He's had to let all but Barnabas and Josie's maid go."

"Tch," Teddy said. "I'll have to hire Barnabas when Shafer's down to his last dime. I wouldn't want to lose Fredik."

"Where would they go?" Graham asked. "Back to Romania? There's hell fire going on there. That's why they left."

"How long have they been here?" Cleo asked.

"Came before the war," Teddy said. "Barnabas first, ten years before his nephew Fredik."

Graham's cheek craned toward Cleo. "Barnabas lives in a tabby cabin on Bellflower. His family works the land for food."

Neill asked, "Shafer that bad off?"

"Bellflower's on the block," Graham said.

"Sad but true," Teddy said.

"Selling it is another matter," Graham said. "These days, who's snapping up mansions on isolated sea islands?"

"Don't be so quick to discount Sago," Teddy said. "The oil and railroad men are looking to build summer homes."

"Unfortunately for the Drakes, the robber barons have taken to St. Simons."

"Don't be too critical of the railroad men," Teddy shot back. "They buy our steel."

Everyone's on edge, Cleo thought.

Graham said, "Steel, oil, railroads, – all genuine capitalist ideals."

"What you went to war for, son," Teddy said.

"Oh don't get me wrong, I'm a capitalist through and through. I'm no Commie. It's just I think immigrants get a raw deal."

What Graham said interested Cleo. Graham went on, "They're slaves to people who have money to spare, and those adventurists who dream big and live life to the fullest."

"Graham, darling," Teddy said, her tone cutting, "I believe you're talking about your dream to fly the Atlantic solo."

"I know what you're going to say, Mother, and I credit I cannot do it without family money, which comes straight out of the hearths."

Teddy looked at Cleo. "To be fair to Graham, he saved the money he earned in the war and used it to help refurbish our Negro village. We all pitched in, even Shafer before Prohibition ruined the Drakes, but it was Graham's idea to smarten the cottages."

Neill said, "Good old Graham, like he kept the English children in chocolates and the old women in cigs."

To get away from good old Graham's goodness, Cleo asked, "Didn't the Drake's have any interest in the steel mills?"

"Not one penny's worth," Graham said. "Teddy's sister married Shafer's daddy. They never had an interest in Henry Steelworks; they were always in booze."

"Shafer could go to work for us," Teddy said.

"Fat chance," Graham said. "What could he do all day but sit on his arse and drink?"

"Graham," Teddy said, "that will do."

For the last mile to the wharf, an annoying silence filled the car.

The cover was off the boat; Cleo and Teddy climbed in what Teddy called the aft cockpit. The boat's bow rose, and soon they were flying across the waters of the sound. Cleo looked up as a flock of birds flew overhead. She tilted her head way back to see if a long-winged raptor climbed above to plunge downward. She grinned to herself. The unsuspecting birds could feed peacefully. Billy was free-lofting in his mews.

CHAPTER NINE

Graham played the part of the gentleman and held his hand for her to disembark the runabout's cockpit. "Did you enjoy the ride?" he asked.

"Yes," she said, walking past him to where Teddy stood.

Teddy said, "The King's Inn is where everyone meets to spread gossip and news. We'll go there first and wet our whistle."

The King's Inn was a two-story structure with columns on three sides. It had been built across the street from the Port Maria Docks where commercial schooners, shrimp boats, steamboats and small flat-bottom boats were floating about haphazardly.

"A rum-runners paradise," Graham said.

"I never thought of that," Neill said. "Where from?"

"Barbados and the West Indies."

"Some day I'm going to the islands," Neill said.

Graham skip-stepped to Cleo's side. "How about you? Would you like a sail to the islands?"

She didn't look at him. "I haven't the clothes to go native."

"I'll weave a grass skirt for you."

Neill laughed.

She breathed in, trying to look bored, but her rage threatened the boundaries she'd carefully built.

"Don't be mad at me," Graham said softly. "We need to talk."

She flicked her elbow. "Get away with yourself, silly."

Inside the hotel, ceiling fans ringed lazily overhead. The wide oak floors and booths were stained with decades of human habitation. Teddy led through a swinging door into a room that had been a saloon. The sign above the bar said, "Welcome to the New King's Tavern. No spirits served By Law." In front of a beveled mirror, where whiskey and rum had once held sway, root beer extract and fruit juices in fancy bottles were on display. Big pull taps had placards that proclaimed they poured lemonade and colas.

The man at the bar beamed. "Welcome Miz Henry."

"Good morning, Lester."

"What brings you across Sago Sound?"

"We'll get to that. What's potable in here?"

Although they were his only customers, Lester's eyes roamed into the far corners as if ears were attached to the walls. "Just rum."

"Rum's fine," Teddy said. "Got any of that peach juice you had last time?"

"Beulah just made a batch."

"Pour some rum in it for us," she said, leading Cleo and the men like a mother hen to a table in the middle of the room. She called to Lester, "Get yourself one and sit with us."

He grinned. "Yes, ma'am."

So much for Prohibition, Cleo thought, as Lester brought their tall peachy drinks with sprigs of mint. The first sip was nectar for the gods.

Teddy said to Lester, "You'd tell us if Josie was here, wouldn't you?"

Lester paused, his glass half way to his mouth. "Why sure."

"Is she?"

"No, Miz Henry. I ain't seen Miss Josie since last week when she came in with ..." His eyes flashed at Graham, then away.

Graham placed his glass on a coaster. "I rode her over in the runabout. She wanted to visit Seymour's." His throat seemed to have grown a frog. "Lester, why don't you tell Mother what we did when we were here."

Lester answered readily, "Came from Seymour's with a bag of goods. Ate a noon day meal and left."

The look on Graham's face seemed to say, *There!*

"And that's the very last time you saw Josie?" Teddy asked.

"The very," Lester said.

"Have you heard the latest news about her?"

Lester's mouth twisted. "I heard tell from Mr. Thompson, when they was here yesterday morning, that she came to the mainland to get a ..." His laugh was more a hiccup. "I guess it's not true."

"It isn't," Graham said.

"I don't know no more."

"Let's do some supposing," Teddy said.

"Okay," Lester said, wariness shifting his eyes.

"Suppose a girl wanted to run away, say get married without her daddy knowing. What would she do?"

"Well, if her intended had a car, they'd head out for Savannah. Or even Charleston up a ways. It's a big place to get lost in – you know, for mad daddys – and they give out marriage licenses without even asking for your age. 'Course everybody knows that, so if it were me, I'd go over to Seminole County that was just begun. They don't have much in the way of record-keeping yet, and you could hide down in the Panhandle of Florida." Lester got a confused look on his face. "Isn't Josie and Shafer still married?"

"That was a for-instance," Teddy said. "Josie didn't run off to get married. Where would she go to get a quick divorce?"

"I reckon that's a different story. A soul's got to have grounds, like abandonment and alienation of affection." He eyes didn't quite reach Graham.

"When was Shafer last here?" Graham asked.

"Shafer came the day Graham and Josie was here."

Graham asked, "What did he want?"

"Wanted to know if you and Josie stayed long?"

Cleo knew what that meant.

"And?" Graham demanded.

"I told him just what I told you." He spread his hands apart. "Look, I don't want to get in the middle …"

Teddy interrupted, "Telling the truth isn't getting in the middle. We'll all have another of these angel juices."

"It's on me," Lester said, jumping to his feet. He hurried away looking relieved.

The saloon doors swung open, and a short, portly man walked in. He carried a walking stick and wore a bowler. He removed his hat, and placed it in the crook of his arm. His cheeks were bright red as if he'd spent too much time in the sun, or was about to have a stroke. His eyes were small and of indeterminate color. "Good morning," he said. "May I have a word with you folks?"

Teddy glanced at Graham, and then at Cleo and Neill. "Don't see why not," she said. "Pull up a seat."

"Let me introduce myself." He reached into his vest pocket and pulled out a case. He extracted a card from it. "Lionel Murphy is my name." With a flourish he handed the card to Teddy.

Teddy rose and stuck out a hand. "Theodora Henry."

He laughed. "Not often a fine lady stands for a man."

"I don't intend to stay standing," she said, and sat. "Pull up a chair. My neck will hurt looking up at you."

"I shall, then," he said.

Teddy studied the card and handed it around. It came to Cleo and she read out loud, "Pinkerton's National Detective Agency." She looked at the man. "The words are written around an eye."

"We never sleep, miss."

"Are you on the trail of someone?" Graham asked. Most of the time, Cleo avoided meeting his eyes, even looking in his direction, but something in his voice caused her to stare at him. Involuntarily, her tongue slipped from her lips, then she pressed them tight.

"I am that," Murphy said. "I am asking the good citizens of this county to help me apprehend a dangerous man."

"What has he done?" Graham asked.

"The list is long," Murphy said. "The worst of it is he shot a man."

"Killed him?"

"Put him in a chair with useless legs. Might as well have killed him, my opinion."

"When did this happen?" Graham asked, having taken over the questioning.

"A couple of years ago."

"And you're just now getting around to looking for this villain?"

"My patron hired our firm six months ago after his father couldn't locate the man."

"What did your man do to get himself shot?"

"He may have cheated at the card table."

"Well, by God," Graham said, "every fool knows cheating at cards can get you shot, maybe killed."

"My patron denies he cheated. He says the man had a bone to pick with him and used the card table as an excuse."

"What was the bone?" Teddy asked.

"A woman."

"What's the name of the man who hired you?"

"A gentleman who will remain anonymous until I apprehend the man who wielded the fire arm to answer the charges."

"Who is this scoundrel?" Teddy said with a touch of sarcasm.

"He goes most often by the name of Harry Hepplewaite."

Graham sat back. "Never heard of him."

Neill piped up, "Was this Hepplewaite in the War?"

"The lottery missed him."

"Damned draft-dodger," Neill said.

"He uses other aliases," Murphy said.

"Which are?"

"Robert Horn and Joseph Tindale."

"I for one have never heard those name," Graham said. "Teddy?"

"Never," she answered. "You talk to the sheriff?"

"He's acquainted with my mission here. We always work with law enforcement."

"Where's this Harry Hepplewaite from?"

"Atlanta, Georgia originally, but he's travelled a lot. By trade, he claims to be a dentist, but we want to question him for fraudulent practices as my client also alleges. Several of his patients are worse off after his ministrations. The police have his name on their fraud rosters."

Despite the heat in the tavern, cold air skimmed Cleo's skin as pictures of a gentle man and a smart bird floated through her head.

"A dentist who plays cards, and shoots someone who cheats him," Graham said. "Never known anyone like that. Might make our little society down here interesting if he were to come for a visit."

"You folks don't sound Southern," Murphy said.

"We're not," Teddy said.

"Are you travelling?"

Teddy said, "Mr. Murphy, I get the idea you came in here for the purpose of speaking directly to us."

He cast his eyes so that he looked sheepish. "I am acquainted with Henry Steel Company and the fact that Mrs. Theodora Henry resides on Sago Island most of the year, yes."

"Why didn't you say so at the beginning," Teddy said.

"You didn't ask, madam."

"Your tactics remind me that years ago your agency helped a steel competitor of ours break a picket line. Innocent people got killed by your strikebreakers."

"We lost men, too," he said.

"I can tell you this," Teddy said, "I have no knowledge of a fake dentist who shot a man that might have cheated him."

"I have trailed him to Timican, just seven miles inland from here. From descriptions, I believe he was there for a month before he disappeared."

"Why do you think I might know him?"

"He is known to hire himself out in some medical capacity."

Like a vet, Cleo thought.

Teddy said, "I have a doctor in Pittsburgh, also a dentist. There's a hospital in this county if I need emergency help."

"I see," Murphy said, getting up and picking up his bowler. His voice hissed like a gas leak. "Thank you for your trouble."

"Before you go," Teddy said, "we're looking for someone. While you were snooping, did you come across a Josie Drake?"

"Josie Drake? Can't say I have. She gone long?"

"Two days."

"You want Pinkerton's to look for her?"

"Not at all, thank you."

He left and Teddy said, "Presumptuous toad." She stood suddenly and made a dash for Lester, who had been ignoring them by turning his back and polishing the already highly polished mahogany back bar. Cleo caught her shoe on a chair leg going after Teddy. Graham caught her arm. She pulled it away.

Teddy stopped at the bar and Lester turned to face her. "You ever see that Pinkerton man before?" she asked.

"He's been staying at the hotel, three days now."

"Is he asking these questions of everybody who walks in?"

"Just about."

"You acquaint him with my family and Sago Island?"

"No ma'am. I value your custom. He asks questions, I told him I'm the only game in town and I don't talk folks' business."

"Who's been telling him about us?"

"You ask me, old man Seymour. He's like a clothesline lady."

"Thanks, Lester." Cleo trooped after Teddy with Neill and Graham behind her. Once outside, Teddy said, "Forget Seymour. It's too late. Let's get back on island. We'll discuss this then."

No one spoke on the way back which suited Cleo. Racing the boat across the sound seemed to express Graham's acute anger. Teddy's arms hugged one another for dear life, and Neill rolled his thumbs in nervous jerks. The racing blur of gray water running alongside the boat cast her in a different film, one so very unlike her own. Nursing had brought her into contact with the good and bad of humanity. Out in the wide world, what were the odds of being taken in by two dishonorable men in the space of two days?

They reached the docks, and, once seated in the Ford, her own small world having been further diminished, she closed her eyes to withdraw for the ride.

CHAPTER TEN

Drinks were poured in the drawing room. Teddy paced while Graham leaned on the mantle. Cleo and Neill sat on the sofa. "I sent for Sam Holliday," Teddy said.

"If that's the bugger's name," Graham said.

From some level, Cleo summoned up some spunk. "How dare you. You don't know that he's Pinkerton's man."

Teddy snorted – from what emotion Cleo couldn't imagine – and strode to the end of the room. Clasping her hands behind her back, Teddy appeared enthralled with the sea or the shore or the gardens. Maybe even the lighthouse.

"It's a good assumption he's Pinkerton's man," Graham said.

"You assume a lot on short notice," Cleo said.

Shaking his head, he said, "Doc's always been a cipher."

"What's a cipher?"

"A wrong number."

"Proved guilty before the trial, eh?"

"I'm not the only judge and jury in this room."

Teddy swung around. "Kids."

Cleo wanted to laugh. *Kids.*

"How did this Doc wash up here?" Neill asked.

Graham and Teddy glanced at each other. Teddy answered, "Just walked up the trail with a knapsack on his shoulder and asked if anyone needed a man who worked with animals."

Cleo asked, "Did he call himself a vet?"

"I don't believe he did," Teddy said.

"Did he call himself Doc?"

"He introduced himself as Sam Holliday. Shafer's the one who started calling him Doc. It came out that the gunslinger was an ancestor."

"So," Cleo said, "maybe he's not Murphy's criminal."

Teddy said, "He offered to work for food and a place to hang his hat. I paid him a pittance at first, and then raised his wages when I saw his work." As she moved, her fingers twisted together. Cleo watched the subtle wonder cross her face. "It might be a mare's nest, for all we know, and he is who he says he is."

"Let's don't forget Josie is missing," Graham said.

"Josie?" Teddy said. "Why would you think Doc has something to do with Josie's disappearance?"

"Josie was always going off island to hang out at the King's Inn. Here's a thought. She could have talked to Murphy. Probably did. She confronted Doc and demanded money."

"Blackmail?" Teddy asked.

"You need money. Somebody has a secret. Bingo."

"For crying out loud," Cleo said.

Mitty opened the door and showed Fredik into the room. Fredik bowed. "Afternoon."

Cleo said "Afternoon," along with everyone else.

Fredik said, "Mr. Sam is not in his usual places at the stable. The horses are in their stalls and accounted for."

"*Merde*," Teddy said.

Graham snickered, "When Teddy curses in French, it's not cursing." Teddy shot him a look that wiped the smile from his face. He said, "So now we're looking for two missing persons."

"When do you call in the authorities about Josie?" Cleo asked.

Impatience in every move, Teddy said, "It's no crime to go missing. The sheriff won't be pleased if he motorboats over here, and she turns up hiding out." She addressed Fredik. "Keep looking for Doc. Meantime, I'm going to change for swimming. Who's game?"

Graham and Neill looked at Cleo. She said, "No, thanks. I think I'll sit in the sun."

Graham said, "Neill and I will be out looking for our *vet.*"

So will I, Cleo thought.

*****

She wore the beach pajamas Eurella said looked best on her. The one-piece chemise had a shawl collar and wide legged pants that appeared to be a skirt. The lobster print was divine. She'd never felt so free and easy in a style before. When she got home, she would hide it in a drawer and hope her mother wouldn't snoop that far back.

At the top of the terrace steps, she spotted Shafer below, rounding the shrubs. He looked up, halted and waited. Going down, she said, "Good afternoon."

"Not so good," he said, puffing a cigarette. "Josie's not back, not coming back probably."

She smelled whiskey, but he wasn't falling down drunk. "You don't know that yet."

He spoke as he exhaled. "I'm a poor sap, falling for her."

"Where are you off to?"

"Just walking around, looking. I'm lost, Cleo."

"I can see. Want to walk down to the sea with me?"

"Why not?"

He meandered alongside her, over the boardwalk. When they came to the tallest dune, he had a hard time scrambling up the slippery sand. He appeared to have no strength in his legs and collapsed in the sea oats. His response was to laugh like a maniac while he struggled to his feet. At the shore, with the wind flapping her pajamas, she watched the terns flock above the bloated sea.

"Gonna rain," he muttered, fishing cigarettes out of his shirt pocket.

"Those black bottoms above the horizon look full to bursting," she said.

He grunted an acid laugh and offered her the cigarette pack. When she shook her head, he pocketed it and cupped his hand to light his fag. Taking a deep drag, he cocked his head. "I say, that's a sporting dress you have on."

"Beach pajamas, Teddy calls it. Did Josie wear beach pajamas?"

"Sure." He was already listing when a gust hit him. She grabbed his arm in case he toppled.

"Bet Josie liked wearing daring clothes," she said.

"It went along with her idea of fun. Crazy Josie." He put the cigarette between his lips and inhaled deeply. "And, gee whiz, how I loved – love – her." He knelt to pick up a shell and toppled on his side.

She sat down beside him. "I'd like to know more about her."

"Why?"

"So I can understand her when she comes back."

"She won't."

"How can you be so sure?"

He waved the cigarette. "I'm stony broke."

"My mother says Prohibition won't last forever."

"It's lasted more than a year, long enough for us to lose our shirts."

"Try something else. I saw root beer on tap at King's Inn."

When he guffawed, despite the wind, an old barroom smell flowed from his mouth. "If people swilled root beer like they did whiskey it'd be fine, but root beer don't give you that zing. Besides, people are still getting all the booze they want – just not from Drake Brewers and Distributors."

"Where's Lester getting his rum from?"

He glanced at her. "The Islands, where every body gets it."

"You done any bootlegging?"

"I wouldn't say if I did."

"I'm not the law, besides you've seen me drink Teddy's cocktails."

"Bootlegging doesn't pay, unless you haul it in quantities, and Drake's is number one on the Prohibition Bureau's list of firm's to watch. The minute the law passed, they came to our warehouse and seized everything. Two months later, they seized our trucks and boats on the pretense booze was still in them. Said they smelled of alcohol. Sure they did; we been hauling legal liquor up and down the east coast for seventy-five years. They're itching to throw me, my brother and father in the klink."

"I see how you'd be suspected."

"Things are going to get worst. The gangs out of New York and Chicago have organized smuggling operations. They saw the writing on the wall before January of nineteen-twenty. Once you get the mob in a business, no law in the land is going to stop them."

"Could Josie have gotten caught up in this activity?"

"Josie's only association with hooch is a glass in her hand. No merry band of mobsters would let Josie in on their routes. Her mouth outruns her brain."

"How well do you know Doc Holliday?"

"Doc? You thinking Doc has something to do with Josie going missing?"

"There's a man at the King's Inn who's looking for a criminal. The crime happened before Doc showed up here."

"What's that got to do with Doc?"

"Don't know," she shrugged. "I'm curious about what you know and think about him?"

"You sweet on him?"

She laughed. "Not him. His falcon."

"Billy's a wonder. Over in England, they got falconers everywhere. Not one as good as Doc with Billy."

"Can I ask you a question that might make you angry?"

He ground his cigarette butt in the sand. "I can 'bout guess what it is."

"Graham and Josie."

"Thought so."

"Why would she leave that note?"

"Things must have gone beyond what I thought was going on with her and Graham." He scratched his scraggly whiskers. "You know what I mean?"

Although she did, she shook her head. "I don't."

"They were together a lot, they like the same things, things I didn't go for. They liked Cole Porter and some of his racy lyrics. They liked to dance and cut up. I'm just okay with the fox trot, but Graham's a swell dancer. You, too. I was going to ask you to cut a rug with me the other night, but then, things got haywire."

"Why did they go haywire?"

"Josie took a notion. Jealousy. Graham dancing with you."

She opened her mouth to speak, but he went on, "You showing up and monopolizing Graham like that – it got to her." He ran his hand through his hair as if to tame the wind in it. "She ran out on me because I'm busted."

"Where's Josie from?"

"Cincinnati, but Graham and I met her at the Ziegfeld Ball in New York."

Surprised, she asked, "Josie was a Ziegfeld girl?"

He laughed. "Sure was. Came from Cincy. Her father owned a drug store. She struck out for New York in search of fame. She's quite a dancer and singer."

"She'd have to be. So you and Graham met her at the same time. She must have wowed you both. How'd you get her?"

"You mean, since Graham's better-looking than me?"

"Come on, Shafer, I didn't say that."

"You know, I thought you and Graham might get sweet on one another. I could get sweet on you."

"Like you said, Graham's a swell dancer."

"You dames are all the same, money and fun."

She resented that like hell, but let it go. "I can't understand the note she wrote."

He reached in his pocket. "Tell the truth, neither can I." Out came the cigarette pack. "I know Graham pretty damn good. He always wanted to be an aviator. He gets single-minded about what he wants, and he's pretty free and easy. You see, Josie gets to clinging and that don't do with Graham. But me, I like my girl close to me. She can cling all she wants." His bleary face took on a blissful look for an instant, then his eyes stared off. "I got to meet with my old man in a month. He wants me to go into insurance." He lit the cigarette. "I lost my wife, my job and now I have to go into god-damned insurance, all because of some temperance nuts like Carrie Nation."

CHAPTER ELEVEN

She stayed close to the sea, away from the cabanas, but conscious of the bank of black-bottoms hanging above the slate sea. It smelled like rain, not like the promise of rain in the city, but like the threat of a drenching downpour on sand and marsh. Hurrying along, she came to a path that led up a sharp rise. Was this the bluff Doc spoke of? Not much of a bluff, but certainly a tall sand hill. Ascending, she noted it was more silt than sand. At the top, she gazed out to sea. The angry clouds coiled in on themselves, the sea bulged like an inflated dirigible and waves smashed into the shore before they were sucked beneath the breakers.

"It's high tide," the voice said.

She spun around. "Doc."

"Won't be flying Billy this afternoon."

"No doves for dinner?"

"I got some salted." He looked at her, his expression trying to guess her mood. "Ever eat salted bird?"

"Pheasant, but I think it was smoked."

"Another good way to cure."

"Ummm." She looked back at the sea.

"You got something on your mind, don't you?"

She nodded and looked at her beach shoes.

"I could tell by the way you came up here," he said and sat on the dirt. "I'm listening."

She folded the pajama material under her and sat beside him. "You know – we went searching for Josie."

"I know."

"We went to Port Maria."

"Saw you come back."

"There was a man there …"

"Go on."

She turned to face him. "Pinkerton's."

If that struck fear, he didn't give it away. "And?"

"He's looking for a fugitive."

He folded his arms. "Why does that bother you?"

She was afraid of blundering, of hurting him. "It … really … doesn't."

He looked at the sky, then at the beach. He pointed downward. "See those gulls."

Hundreds were gathered on the beach. "I see them."

"They're on the land. Storm's coming. Maybe a strong one. Let's get back." He got up and extended his hand to help her rise. Once on her feet, she started for the path down the bluff.

"We'll go along the road," he said.

"I can't, not in …" She reached down and pulled at the legs of her suit.

He laughed. "In that, you'll balloon and be blown out to sea. I say we got ten minutes before the storm hits."

"Let's go then."

He ran-walked, pulling her hand over the paths and lanes, through the maritime forest. There wasn't time for thinking, just watching where her foot landed.

Thunder quaked in the east. "Squall," he said.

Lightning punctuated the word.

They were almost to Oystercatcher Trail. "No," she shouted above the rumble.

He stopped. "What?"

"They're trying to find you."

"Find me?"

"The Pinkerton man. He described … what he said … it might have been you." I was hard to speak against the wind.

"Me?"

Thunder broke behind her. She looked up at him. "Let's please not take the road. Graham and his family are looking for you."

He shrugged and laughed. A streak of lightning lit his face. Could this crooked-mouthed man be as dangerous as Murphy said?

Doc said, "They haven't been looking hard."

"If we go on the road, they'll be in cars."

"Probably not anymore." Raindrops fell, fine and pitting. "C'mon, it's just a sprint more."

"I'll be drenched," she yelled.

"I can get you a shirt," he called, catching her hand. "Unless you want to go to the big house."

She needed to ask more of him, whoever he was. "No."

They rushed over the uneven ground, rain pelting her face, soaking her headband, ruining her carefully crimped waves. Worse, she was in soaking wet beach pajamas that clung to her skin, outlining her bubs in the sidelacer.

Once they reached the lodge's vestibule, he shook water from himself. "Be right back," he said and strode deeper into the lodge, leaving her shivering in the dark hall. Next thing she knew, he was next to her, draping a quilt around her shoulders. For a moment, his closeness in the small black room interfered with her ability to think straight. He took her elbow and guided her inside the main room. "Stay right here," he said. "Don't want you tripping in the dark." He lit two lanterns and then took the narrow steps by the fireplace two at a time. A light came on and shone down the second story stairs, and, not more than a minute later, he returned. "I've laid out some clothes. They're too big, but they're dry." He motioned toward the stairs. "Go on, but watch it, the steps are slick when they get wet."

His bed was an iron bedstead with a feather mattress on top of straight springs. On the spread, lay a checked shirt and trousers that buttoned in the front, along with a pair of socks. She put the dry shirt over her sidelacer. She wouldn't dream of slipping men's pants over her naked bottom, so she plied them over her wet bloomers. After she put his socks on her feet, she took the headband from her head and finger-combed her hair straight back.

He watched her come down the last step, holding the pants at the waist so they wouldn't fall around her ankles. He grinned. "Everything all right?"

"Fine." She shivered. "A little big."

"Don't worry," he said.

He had pulled the shades and lit a fire in the fireplace. The kettle began to rattle on the andiron. "Coffee or tea?" he asked.

"Coffee," she said.

He went to an oversized easy chair and pulled the padded arm close to the fire. She curled herself into it, and he covered her with the quilt. The fire and the quilt made the wet undergarments bearable. She breathed in the comforting smoke and the lodge's masculinity while he made small sounds behind her. Coming from the shadows, he carried a scoop and poured the coffee beans into the tea kettle that steamed over the fire. He pulled up a straight chair. "Best coffee in the world in there," he said. "Comfortable?"

"Yes."

"Worried?"

"A little."

"I suspect."

"What will the Henrys think when I don't come home?" she said, her voice sounding childish. Then she laughed. "What will they think when I come home in these?" She touched the collar of the borrowed shirt.

"We can get you in without being seen."

"You can?"

"Think about that place."

She grinned. "It's big. It's got lots of door I discovered."

"When the storm's over."

"They'll all be gathered in the Blue drawing room," she said.

"There are three other wings; two never get used unless they bring down parties."

"I can get to my room in the main wing by the servant stairs, but I have to go through the rotunda."

"That's not the way we'll do it."

"How?"

"You'll see."

"I'm feeling better already."

He got up and checked the coffee. The steam added its aroma to the room. He went to a cabinet and took out two cups and saucers. "I don't want you uneasy being here."

"It's not that. It's the circumstance."

He brought a small table to place between their chairs, sat the cups and saucers on it, went to the kettle and brought it steaming to the table. He poured two cups without spilling a drop. He added cream and sugar to hers and stirred.

He sat and said, "Now we can talk about this Pinkerton man."

"His name is Lionel Murphy." Thunder convulsed outside, followed by a shockwave of lightning.

"Never heard of the gent," he said.

"He approached us at the hotel."

"A place to start if you're looking for someone other than the sheriff."

"He said the sheriff knew of his mission. Have you heard of Pinkerton's?"

"I have." He sipped his coffee.

She said, "They never sleep, isn't that an odd thing to say?"

"Not if you're on a manhunt."

"He said he was."

"He say the name of this villain?"

The hot coffee was a treat, going down her throat and warming her hands. "Harry Hepplewaite."

"What did Hepplewaite do?"

"Shot a man over a card game and a woman."

Thunder reverberated over the rooftop; the following lightning lit Doc's face. There was a curious expression on it. He said, "He killed this man?"

"Put him in a wheel chair."

"When?"

"A couple of years ago, but Pinkerton's just got hired six months ago."

"He tell you the name of his client?"

"No."

"He told you Hepplewaite's name, but not the card cheat's?"

"He said Hepplewaite had other names. Aliases."

"He say what?"

"Robert Horn and Joseph Tindale."

"Where'd this happen?"

"He didn't say, but he said Harry Hepplewaite was from Atlanta."

"He tell you anything else about the man he's pursuing?"

"He travels. He claims he's a dentist. He hurts his patients. He's wanted for fraud."

Doc's face was in shadow, hard to make out. She squeezed her hands around the cup and became conscious of the fact the thunder had moved away.

He said, "I think all dentists hurt their patients. When you yank out a tooth, that's the result. I don't know that Doc was ever wanted for fraud. Murder and bank robbery, yes, but not fraud."

"But," she said, "we're not talking about your Doc Holliday. He died out west."

"Somebody's having fun," he said.

She thought he made sense. "Murphy knew all about the Henrys and seemed to accuse Teddy of hiding this imposter."

"And, so, the family believes I'm the mysterious Mr. Hepplewaite?"

"I …" She heard Graham's sneers echo in her head. "They want to talk to you."

"Do you want to ask me outright?"

Sitting not six feet away, the familiarity of the moment snatched coherent speech from her mouth. "I … wanted to … to warn you. I …I didn't want you to be surprised."

"Do you want me to tell you if it's true or not?"

She leaned back. "If you want."

"Did you want to warn me, or help me get away?" His voice was hoarse, like rubbing cloth on a washboard.

She met his eyes. "Yes to both."

"Thank you for that."

"Graham, Neill, they went out looking for you. The horses were all in the stable. They didn't know where you were."

"And you knew I was planning on flying Billy from the bluff?"

"Yes."

"But a storm was coming. How'd you know I'd be there?"

"You wouldn't let me come to see Billy and not show up."

"No, I wouldn't. I didn't."

He got up and picked up a poker. He stirred the embers into small flames. "Storm's dying," he said. "It's dinnertime. You want some salted dove?"

"I don't …"

"Didn't think so." He sat back down. "What did Teddy have to say about this Murphy?"

"She called him a presumptuous toad. She said she didn't know of a fake dentist. It was interesting, though. She had a beef with him. It was about their steel plant and strikebreakers. Innocent people got killed when Pinkerton's broke up a picket line."

"Murphy say what brought him to this part of Georgia?"

"He followed his suspect to Timican."

"Why would the Henrys know Hepplewaite?"

"Murphy says he hires himself out in some medical capacity."

"Like a veterinarian?" She dry-swallowed, and he apparently noticed. "Is that what you thought?"

She lowered her lashes and shook her head.

"Do you wonder if I had anything to do with Josie Drake's disappearance?"

She looked at him and shook her head more vigorously. "I never did, no."

"Who does?" he asked.

She hesitated and took a sip of coffee.

"Makes sense, if I'm a dangerous man."

"But you're not that man."

"Do you truly believe that?"

"Would you shoot a man in a card game, just because you wanted his wife?"

"If I shot a man in a card game for his wife, he'd be dead."

"You could kill?"

"We all can kill."

She thought about Neill and Graham in the war, shooting down Huns. "Were you in the war?"

"Bum legs."

With the black storm's passing, what was left of daylight came through the shaded windows. She stirred and sat upright.

He said, "Ready for a hike?"

She looked at her clothes, at her stocking feet. "No."

He began to laugh, and, laughing with him, she gathered her wet chemise and shoes. "Can we meet at eight in the morning?" she asked, crossing the laces.

"Later than that. I have some things to do. After noon."

When they got to Southerness, he said, "We're going in by way of the Red Wing." He slipped the lock and opened the door to the servants' entrance. He held out a hand, and she took it. He said, "I like your hair unencumbered and curled by the rain."

Unsure of herself, her hand went to her damp hair. "It'll take days to get the curls into waves."

"Don't even try," he said and let go of her hand. "Have a good night."

"I will."

He disappeared into the twilight.

The eerie stillness told her there were no servants about, and all the furniture in the Red Wing was draped in white. She wound through halls, backtracking at dead ends, and found the door to her rooms. When she opened it, Eurella was sitting in a straight chair under the rope pull. Her face didn't smile nor frown at Cleo's outfit.

"Evening, Eurella. Quite a storm."

"Yes, miss."

Eurella pointed to garments on the dresser. "Miz Teddy says you might be needing some relaxin' clothes."

"Teddy always has the appropriate clothes for her guests, doesn't she?"

"Sure do," Eurella said, standing. "People don't have to pack none when they come here."

Cleo fingered the lovely cotton material. A straight line dress had been fashioned in white eyelet and another was mauve muslin with ecru lace. She knew they would fit perfectly. "Eurella, did you sew these dresses?"

"No, miss, Canada did."

"Who is Canada?"

"Our seamstress."

"I want to meet her."

"Surely, miss. I'll let her know."

She began unbuttoning the plaid shirt. "I'm going to wash and go to bed." Eurella was at her side, doing the unbuttoning. "I'm exhausted."

Eurella's strong hands landed on her shoulders and began to work into her muscles. "You got to work out the troubles, miss."

Feeling anxiety melt, Cleo said, "Feels good."

Eurella left to run a bath. Standing in a robe, she looked at herself in the cheval mirror. Her eyes were smeared black like raccoons' eyes and the powder had washed off her face. She wondered what Eurella thought and what she knew. Servant gossip sped faster than Morse code.

Eurella returned from the bathroom. "Water's just right, miss."

"Thank you. I'm desperate for it."

Cleo held up the mauve dress. "Is tomorrow going to be a mauve day, you think?"

"'My, tis lovely on your skin."

"Mauve, it is."

"Miss?"

"Yes?"

Eurella went to the door, opened it and peeked outside, as if looking for listeners. She closed it firmly. "I'll send a tray right up with hot chowder and cheeses."

"Oh, Eurella, you're a dear. And I'd like to sleep in until ten in the morning."

"Yes, miss."

"A tray of dry biscuits and orange juice would be fine."

CHAPTER TWELVE

They were gathered in the morning room, waiting, ready to pounce. There would be no dancing in a new frock tonight. "Good morning," she said and went to sit by Neill on the sofa. Graham sat in the blue chair and Teddy stood at the mantle.

She anticipated the question. Graham and Teddy let Neill ask it. "Where have you been, Bearcat?"

"Sleeping."

"And yesterday afternoon?"

"At the shore."

Graham leveled his eyes at her. "In a storm?"

"The cabana sheltered me."

Graham stared as if in a sudden trance.

Teddy said, "You must have been soaked."

"I gave Eurella my wet clothes."

Teddy waved a hand as if to make light of the matter. "My dear, Cleo, you are a wanderer."

"I took you at your word ... that we're on our own."

"Indeed." She laughed and looked at Graham. "You need to keep an eye on our Cleo. I don't think my heart can take another disappearance."

"Who has disappeared now?" Cleo asked.

"Doc," Teddy said. "Graham and Neill just got back from his lodge. No sign of him."

Graham said, "His people haven't seen him. Fortunately, they know their work and were at it without him. No horses have been taken out. No jalopies. The fellow wasn't answering our knock."

Neill grinned at Graham. "I had to keep my ol' buddy from busting in. Wouldn't be right."

"No," Cleo said. "You can't go around being vigilantes."

"The damn man found out we are on to him," Graham said.

"About what?" Cleo asked.

"He's Hepplewaite."

"Did you find proof?"

"An innocent man doesn't hide himself/"

"What if he's not hiding, just doing something somewhere else on the island?"

"How'd he get where he's going?"

"I don't know this island, and I don't like hanging a man before he's found guilty."

Graham blue eyes cut into her resentment. "Did you see him on your walk on the beach?"

"He wasn't on the beach."

"He flies Billy from the Petrel's Bluff."

"When a storm's coming?" she asked. "The gulls were huddled on the beach."

"What's that mean?" Neill asked.

Graham snorted. "Someone's been telling our Cleo about seagull's habits. There's an old proverb, 'Seagull seagull sitting on the sand; it's never good weather when you're on the land.'"

Teddy said, "Doc wouldn't take Billy out with a storm coming. Let's hope Doc turns up tomorrow and it's all a mare's nest."

Graham looked at Cleo with something like pain in his eyes. "Neill tells me you got to be pals with Doc."

She looked at Neill, who suddenly focused on the table in front of him. She turned her gaze on Graham. "So?"

"Nothing," Graham said, suddenly interested in his hands.

Neill looked up, his face reddened. "The man didn't enlist to fight for his country. The army needs medics, even if they are frauds."

"The country needs medics at home, too," she said.

Graham leaned back and blew air from pursed lips. "Would you warn him about the Pinkerton man if you could?"

"I would tell him Murphy was looking for a man who might fit his description. He could do what he wanted to about it."

"Ha," Graham said, picking the cigarette pack off the table.

"Where could he hide on this island?" Neill asked.

"No telling," Teddy said. "He knows it as well as we do. Maybe better."

"Caves?" Neill asked.

"We're an island. Sand," Teddy said.

"Of course."

"Some of our thickets could be caves," Graham said, lighting the cigarette and blowing the smoke toward the ceiling.

"I'm not for beating the bushes for him," Teddy said. "If he somehow got wind of the Pinkerton jerk, and he got away, good for him. We'll deliver our own foals and calves as we have in the past."

Graham laughed smoke from his nostrils. "How many calves have you delivered?"

"More than you," she snapped at him. "The Negroes are very good at animal husbandry and they are eager to teach anyone willing to learn."

Take that, Grammy boy.

Graham flicked the cigarette ash into a crystal dish. "Doc found them very helpful, I must say."

"Don't diminish his skills, Graham," Teddy said.

"Hey, I liked the man," Graham said, spreading his arms wide, looking at Cleo. "I just want him to fess up if he's Pinkerton's man. We'll tell him to move on, that's all. Hell, Teddy, if you want him to stay, he stays."

Mitty came to the door. "Luncheon is served, Miz Henry."

Teddy rose. "No more talk of Doc."

She meant it.

*****

Good manners prevented her from begging off lunch; thus she took her accustomed place next to Graham. Eagan and Linith were at school on Amelia Island so the meal began quietly.

For starters, there was corn soufflé. The first bite was sweet and creamy, but she found swallowing difficult. She looked at Graham and pitched her voice low. "Please, I can't eat with you staring at me."

"Sorry, I can't help it."

"Pretend I'm not here."

"But you are." He looked at his bowl. "Okay, I'll mind my own business."

Next came beef rib roast and sweet and sour cabbage. Utensils clanked on china and there were a few throat clearings. Then Neill said into the silence. "Quite delicious, this beef."

"Ummm," Cleo agreed half-heartedly.

The Waldorf salad came. Teddy said, "We make it with raisins until grapes come in in summer."

"I like raisins," Neill said. "Cleo makes smashing raisin pudding."

Teddy smiled. "A woman of many talents."

Graham's looked at her. "I adore raisin pudding."

Trying to smile, her mind slid back to his epic betrayal and slowly she began to shatter. First the short breaths, then the lower lip tremble, finally an eye tic.

She heard Teddy say something to Neill. Neill replied, but she had no idea of what they spoke. Except it was political.

Through Neill and Teddy yakking, she felt Graham's eyes on her bowed head. He leaned closer. "Please, I want to talk …"

She shook her head.

There was a short pall hanging over the table before Teddy commented about last night's storm. Neill said something about debris in the garden.

She glanced at Graham's hands. How they shook. Without meeting his eyes, she asked softly, "What does your mother know?"

"Nothing."

"Liar."

His head went back like he'd been slapped. If only she could. Her hand meeting his smarmy cheek, the sound of insult cracking the air would echo ever so sweetly, especially when her tears started to fall.

Mitty came in, his stately walk gone, his steps quick. "Excuse me, Miz Henry."

Teddy rose. "What's the matter."

"Ummm … "

"Speak freely," she said.

"Fredik reports the villagers saw Mr. Sam getting on the coal boat for the mainland."

Cleo raised her slumping shoulders and tightened her jaw. The threat of tears vanished. Doc gone?

Teddy asked Fredik, "When was this?"

"Last evening. After the storm."

"Hell, he's probably in Atlanta by now," Graham said.

"Watch your language, son."

"What's a hell now and again, Mother?"

Teddy ignored Graham. "Thank you, Mitty. We'll have the rhubarb pie now."

Cleo hated rhubarb anything. "May I be excused, please?"

"Of course," Teddy said. "My waist is too fond of pie. I'll walk with you."

Damn the woman.

She couldn't be late for her rendezvous with Doc. Surely he wouldn't stand her up. Surely not.

CHAPTER THIRTEEN

Teddy wasn't walking with her usual long strides. She set a slow pace toward the stairs and that irritated Cleo, as if Teddy purposely forestalled her meeting with Doc. Although Teddy couldn't know about that.

Teddy said, "It wasn't a nice thing for you to learn, was it?"

"I'm not sure I follow you," Cleo said.

Teddy stopped and looked into her eyes. "Graham and Josie."

Having formed pat answers for this conversation, Cleo said, "It's none of my business."

"It could have been. You two hit it off, any fool could see that."

"He's a good dancer."

"That all you can say?"

"He's always been a gentleman as far as I can tell."

"He's also a man."

Cleo's hand rested on the banister post. "Do all men deceive?" This was a departure from her preconceived script, but she couldn't help ask.

"Did Graham deceive you?"

Her brain clouded with remembrance. "Why would he?"

They walked up the wide staircase. "Graham's twenty-four," Teddy said. "A man of twenty-four is bound to have experiences."

"I understand biology," Cleo said. "I work in a hospital."

Teddy hesitated, then said, "If men are to pursue women, or women allow them the pursuit, they should have a bit of knowledge and skill, don't you think?"

Graham had both, but she wasn't about to say that to his mother, or, for the love of God, give herself away.

Teddy went on, "From the beginning, it was clear you two would be attractive to each other."

Teddy, the matchmaker.

Teddy said, "Your dark hair and fair skin, wonderful green eyes and rather shy nature would attract any man."

They came to the top of the steps. "I haven't cornered the market on those traits," she said with a little smile.

Teddy ambled down the hall. "Girls have fallen over Graham since he was a child. But I've never known Graham to fall in love. Of course, I don't know what went on in England, or France, but if he fell in love with an English or French girl, she would be here now. I'm going to tell you something I've never told anyone else."

I don't want you to.

"Graham is not like his father. Edgar was utterly faithless, and Graham despised him for it." She paused to let this sink in. Inwardly Cleo shrugged *so what*? Teddy continued, "I looked the other way for years, but looking the other way just made Edgar bolder. After Eagan was born, I gave him one more chance to change his ways, but he didn't and we separated. We never divorced for the children's sake." She paused again, then resumed. "Edgar died in Paris last year. The official cause of his death was pneumonia. Graham went to Paris to learn the truth. Don't know how much of what he learned is true, but the story goes that Edgar kept donning his top hat at the ladies who past him on *Rue de la Paix* while he stood outside Cartier's waiting for his mistress to purchase some baubles. It was raining and he had lung trouble. After his death, I saw the receipt for Cartier's – ten grand for a diamond and pearl set."

Teddy stopped at a marble chest under a mirror in the hall. An oil lamp gave off muted light. She opened a drawer and drew out a handsome box. Inside was a pack of cigarettes. Next, she reached inside for a long gold holder and matches. She offered the holder to Cleo, who, not being in the mood to smoke, shook her head. Replacing the holder in the drawer, Teddy lit the cigarette like a man would and flicked the match dead. "I know my son. There's no like-father like-son in Graham."

They approached Cleo's door. "Neill and I should leave here."

Teddy coughed sharply, whether from smoke in her lungs or disagreement. "You won't be restrained, but please, I beg you, don't."

"It's a bit awkward."

"Don't leave." She aimed piercing eyes at Cleo. "For Graham's sake."

Which is precisely why I should leave.

Teddy said, "Wait until Josie turns up."

"That could be never."

For the first time Cleo saw Teddy's extreme anxiety in the shifting of her eyes, the blink of her lashes. Had Teddy deliberately revealed her emotions for an instant before she put on the bright smile? Waving a hand, Teddy said, "Hot weather sends most of us northerners home. A few of us stalwarts don't want to go back to our civic duties. Josie wanted to go back to her old life. We may learn she's in New York living it up. Graham and I have started inquiries in that direction. Shafer's too distraught to think straight."

Cleo said, "Josie's what my cousin would call a pocket twister."

"I can't disagree," Teddy said. "But just so you understand. Shafer says she stayed downstairs after he went up to bed. I talked to Barnabas myself. He swears Shafer never woke up once he passed out, and Josie never came upstairs. Barnabas doesn't know when Josie left the house. He said when he and Shafer came down next morning, they found the note."

"Did you see the note?"

"I did."

"What did it say?"

"To the best of my recollection, it said, 'Dear Shay, Am so sorry, darling. Can't help myself, I guess. Am a sucker for the bucks. I'll miss you. Nothing but divorce for it. Hate me. Don't hate the flyboy for this. Love XXOO.'"

Cleo said, "It doesn't say out right that she was leaving Shafer for Graham."

"Who else?"

"Neill's a flyboy, and he's rich."

"My dear lovely idiot," Teddy said, blowing smoke upward and smiling. "We love Neill, but Josie was crazy for Graham." Cleo opened the door to her rooms and waved a hand for Teddy to go in first. Closing the door, Cleo had disturbing thoughts of Graham with Josie, herself leaving here and never knowing how it would all turn out.

Teddy went to the window. Cleo followed, and, side-by-side, they looked upon the sea. The ruthless swells made the blood hammer in her veins.

Teddy said, "Graham would not carry on a romance with a married woman, nor propose marriage to his cousin's wife. It's preposterous."

"I'll take that cigarette," Cleo said, extending a hand. Teddy offered the pack and Cleo put the cigarette on her lips and let Teddy strike a match to it. After inhaling deeply, Cleo asked, "Why are you worried if the note is a lie?"

"What if we don't find Josie, or what if the unthinkable is true?"

"That Josie is dead?"

Teddy shook her head. "I can't give up hope. She's so young."

Cleo inhaled slowly from her cigarette. "Young people die, too."

Teddy made a noise close to a gasp. "Sorry, Cleo, that was tactless of me. I understand your grief over losing your fiancé." She turned and went for a Waterford ashtray to snuff her smoke. "I like you, Cleo, so I'm going to do all I can to get you out of the past."

Despite the upheaval in her head, she managed a smile at Teddy.

"Now we must concern ourselves with Graham," Teddy said, back to business. "Who knows what the authorities will think up? Graham is known to like his liquor. So's Josie. When he's down here, they drink together at The Dolphin and in Port Maria. The authorities overlook that it's illegal. But with a missing person and a mysterious note, they'll be remembering how the two of them were often together. They swam, played tennis and golf when her husband was away on business. It's been gossiped they were having an affair, but Graham said they weren't, and I believe him. For him, she was a diversion. She, however, was infatuated; in love, probably. There was that scene on the dance floor."

"Maybe Shafer got tired of being treated like he was."

"You can't think Shafer … No, he wouldn't hurt Josie."

"The women's wards are full of wives with black eyes and broken bones."

"But you've seen him, how nervy he is. Besides, Barnabas was with Shafer all night."

"Doesn't Barnabas sleep?"

"Not when Shafer has too much to smoke and drink. He's an asthmatic."

"The flyboy reference is certainly telling," Cleo said, as mildly as she could.

"That's Graham, of course, but I think it's all a ruse. She's playing a shell game. It's someone else. Shafer considered Doc a threat when Graham wasn't around."

"Doc?"

"Cleo dear, you've been around him. He is quite a fascinating man."

She tapped her cigarette in the crystal dish and took another drag. It gave her an excuse to think. "The note is what interests me."

Teddy asked, "What would you like to do this afternoon? How about a swim?"

"I think I'll read, or maybe walk on the beach, if that's all right with you."

"Sure. Don't, please, get lost."

"I won't."

"And, please, think about this. If Graham was with *someone* that night it would make all the difference."

Cleo walked back to the window. *Teddy knew* – she saw or intuited what happened. Cleo couldn't believe Graham would have told her.

She wanted Teddy to leave the room. Now. She was sick at the very suggestion of confessing to lying with a man after knowing him only two days. Oh yes, Teddy knew, but Teddy wasn't going to get her way. No way in hell would she confess that humiliation, that degradation.

Absurd, Cleo thought. I'm being paranoid. She doesn't know. She turned to reply and saw the door close on Teddy's back.

*****

Eurella came into the room thirty seconds after Teddy left. She said, "Mr. Graham is looking for you to come down."

"Hell's bells."

"He's waiting at the last step."

She put a hand to her forehead.

"He knows his mama just come down."

"Can I tell you a secret?"

"I been in your confidence since you comes here."

"I know how to get out of the house another way."

She laughed. "Ever body does."

CHAPTER FOURTEEN

At the stable, the air smelled of burning metal. Walking up the wide aisle, she saw a giant of the blackest hue she'd ever seen banging on the hoof of a horse.

"Hello?" she called. "Hello?"

He let go of the horse's leg and looked up. "Af-noon, miss."

"Afternoon. I'm looking for Doc."

He shook his head. "Many are. Not 'round here."

"Is he at his cabin?"

"No tellin'."

"Thanks."

"Wait, miss."

"Yes?"

"I'd see in the mews, I was you."

She grinned. Doc had his friends.

When she saw him standing next to Billy's hoods, she started to apologize for her lateness, but he held up a hand. "Want to pick out one?" he said.

He looked leaner, more rugged, like he'd been camping out all night, sleeping with the bears and wolves. When she walked closer, she detected the smell of leather and the electric aroma of tension. "I like the one with the oriental dome on it."

"Billy does, too."

In taciturn silence, he hooded Billy, ensconced him in the back of the truck, and they got into the cab. When he got to Oystercatcher and turned south, she assumed they were going to Petrel's Bluff, but she kept quiet, not sure how to ask questions that didn't slide easily from her brain to her tongue.

With his arms straight as sticks, he clutched the wheel like it might, at any moment, wrench from his hands. "Aren't you going to ask?"

Had he meant to sound so harsh? She cleared the knot from her throat. "You went to the mainland yesterday. Did you find Murphy?"

"He left town."

"Did you talk to the sheriff?"

"He got straightened out."

"Did you tell him about Josie?"

"Her name never came up."

"It's been three days."

"Not my business. Shafer's."

"Neill and I have been caught up in this mess. Someone has to go to the sheriff."

"Shafer needs to resolve it."

"He's drunk ninety-eight percent of the time."

"There may be a reason."

She stared at his profile. "What are you thinking?"

He let his elbows relax, and took one hand off the wheel. "Takes a while for a body to wash up."

"You're saying Shafer did something to her?" Doc twitched his shoulders apparently to suggest the possibility. "He'd had too much to drink that night and his man watched him like a hawk."

She almost laughed at the thought of hooded Billy (who wasn't a hawk exactly) in the back, but Doc was in no laughing mood. "Barnabas is an old man," he said. "Old men must sleep"

He didn't slow at the sandy road to Petrel's Bluff. "Where are we going?"

"The village."

"Teddy is afraid for Graham."

"Natural. The boy's got a reputation."

"I know."

"I know you know."

Exasperated, she said, "Does everybody know about everything on this island?"

He glanced at her. There was something feverish in his crooked smile. He looked out the wind screen, both hands straight out on the wheel again. "Just about."

"Tell me about Graham."

"You know already."

"Not what I know, what you know."

"Think about it."

He sure liked to speak in circles. It was hard to rationalize why he was making her apprehensive, and was he doing so on purpose? They rode for a while with anxiety for company. She tried to concentrate on a small herd of horses on one side of the road, and, a little ways up, on the wild hogs foraging the ground. By the time they reached a grove of small orange trees, her nerves were at their jittering worst.

The truck burst from the trees into the center of doll-like white buildings that shimmered in sunbeams. The village clearing – with no discernible roads or streets – was shell-strewn. The tabby structures were arranged in a ring and reminded her of tombstones. Dead in the middle of the circle, a small pitch-roof church with a steeple asserted its importance to the village. On the right, a structure sported a sign proclaiming it to be, "The Food Store and The Post Office". Next was a longer, lower shop that had a sign, too. "For sale. Feed, seed, horse-shoeing, plows, harrows, cows, chickens, season produce, melon and tomato. Breakfast served. Supper on request." Offset from this general of general stores was a small low edifice. It was surrounded by enormous trees with tire swings hanging from massive limbs. Such was the town's commerce center. On the left of the church, a dozen or so wooden houses had been built, some in pretty bad shape, maybe even abandoned. Through the trees, she could see other small cottages.

There was nobody about. "Where is everybody?" she asked.

"School, working, fishing, crabbing," he said. He pulled under a tree in front of the building with the tire swings. "The school house," he said.

"Millionaires kids go here?"

He cracked what was supposed to be a smile. More like a grimace. "Tutors," he said. "Some, like the Henry kids, go across the channel to private school on Amelia Island. This is the Negro school."

At that moment, a group of children ran from the building. They carried burlap sacks. Doc got out of the truck and walked to where they'd gathered around a white woman. She waved to Doc and nodded at Cleo. The children left her side, ran to Doc and danced and clowned around him. Cleo stood by the truck and watched him gesture the kids quiet by putting his finger against his lips. They mocked him by doing the same.

One of the kids said, "No spookin' Billy."

"Wouldn't want to do that," Doc said.

The kids followed him to the truck. He said to her, "We're going to the point where the great marsh starts. I promised the kids a hunt. They get fresh meat for dinner and their teacher gets a break."

"Just one teacher?"

"She teaches all grades."

Cleo surveyed the children. She counted twelve of all ages. Doc singled out a girl of about eight or nine. He spoke to her briefly, then he gloved his hand. The girl reluctantly moved away from the rest of the group, each child about to sizzle out of his or her skin. Doc got Billy out of the truck and on his gauntlet. Billy stayed calm when the hood came off, and, looking into the sky, eyes darting for prey, danced on the glove.

The young girl approached Cleo a thumb knuckle between her teeth.

"Hello pretty girl," Cleo said.

The girl smiled and dropped the hand from her mouth. "My awunt does for your people."

Doc obviously told the child to talk to her. "Who is your awunt?"

The girl twisted her hands. "Aunt Eurella."

"A fine woman. She helps me in the house."

"I knows."

The teacher had walked up. "Nora. The correct English is, I know.'"

"Yes um." Nora twined her fingers and jumped up and down. The teacher, who was early thirties, thin, but pleasant-looking, introduced herself. "I'm Ruth. Nora needs to learn good English to go out into the world."

"I'm Cleo." She let her gaze travel over the village which oozed complacency. "This doesn't seem like a bad life."

"Families are close and need new blood."

"How many families?"

"Twenty. Most are old folks. When the Civil War began, the plantation owner here freed his slaves. There were almost four hundred then. Most left for towns in Florida and Georgia to work as freemen. But some stayed. They were free, of course, but still did the work they'd done before the war. Over the years, more left, but none moved back." She took a deep breath "The life is good for young folks who like fishing, hunting, and working the orchards and rice fields, milking and caring for the livestock. But some are more ambitious, and they should have the education they need to go on if they want to."

Cleo watched Nora, who listened to her teacher. "Is Nora one of them?"

"Yes, she's a very smart girl." The teacher looked at her pupil. "Aren't you Nora?"

Nora sparkled with curiosity. "Smart as Aunt Eurella."

"Hey," Cleo said, pointing at Doc and his followers disappearing down a hill, "our falconer is getting ahead of us."

The teacher waved and walked away.

"Shall we catch up with Doc and Billy?" Cleo asked Nora.

"Yes um."

They walked side-by-side, she and the little colored girl. "It's nice to live on a beautiful island, isn't it?" Cleo said.

"Teacher says I go to Port Maria."

"That's a nice place, too."

"Aunt Eurella wants me to live at Southerness and be a servant like her is."

"She is," Cleo corrected. "You're too smart to be a servant."

"Awunt Eurella say I get uppity ways. She say I should go to Port Maria and find me a husband and bring him back to here."

"First, you must get an education."

"Aunt Eurella say the more I knows, better I chose." She giggled.

"Aunt Eurella is a smart woman."

"She likes you, she say."

"Miss Eurella is my friend and confidant."

"Con – fee – dant?"

"We keep secrets."

"Secrets," Nora said with a sly smile. "I likes secrets."

"What kind of secrets?"

"'Bout people."

"Everybody on this island whispers about each other," Cleo said. "You couldn't have a secret if you wanted to."

"You find some if you sneak 'round."

They'd reached the down side of the hill, and Cleo's foot slipped on the damp sand. "Dog gone it," she said.

"I like sneakin'," Nora said, getting back to the subject.

"It would have to be dark outside," Cleo said.

Nora's eyes shone. "My brother punches me out the bed, so I go out."

"Oooo, snakes."

"Them's in the woods."

"They are in the woods," Cleo corrected.

"Yes um."

"Where do you go when you sneak out?"

"Southerness. See parties and dancin'"

Her heart upticked. "Where do you live?"

"By the beach. Go along this here road, like we're goin', and you turn where the river runs into the salt." She waved her hand toward the sea. "You comes right out by the lighthouse and go up the boardwalk."

Cleo's nerves flicked like flames. "When were you last at Southerness?"

"Um ..."

"Last night?"

"No ma'am."

"Night before?"

"Um, 'fore that."

"Tuesday?"

"Um yes ma'am. I knows my days."

They were about to catch up with Doc and the other kids. She stopped and said, "I was at Southerness that night. Did you see me?"

"No ma'am. Saw Mr. Barnabas."

Cleo had begun to get her island bearings. Coming from the village, down the beach, the Drakes mansion, Bellflower, came before Southerness. "Where was Mr. Barnabas?"

"Sittin' on steps with Miss Josie."

At least one somebody lied. "Was she okay?"

"She be ... was crying. Drinkin' prolly. Aunt Eurella says."

"Did you speak to Mr. Barnabas?"

"No ma'am." Her eyes were saucers. "He'd be mad at Nora."

"Did you see Mr. Shafer?"

"No ma'am."

"Did you hear anything Mr. Barnabas said to Miss Josie?"

"She was cryin.'"

"Did she say anything."

"Something about money. Awunt say they got no money. It's that pro – probishon got them."

"It got a lot of people, Nora."

"Don't bother us none here."

Doc yelled, "Hey, you two. Billy's waiting."

Near the edge of the marsh river, Doc stood on a rise with Billy on his arm. The fresh waters of the river flowed through the great marsh, mingling with the salt of the sea. The air smelled of brown earth and dead fish.

Billy put on quite a show – diving for sea birds, catching them as they fell, releasing them at Doc's feet, giving them a *coup d'etat* to the neck. The kids all cried, "Ooooooo. Eeeeeeeee." Then Billy would take a bow by swooping over their heads and landing on Doc's arm.

"Here we go again," Doc cried, and off flew the fabulous Billy. Cleo said to Nora, "He's a live wire, don't you think?"

Nora looked uncertain. "Them's jesses, not wires."

Cleo laughed. These kids, bless them, were as far away from the jargon of the city as they could be. But she thought the cadence of their peculiar jargon was just fine, too.

*****

Billy had massacred a lot of sea birds. Doc portioned out two for each child's burlap bag, and then it was time for Billy to eat. Cleo winced watching him tear apart a small seagull. The children wandered away, pushing sticks into the marsh, kidding each other, playing tag, just being children. Billy finished his meal, and Doc held up his arm. Billy obliged with uplifted wings and a perfect landing. She would miss this bird when she was back in Philadelphia. Perhaps Doc would photograph him and send pictures. She would ask.

At the truck, the children said goodbye, and Billy raised his head for the hood.

Scooting under the steering wheel and closing the truck door, Doc said, "Billy had fun. Did you?"

"I've got a crush on Billy."

"Lucky Billy."

She daren't look at him while her brain processed his words, his inflection.

The truck crept down the sandy road, the dense woods on each side, while her thoughts whispered among themselves.

He said, "Was Nora helpful?"

"You thought she would be, didn't you?"

"I thought she'd talk to you. She gets on with her teacher."

"She's in the habit of sneaking out at night."

"I've seen her. She doesn't know it, and I won't interfere."

"Barnabas sat on the steps with Josie Tuesday night. Josie was crying."

"Nothing new. Josie cried a lot."

He sounded like a man who knew her well and he'd used the past tense. Cleo said, "Apparently she had crying jags after too much gin."

"Anything else?" he asked.

"How old is Barnabas?"

"Late seventies, I expect."

"Teddy told me he stays up all night when Shafer has too much to drink because of Shafer's asthma."

"I had a few conversations with Barnabas. He's a tough old bird from the old country. He says when his time comes, he'll sleep."

"Do you think Josie's dead?"

"It's looking like it."

"Could she have killed herself?"

"No." The word was a small explosion.

"The Thompsons were at Southerness that night."

"They're always there. They left to go north the next morning. I saw their jitney leave."

"Swinny was also there. Terrible dancer."

"Not like Graham, huh?"

She thought back to the last time Graham's name was in her head. She didn't appreciate Doc's bringing it in again. Had he deliberately done it? To torture her? What did he know of that night? Well, she wasn't going to shy away. "Graham's a swell dancer."

His eyes narrowed as he stared out the wind screen. "Things are changing, Cleo."

"How?"

"More like why."

"Tell me."

"Graham comes home a war hero, but with no notion of going into the steel business after his father died. He's an aimless young nitwit." He looked sideways at her. "Don't get me wrong. He's a fine fellow. I'm not talking against him. If I did, you'd think I was jealous, wouldn't you?" His eyes hadn't shifted from their level gaze.

A curious sense of time slipped by like fog dissipates, when all of a sudden the truck jerked sideways, and he broke eye contact. His inattention to the road caused the truck to veer with the left front wheel climbing a log near a thicket. He fought the wheel but the truck slid into the shrubs. "Damn," he said and shifted the gears, back and forth, back and forth, the truck grinding away until it broke free and skidded back onto the road.

She had these moments to sort through the reality of his emotions, and hers, which battered against the shores of her resolve. How could it all get so crazy?

He stopped the truck. "Check on Billy," he said.

Moments later, he climbed back under the steering wheel. "He's all right." He laid a hand on her knee. "How about you?"

"Fine, fine." She looked at his hand. So much flew at her now, her chest expanding and contracting to her breathing. She glanced up. "You were saying things were changing."

He took his hand away, and, clutching the steering wheel, pressed the gas. "The war over. Prohibition. Josie going missing. The Pinkerton man showing up. The whispers are growing louder."

"They would, wouldn't they?"

He grunted, and she waited for him to go on. "I don't know what I'm talking about sometime. We all have our disappointments in this life. You got to move on. Get your mind off it."

"I feel like I'm in quicksand, being sucked down by inches, just watching myself, doing nothing about it."

He put his right hand on her shoulder, giving it a shake like a buddy would. "You'll be all right."

"Will you?"

"I'm always all right."

She didn't know how to handle Doc's shifting moods. He'd always been aloof, but today he seemed like someone had punctured his reserve, and he was winding down. No doubt he was telling her he cared. He was as fascinating as a movie star, but she had no idea how she felt about him. His presence didn't touch her in the intimate places like Graham had when he looked at her and spoke. Yet she'd enjoyed being with Doc. He wouldn't take kindly at being compared to a comfortable pair of shoes, but he was that. And, seized by guilt, she added that he was so much more than comfortable old shoes. Criminy, the more she tried to sort through it, the more her brain waves sloshed in her numb skull.

He turned on Plover Road before he spoke again. "You in the mood for some roasted seagull?"

She thought of Graham's proverb. *Seagull, Seagull sitting on the sand…*

"Um …"

The ticking silence lengthened.

Doc's laugh was like a rattle in a bucket. "We got some other choices. I'm starved."

*****

She drank beer and watched him roast the gulls. Funny how skinny they turned out to be once their feathers came off. He lined five birds, with an onion between each, on a stick he called a spit, and placed it on a grate over the fire.

He said, "Here you are drinking home brew and watching seagulls cook while folks at Southerness are into their second gin rickeys and looking forward to lamb chops."

"I like your home brew," she said. "Don't know about the gulls."

"Alcohol's alcohol and meat's meat," he said. "It's not fashionable to eat gull, but it's on par with dove and quail."

"I guess they taste the same to Billy."

"Rat, too."

She gulped. "You ever eat …?"

"When Billy preys on rodents, he knows not to drop one in front of me, unless it's squirrel or possum."

Possum? She calmed her gag reflex. "What are we going to do about Barnabas?"

His eyebrows lifted at the sudden change. He went to get two thick white plates from a cabinet and two knives and forks. "I been thinking about that."

"Just so you know," she said, "I won't divulge that little girl's confidence. She might get punished."

"I wouldn't expect you to. Nor will I." He brought salt and pepper to the table.

"Somehow we've got to make Barnabas tell us the truth."

From an icebox, he fetched a plate of sliced raw carrots. "I got an idea you might consider?"

"You sound hesitant."

"You might not like it."

"What?"

He removed the long spit from the flames. On the sink, he raked the birds off the spit and cut them in half. "You game?"

She wriggled her shoulders. "I'll bite."

He set plates on the table with two white napkins.

A half a bird lay on her plate. "It looks like squab," she said.

"Sure does."

"But it isn't."

He tapped his head. "All up here."

She picked up the knife and fork. "What might I not like, Doc?"

"Ask Graham to talk to Barnabas."

"Ask Graham?" She'd almost choked on his name.

"Convince Graham he's got a lot to lose if Josie's not found."

"Surely the fool knows that."

"Rich folk like to hide their heads in their silks and top hats. Make it go away. And they think they can get away with anything."

She thought about the truth in that, about a couple of famous Philadelphia cases of debauchery buried in gold and diamonds. "I thought maybe, maybe you and me could somehow tackle Barnabas."

He chewed steadily, like the bird might be tough. He swallowed and drained half a glass of beer. He wiped his mouth with the napkin. All acts measured and controlled. "It's not the best way. We're outsiders. Besides …"

"Besides what?" she asked, nibbling on a carrot.

"I got some things to see to."

She thought about the Pinkerton man, but didn't want to go into that again. "I never told you something."

He started to bring the fork to his mouth, then halted. "What might that be?"

"Fredik took trunks to the *Monongahela* on Wednesday morning, right at dawn."

"Teddy's going north soon."

"Josie could fit. Burial at sea," she said.

"That would leave Graham under suspicion for the rest of his life."

"Like you said, the rich think they can get away with anything."

"Be a shame to besmirch a fine military career," he said, chewing. "But better than going to prison." He aimed his fork at her plate. "You promised a bite."

"I changed my mind."

"Think on it. About Graham, I mean. He's a fine man, about as fine as you'll find for his breed."

Without considering his words, she said, "I can hardly … it isn't something we would talk about."

"Think of a way." She heard the subtle suggestion in his voice.

"You're asking a lot, Doc."

"I'd ask a lot more of you, if I could."

She couldn't think of anything to say, so she rose and took her plate to the wooden sink, pushed the half-bird onto the platter, then ladled water from a tub into a porcelain bowl. He came up with a washrag. When she took it from his hand, his mouth turned up in a puzzled smile. She said, "I'm not rich. I just pretend to be."

His eyes held hers. "I am rich, and I pretend not to be."

Rolling her lips inward, she tied a towel around her waist. He picked up another towel. They finished washing up in the kind of silence that makes you feel jumpy as a new kitten in the home of nervy dogs. She took off the towel and went for her hat.

He said, "Saved yourself room for some Southerness lamb."

She placed her cloche on her head and looked up at him, the tops of her eyelashes skirting the brim. "That was unworthy of you."

His mask of control slipped a little. "I have more unworthy thoughts than I can ever express." He looked at her shoulder. "I'll be going away for a while."

"Promise you won't go away without saying goodbye?"

He took one of her hands and kissed its knuckles. "I'm not ready just yet."

It was one of those unthinking impulses – perhaps meant to make up for her unease and his anxious state – that caused her to stand on tiptoes and kiss his cheek. He turned his head in time to get her lips. His whole body tensed when he wrapped his arms around her in a tight hug. A second or two longer and she moved her head to the side. When she looked at him, his eyes changed from hopeful to reflect an ache throbbing deep inside. Her heart reacted by doing a little flutter step in her chest. "I must go."

"I know," he said. "I can't keep you here."

*****

Predictably, they were gathered in the drawing room. When she walked in, Neill hurried toward her so fast she thought he might tackle her. She sidestepped. "Whoa."

The short sprint winded him. "We've waited. Cleo." His eyes were like big question marks.

She gazed over the room, nodding to everyone. "Sorry. I was at the village. The school. I met the teacher, the children."

"That's commendable," Teddy said, her intonation belied the meaning of the word. "Next time give us fair warning."

Cleo clamped her jaw against a retort.

Mitty, the master of impeccable timing, came to the door. "Dinner, madam."

Teddy rose and took Neill's arm. Graham moved forward and offered Cleo his. She had no choice but to lay her palm on his forearm. He said, "I had an idea for this afternoon, before you escaped."

He had a nerve to scold. "Escaped to a school? Shall I tell you how thrilling it was?"

"What are your plans later?"

"Rest and reading."

"Swinny's coming over for Mahjong and a night cap."

"That out-thrills reading."

"You've not been very sociable, Cleo."

"Dare I say what you've been?"

"I'm trying, Cleo. I want you to …"

"Shhhhhhh."

Teddy turned her head at the hissing sound.

For the adults at the table, conversation was somewhat strained, but Linith and Eagan filled the silence with their exploits on the tennis courts. Eventually, they were excused.

When dessert was served, Cleo felt bold enough to ask, "When do we go sailing?" The wine had gone to her head, firming her spine in the face of Teddy and Graham's stoniness.

Teddy stopped chewing. "We had planned to sail this afternoon."

"How about tomorrow?"

Graham tapped her hand. "All of us? Or you alone?"

"Graham," Teddy warned.

"Sorry," he said, conferring a dim smile on Cleo.

Teddy said, "Depends on the weather, but yes, tomorrow would be good." Her thoughtful eyes observed Cleo. "What time shall we expect you to meet us?"

"I'll do my walking in the morning unless you want to leave then?" She was feeling quite breezy.

Teddy waved her fork. "Wind is better later. Tide will be right at eleven."

"Eleven it is."

Dinner over, Graham followed her out the door and down the hall. "Cleo, will you play Mahjong tonight?"

"It's a game for four players. Besides I'm not fond of Mahjong," she said, telling a bald lie. She adored the gambling tiles. Heading for the staircase, she looked over her shoulder. "See you at eleven tomorrow. My best to Swinny."

How intractably rude she'd been. Yet she high-stepped all the way to her rooms.

CHAPTER FIFTEEN

Although Teddy had severely challenged her own motto of guests going off on their own, Cleo knew her hostess wouldn't leave her guests without the proper attire for the event du jour, in this case sailing.

Eurella arrived as she was fiddling with a sidelacer. "Miz Henry suggests knickers for sailing," she said, taking hold of the laces.

"Excellent, Eurella. I was at the school yesterday. I met your adorable niece, Nora."

Eurella tugged hard at the camisole laces. "That chile. She chattered all night long about the pretty lady with green eyes and nice smile."

"She's sharp," Cleo said. "Her teacher said so, too."

"Her teacher be filling her head with daydreams 'bout education."

"Nothing wrong with education."

Eurella didn't exactly bristle. "No, miss for them's can afford it."

Time to placate Eurella. "Good way to get an up-and-coming husband, don't you think?"

"You got to find an up-and-comin' man first."

"An idle mind can get a smart girl in lot of trouble, I always say."

"Ain't that the truth. Nora's got no idle mind."

"But at her age, she has to guard against imagination."

"Nora don't imagine nothin'. Like her awunt, what we sees is what we knows and what we says."

The outfit she chose was a sleeveless, swing collar tunic in duck cloth with a broad navy stripe up the bodice to the neckline. A sailor's emblem was embroidered in the center. The trousers were navy and banded. The band snapped together right above the ankle. "Quite smart, don't you think, Eurella?"

"Yes, miss."

She wondered what Doc would think and smiled. Probably nothing; he didn't seem to notice her wardrobe. *Doc, Doc, oh Doc* But for the boundaries she'd built, maybe … *Oh, don't think about it.*

In the gingham blue breakfast room, Teddy and Graham were discussing politics; both were high on Warren Harding. Neill read a three-day-old newspaper. Cleo went to the buffet and forked a waffle on a plate, smeared butter and raspberry jam on it and walked to the seat next to Neill.

Neill looked up for the first time and spent several seconds looking her up and down. "Whew! Spiffy. What would Aunt Amelia say?"

Cleo scooted into her chair. "I'll tell her how comfortable trousers are."

Neill shrugged. "No different than her going around the house in her bloomers."

Surprised, she looked at Teddy and Graham, who were praising the president over some bill he proposed in Congress. She said to Neill, "Who told you about Mother?" It was true Amelia ironed in her bloomers, but only when women were in the house. They had one servant, old Flossie, who was nearly seventy and had bad knees and ankles.

"I saw her," Neill said. "I came through Philly last year. The flivver got a nail in one of her dogs so I got a rental fliv to your house. No one answered the dong, so I went around to the side. Peek-a-boo in a window and there was Auntie in her bloomies." He laughed. "Rhatz, I vamoosed before she ogled me."

Suppressing a grin, she cut into the waffle. "Mother would not be pleased."

Graham rattled on about the new president. "Charming fellow, I met him last year when I went to the polo matches in Dayton."

But Teddy had heard Neill's discussion about Amelia in her bloomers. She said, "Cleo's mother was overdressed for ironing – dreadful chore. If I didn't have Juanite, I'd go around in wrinkled clothes."

Cleo thought Teddy probably shed more than her tunic and skirts when she got hot. She pushed her plate aside and rose.

"Where's our girl off to?" Graham asked.

Trick question. "Can't decide."

"I thought I'd take myself up to Petrel's Bluff," Graham said, rising. "Watch Billy. Haven't seen him perform for a while."

Drat

"So," Graham continued affably, "if that's where you're off to, care for a ride?"

She looked at Teddy, feeling reticent, but forging ahead with an improvised alternative to Graham's plan. "I wanted to ask if I can drive one of your automobiles to see the whole island."

Teddy looked at Graham, who seemed torn between anger and resignation. She shrugged at Cleo. "Okay by me. Get Fredik to help with instructions. What can you drive?"

"My fiancé taught me to drive his Model T Touring car."

"Got one. It's yours. Don't hurt yourself." She got up from the table.

"I'll start you off," Graham said.

Neill rose. "Bearcat, the Roller needs an outing. What say?"

She wanted to go alone, and nobody drove Neill's cars but Neill.

She said to her cousin, "Read your book, I'll be fine." She headed for the door. "Thank you all, but I'd like to see the island on my own."

In the hall, she blew out a long breath. Getting away from that mare's nest took swift thinking.

*****

Nattily clothed, Fredik walked from the garages toward her – large, muscular, sure of himself. He wore a straw fedora. His smile blossomed, but didn't reach his eyes, which looked above her head like flies buzzed it. His eyebrows came together over his nose and one of his incisors was gold. Pirate, she thought, and a chill flicked across her shoulders.

"Good day," he said, his voice soft, insinuating.

"Morning. I've permission to take out the Model T Touring."

"I zee."

"Mrs Henry has given permission."

"Miz Henry's wish is mine command." He looked away, sly as a fox. "Top down?"

"I don't think so, no."

He walked off like he was on the leisurely stroll of his life. He glanced back once to see if she followed, but she waited until he drove the car around and opened the door for her. "Do you know to crank?" he asked.

"If I have to."

His dark eyes darted, the corner of his upper right lip curled. "Hope you don't have to. Hard starting."

"I won't be long."

"As you say."

"Thank you."

*****

Doc wasn't at the stable, but several men were busy with the morning chores. He didn't answer her knock, and he wasn't in the mews. Billy was, however, perched on a fat tree branch that had been nailed to the wall and protruded into the middle of the room. He sidestepped, talons to talons and said, "Kek."

"Kek to you, too, Billy boy." She blew him a kiss. "See you later."

She turned and almost smacked into Graham. Damn him.

"So you, too, are taken with our Billy."

Furious, she said, "Doc's Billy."

A muscle in his jaw twitched. "What Doc found on this island, stays on this island."

"You followed me."

"I did."

"I'm going."

"Cleo."

"Graham, how much plainer can I make it. I don't want to be alone with you."

His shoulders slumped and he held his hands out like a beggar. His eyes bore into hers, and she was unable to break the stare. All her muscles, tendons, nerves froze in place.

He said, "I'll say this quick before you run away to wherever. I'm sorry. I want you to believe what we had was … came from my heart."

She swallowed to break the tension, thinking that love and hate really do share a common border.

"I want you to believe …"

"Sure." She juggled past him.

When she left the mews, she skipped away, telling herself, don't look back.

Ahead – Hallelujah – Doc emerged from the palmettos. Her heart gave a little lurch at the self-confident way he wore the wide-brimmed straw hat. Seeming amused, he stopped five paces away, his crooked, sensuous smile a balm on her raw nerves. "Morning," he said, removing his hat.

"Morning," she said, happy there were no ripples of unease between them like yesterday.

Whispering   135

Something caused Doc to look past her shoulder. "Graham." he said. "Anything the matter in the mews?"

"Not with Billy," she said.

She watched Graham walk toward them. "Morning, Doc," he said.

"Morning. Everything all right?"

"Fine. We came to get a gander at Billy."

"Won't be flying this morning," Doc said, glancing at Cleo.

"Looked forward to it," Graham said.

"Mare's down, over in the pasture."

"You have to put her away?"

"Keeping an eye for now."

"Good work, man." Graham looked at her. "Cleo?"

"Don't wait for me."

Graham saluted. "Be seeing ya." His steps were slow. It appeared any moment he might turn and backtrack, but he got in the single door and started it.

"What was that about?" Doc asked.

"He's dogging me."

Doc leaned his head toward his cottage. "You want a cup of coffee?"

"I better do what I said I was going to do when I took the car."

"Which is?"

"See more of the island."

"Wish I could go with you," he said, the words catching like he spoke around a bubble of air.

She wished she had a comforting cigarette. "I know, the mare. How bad is she?"

"It's fifty-fifty. I don't want to lose her. She's a good brood mare. The foal made it. We'll see about her."

"I guess I'll get along." She placed her hand in his and felt his knuckles tighten. "Good luck with her."

"Cleo …?"

"The Henrys are taking Neill and I sailing later this morning." A breeze ruffled his hair. He nodded.

"I thought I'd discuss Barnabas with Graham then."

He nodded again.

She let go of his hand and turned away from the frustration he blinked from his eyes.

*****

Thank goodness for trousers.

The launch was an open boat with four benches. Teddy got in the launch first, then held out her hand to Cleo. "Remember," Graham said, holding her at the waist to guide her step down. "Foot in the center of the boat. Wouldn't want to swamp the dinghy. Sit opposite Teddy."

Cleo found herself standing in the middle of the waddling boat.

"I'll take the stern bench," Teddy said. "You take the bow. Be careful. Don't rock us."

Cleo nodded and stepped over a bench to the single-seater in front. Neill boarded next and sat on the middle bench. He lifted a pair of metal things that looked like stirrups and placed them in holes at the side of the boat. Graham untied the line (not rope, as she was told) and climbed in. Sitting in the other bench, he mounted another set of stirrups, then he and Neill threaded oars into the stirrups and began rowing. After a few strokes, they developed a rhythm and the boat moved swiftly through the choppy waters.

Cleo looked beyond their skiff at the sailboat's glistening bow slapping the water. "How long is the *Monongahela*?"

"Overall, she's forty-eight feet," Graham said. "Her length at the waterline is thirty-seven feet. She has a thirty-thousand pounds displacement to nine-thousand pound ballast. Her mast is thirty-eight feet and her draft is six-feet, four-inches."

"Why doesn't she float away?" Cleo asked.

"She moored at permanent anchor," Teddy said, "marked by that buoy." Teddy was fooling with something on the back of the launch.

Neill stopped rowing and pulled in his oars. Graham kept his oars in the water and maneuvered the launch alongside the sailboat. The *Monongahela* bobbed as if welcoming the skiff passengers. Graham dumped life rings attached to the dinghy into the water and drew the boats together. Neill stayed seated so the skiff wouldn't become unbalanced and Teddy stood. Fredik was already on board extending his hand. Teddy stood, and, in one swift motion, planted her leg against the side of the sailboat, grabbed Fredik's giant hand and swung the other leg on deck. Cleo couldn't picture herself doing that.

Grinning, Graham rose and held out a hand to her. "The best way to climb aboard is to face me, I'll hike you up the side to sitting position and Fredik will catch you." *Imagine doing that in a dress and showing your bloomers.* Graham's grin seemed painted on his face and had been since they met at the bottom steps of Southerness.

She faced him, her body stiff. He put his hands around her waist, then slipped them into her armpits and hoisted. Her legs dangled and swayed. Her heels hit the side of the sailboat.

"Won't be long, you'll get some sea legs," he said.

Fredik caught her, and, like a feather, she floated to the deck where he held her two seconds longer than it took to firm her feet against the rock of the boat. Fredik gave a hand to Neill who sprung over the side onto the deck. Graham attached the little boat to the buoy, where another small boat bobbed, and climbed aboard like his mother.

Being on a sailboat was a brand new experience, and Cleo rubbed the polished wood of the deck with the toe of her shoe.

Graham said, "Carvel planked with cedar on hardwood steam-bent oak timbers. She was originally built in 1902 by my grandfather. We had her refitted after the war. A new cabin, bow-fronted all in mahogony with sky-lightning, sliding hatch and lift door to the cabin. The after end of the cock pit is coach-roofed to match."

She bit her lip. "You could be a salesman."

He dropped his smile momentarily, realizing the implication of her remark. He pointed at bags on the deck. "In there are sails. We're switching from racing sails to cruising ones for Teddy's trip north. "Fredik opened the larger of the two bags. She wondered idly why Fredik never met her eyes.

Graham pointed to the bow of the boat. "We stow sails in the forepeak, that's in front of the cabin."

She made mental note of these terms.

While Fredik, Graham and Neill tugged the canvas sails from the bag, Teddy guided Cleo toward the helm. The big wheel was brass, maybe gold for the way it glistened. Graham winked at her. "Cleo is getting her first sailing lesson." He made it sound thrilling, which it was. He continued, "Okay, here we go, chumps and dollies." The three men pulled the heavy canvas out of the bag and unrolled it. "First thing," he said, "is we locate the clew. Good-o, the last sailor rolled the main correctly with the clew on the outside." He was sticking his finger through a ring at a point on the sail. "Give me a hand, Fredy."

Fredik didn't look like a Fredy. More like a well-dressed Frankenstein without the stitches.

Graham looked at her and pointed to a long pole. "This here's the boom. See it has a groove? Okay, we're going to put this end of the sail, called the foot, onto the boom." Neill held the sail while Graham threaded the foot onto the boom. Fredik moved to the other side, pulling the foot toward the clew. Graham said, "A shackle secures the tack corner. An outhaul – this here thing – is attached to the clew and the foot is stretched tight by pulling on the outhaul line and cleating it."

"What's the outhaul for?" Cleo asked.

"Tension." Looking at her, he let the word hang. "On the foot." He smiled and her hands curled into fists. "Simple?"

This outing was a mistake; his closeness, his very being, sought to overcome and conquer her.

"Now," he continued, "we all get to work putting battens in batten pockets. We start at the tack. While we're battening, we trace the luff, that's the leading edge of the sail, to the head, down the leech to the clew to smooth the entire sail."

Teddy said, "Are we giving you too much to take in?"

"I'm following."

"We give simple tests," Graham said.

Graham, Teddy and Neill went to work noisily huffing as they worked the great canvas sails. She heard terms like: "halyard not fouled," "shroud," "feed it into the luff …"

Graham said, "Now for the gib." He looked at her. "It's a headsail, in front of the main. The two sails work together to play with the wind. It's really quite simple."

"For you."

"You'll see. We'll get the jib ready for Fredik to haul her up when we get underway with the main."

Cleo watched as Graham attached the tack corner of the jib and started snapping. Graham called them hanks. Fredik did a fancy finger thing with a line. Graham said, "We tie her with a figure eight knot, until we need her."

Teddy, standing at the wheel, called, "Prepare to weigh anchor."

Graham began singing, his voice full and lusty:
Stand Navy down the field, sails set to the sky.
We'll never change our course, so Army you steer shy-y-y-y.

Neill joined in:

Roll up the score, Navy, Anchors Aweigh.
Sail Navy down the field and sink the Army, sink the Army
Grey.

Get underway, Navy, Decks cleared for the fray,
We'll hoist true Navy Blue So Army down your Grey-y-y-y.
Full speed ahead, Navy; Army heave to,
Furl Black and Grey and Gold and hoist the Navy, hoist the
Navy Blue

Neill could hardly carry a tune, but he was enthusiastic enough.

Teddy laughed. "It's really an old football song they sing ever chance they get." She pointed a finger skyward. "Hoist the anchor," Teddy called. She looked at Cleo. "That anchor wince is called a windlass. The chain is called the rode."

"Got it," Cleo said, in the spirit.

Neill and Graham stood behind Fredik while he wound the windlass. Fredik leaned over the bow and fiddled with the chain. He called, "Up and down." Graham signaled to Teddy pumping his fist up and down.

Teddy pointed skyward again, doing something with her thumb. "Up anchor."

Fredik wound the windlass until the anchor came into view. It was black and hung with seaweed. "Anchors aweigh!" the three men cried together. Fredik and Graham lugged it on deck.

Teddy said to Cleo, "It goes in the locker, a hold in front of the boat."

They pulled in chains and things that looked like pulleys and arranged it neatly in the locker. The boat began to circle, then move. The wind behind Cleo blew her back hairs forward, over and around her headband.

"Raise the main," Teddy said.

Graham winked at Cleo. "Pay attention. Test coming up. Now, Fredik's going to loosen the main sheet, that line that controls the lateral movement of the main sail."

She looked away, desperate to keep him from seeping back into her heart.

Teddy turned the wheel, and the boat began to arc around until the wind was dead in Cleo's face.

Graham said, "Eye of the wind."

Fredik held the halyard with one hand above the other and pulled downward, hand over hand as the great piece of canvas rose, Neill and Graham on either side, aiding the lifting. Fredik gave the halyard several jerks and pulls until he was satisfied it was properly set, then he rolled the halyard and hung it from the cleat on the mast. Meanwhile, Teddy had turned the boat so the wind wasn't blowing straight at her, and Fredik hauled on the main sheet until the sail filled with air.

"Ready to sail," Teddy said. Fredik stood at the side next to a large round thing with lines wrapped around it.

Graham took Cleo's hand. "Fredik's the trimmer. Let's go to the cockpit. We're going to sail close hauled until we reach open water."

"What's close hauled."

"As close to the wind as we can."

"Diagonally upwind," Teddy said, keeping the wheel steady.

When they reached open water, Graham said, "Time to raise the jib."

Teddy turned the boat directly into the eye of the wind.

Fredik released the jib sheets and raised the smaller sail hand over hand as he'd done with the main sail. Teddy turned the boat away from the wind and Fredik adjusted the sail with the jib sheets. Cleo had never seen a big man move so deftly and quickly.

"He's called the trimmer," Teddy called. "I'm the helmsman, or skipper."

"What's Neill?" Cleo asked.

"Ballast."

Neill laughed. "You, too, Bearcat. Everyone on a sailboat has a position to maintain."

Cleo sat on a bench in the cockpit and looked at the steps going down into the long cabin. She'd need to think of a reason to go down there, where the trunks must be.

The boat skimmed back and forth across the water like a swan leading her chicks. The day was gorgeous. Every one on board was fit and jovial. She supposed she was fit enough, but there was too much churning through her head to be jovial. If only, if only Josie hadn't disappeared, if only she hadn't heard about Graham's womanizing. Maybe Teddy was right. A man had to have knowledge to woo and guide a girl through the newness of love. Hadn't she enjoyed Graham's skill? She looked through her lashes as the sails moved across the sky. She peeked at Graham, but he was looking ahead. The boat itself moved like the sea was a bed of satin sheets, sheets like those in the lighthouse.

"It's awesome, isn't it?" Teddy asked.

"Yes," she answered. How could she not be in awe of the powerful boat, which, unchained from her moorings, could go anywhere if free of these masterful people, Fredik, Teddy, Graham. Her mind played with the analogy of these masterful people who wanted her to go in their chosen direction.

"Graham," Teddy called, "take the wheel. I'll show Cleo below decks."

"Aye," Graham said.

She stood at an opening that led downward. "This is called the companionway," Teddy said, placing a hand on the rail and descending. "The door to it is called the hatch. There are several cabins down here. The cabin nearest the bow is the forecastle. Crew quarters, four berths, top and bottom, and four lockers. The skipper, me, sleeps in the main cabin behind it. We're entering the saloon."

Cleo ducked her head until she reach the last step. The saloon was larger than she imagined. "Mahagony bulkheads," Teddy said.

"Bulkheads?"

"Partitions. Walls. Bulkheads separate the cabins, the head and the galley. Guest berths are in front of the galley, bunks starboard and port."

Cleo surveyed the narrow settees lining the saloon walls. They were lovely in navy blue. One was occupied by a large picnic basket and a smaller one next to it. A square table was fastened to the bulkhead, papers that looked like maps were spread across the top. Next to the table were three trunks, the old fashioned Victorian kind with humps. An anchor lay next to the trunks.

"The head is here," Teddy said, and pointed to a cupboard by the steps.

"Head?"

"The lavatory. I thought I'd acquaint you with it in case you need to use it."

"Maybe I will now," Cleo said.

"I'll be topside. Won't be long we'll be at Nance's Inlet where we'll have our picnic."

Cleo opened the door to the head. The johnny was the smallest she'd ever seen and low to the floor. Fortunately, she didn't have to use it and turned toward the trunks. Hearing voices from above, she looked up to see open ceiling hatches, but no one peered down at her. She crept to the trunks. Two were fastened with large locks, the third was not locked. She bent to lift the lid. It raised easily. It appeared to be chock full of clothes. Teddy's. She reached in to push her hand down the side when she heard footsteps. She dashed to the head and closed the door behind her. She counted to two hundred and came out. Teddy was standing at the open trunk. She didn't look at Cleo, but said, "I swear I closed this thing."

Caught. How stupid. If there was a body aboard, it wouldn't be in an unlocked trunk.

Graham lowered himself down the hatch, and Cleo was grateful he'd saved a possible scene. "Getting hungry, ladies?"

"A little," Cleo said, stepping sideways past a settee toward the steps.

Teddy banged the trunk lid shut and made for the companionway. "I'm topsides." She climbed through the hatch.

"I say, what's the matter with the mater?" Graham asked.

"I think she thinks I was nosing in her trunks."

"Were you?"

"Silly."

"She can think what she wants. Why would you?"

She put her foot on the first step. "Indeed."

"I say, Cleo can we have a chat?"

"I can't think what for. I've learned quite a bit about sailing already." She took a step up.

He caught her forearm. "Please?"

"A short chat topsides. See I'm learning the jargon."

"Can't talk above the wind," he said, extending his hand toward a settee. "Please."

She remained on the step. "What is it you wanted to chat about?"

"Can we sit?"

"Graham, I … it's stuffy in here."

He put his hands in his pockets. "Okay, you want me to get the gabbing over with."

"You don't even have to begin."

He beamed a smile full of warmth. "Oh, my lovely Cleo, what can I say? You have judged me harshly and are trying your darndest to string me up."

"Graham." She looked past him, her eyes fastening on the treacherous trunk.

"I don't go away easily, my girl. You are my girl. I don't give up once I set my heart on something."

She licked her lips with a nervous stroke of her tongue. "You can't put a sail up me and point me where I don't want to go."

He grinned. "I like that, Bearcat. Just say you'll give me a chance."

Blinking, she looked away. "You had it."

"I never had a thing with Josie, I swear it."

She dared to glare at him. "There were others."

His eyes became indistinct as if blurred by pain. "Yes."

She waved a hand. "It's not my business anymore. I don't want to speak of this again.'

He reached out and touched the back of her hand. He whispered, "I meant something to you from the first." He wound his fingers in hers. "Please …"

Her heart floated between wariness and rising desire. "Josie is still missing, Graham."

"It's nothing to do with me."

"Something happened to her."

"I swear on Teddy's head."

"She was seen crying that night. She was sitting on the veranda steps with Barnabas, crying."

"I wasn't sitting there. For god's sake, girl, you know that."

"You spurned her that night."

"I always spurned her. She was a tease. Sometimes I'd go along. But only for so long. You've got to believe that."

"You must have cared."

"Never like that."

"Don't you wonder where she is?"

He ran his hands through his hair. "Yes, dammit, I wonder. I don't know why she wrote that silly note, and I'd like to wring her neck when I see her again."

"*If* you see her again."

"But I haven't the foggiest idea where she went."

"Why don't you ask Barnabas why she was crying?"

Outside shadows from the sails shifted on his face, etching its hesitant lines. "It'd be interfering with my cousin's family."

"Go to Shafer."

"How do you know about her crying that night?"

"A little birdie told me."

His hand jerked. "Ah, Billy."

She walked up the companionway. "It's a great day for sailing, don't you think, Graham?"

"Cleo …"

She walked through the hatch into the dazzling day.

CHAPTER SIXTEEN

Fredik dropped anchor in the inlet of a neighboring island. Neill and Graham lowered a small launch from the starboard side. The large and small picnic baskets had been loaded into the skiff.

Before they boarded, Teddy said to Fredik, "Two beers is all. You must have a clear brain."

"Aye," Fredik said, crossing his hairy arms and showing off his gold tooth.

Cleo whispered to Teddy, "Blackbeard."

"Aye," Teddy said and grinned.

With the baskets sitting on the deck of the little boat, Graham and Neill rowed through the waves to the beach. It was a pleasant sensation, bobbing in the waves after the fierce winds and swift sailing *Monongahela*.

Cleo lent a hand in erecting the mosquito net tent. Her pole sunk into the sand easily. An old canvas sail became the floor of the tent. Teddy brought out silver and china and they ate fried chicken, cabbage and carrot salad, biscuits and jam. To accompany the picnic meal, Teddy served excellent imported wines and ales. Cleo chose wine, so did Neill and Graham. Teddy declared her love for ale. It was a pleasant outing. During the meal, Graham didn't stare at her much. He and Neill swapped war stories and painted word pictures of Paris and London.

Satisfied, she leaned against Neill's back like they used to do at picnics when her mother let her ride the train to visit the Connolly's Rhode Island beach house. Sitting on a picnic blanket on the vast Connolly lawn, she and Neill would prop back to back, each with a tooth pick between their fingers. Digging between their teeth like grown-ups did, they would catch each other up on their escapades.

Now, reclining in the mosquito tent on an island in the Atlantic Ocean, Cleo sighed for long ago days, sweet summer days, days before the war. She closed her eyes. Except for the heat and sand and the sea only yards away, they could have been back on the Connolly's lawn … but not really.

Graham's voice intruded when he said her name.

As if his voice was an intrusion, she straightened and said curtly, "Yes?"

"I've been thinking about what you've ask me to do. Let's walk and talk it out."

"How mysterious," Teddy said, opening another bottle of ale.

"Can I go, too?" Neill asked. "No secrets, old man."

"We'll confide all, if Cleo wants," Graham said, standing and reaching a hand to pull her up.

They ducked under the net flap and started up the beach. Before Graham could get out a word, she spied a sea bird. "American oystercatcher," she said, pointing to a bird in flight.

"How do you know about oystercatchers?" Graham asked.

"How do I know about peregrine falcons?"

"Glad Doc is adding to that excellent education of yours."

"So you've been thinking about confronting Barnabas?"

"Whoa. Confront is a strong word, my girl."

"Call it what it is. Barnabas should have told us about that night."

"Barnabas was not at liberty."

"A woman is missing, his mistress."

"I think he calls Shafer his master, if he calls anyone anything."

"He knows something; he needs to tell it."

"I can't just go up to Barnabas and say so-and-so saw you the night Josie disappeared. She was sitting on the steps crying and you were there."

"Why not?"

"Who saw them?"

"I can't say."

"You won't say. You know, but you won't say."

"Yes."

"Doc."

"Why do you think Doc?"

"He keeps odd hours. He seems to be everywhere, all the time. Especially now that …"

"Don't say it," she warned. In his frustration, he could spout out an accusation, and she wasn't in the mood for his jealousy. She said, "It wasn't Doc, but I don't think he'd mind if you let Barnabas think it was him."

He planted his feet in the sand. "You don't think Doc would mind, eh?" He stuck his hands in his pockets and looked at the mounds of white cotton balls floating across the sky. He looked back at her. "Okay, I can't say it, but you can about guess what I'm thinking."

Maybe she was in the mood for a quarrel after all. She folded her arms. "Why don't you tell me?"

"What's with you and Doc? Is it to him you go when you disappear for hours?"

"Sometimes."

He tried to keep eye contact but couldn't. "You left me standing at the bottom of the stairs waiting for you."

"What are you talking about?"

"Eurella told you I was waiting, didn't she?"

"Leave Eurella out of this."

He made a sound of disgust and whirled away, striding out purposely as if to make her quick-step to catch up. But she refused and meandered behind him, picking up shells, tossing them in the waves. He pulled up, she caught up, and he whirled on her. "I'll leave Eurella out all right. Teddy would have my hide. The servants who take care of guests are sworn to secrecy."

"Since they enter without knocking, it's a good policy."

"How did you get out of the house?"

"Graham, what the hell difference does it make? I don't owe you a damned explanation about anything."

"Fine talk for a lady."

"I'm not lady anymore. You took that away from me."

He rocked back on his heels. It was as if she had hauled off with a roundhouse punch and flattened his nose. Worse, tears brimmed in his blue eyes. "I didn't mean it to be like that."

"Remember, you asked me if I'd made love with my fiance? I told you the truth. I said I wished I had. Then it was your turn. I asked you about girlfriends. From your answers, I believed you were honest and weren't a rake."

"I've never been …"

"I'm not finished. No girl likes to hook up with the joke of the island. Now, stop, okay. Let's get back to Barnabas."

He put his hand on her shoulder, letting the tears rain from his tanned cheeks. His breathing was shallow, quickened by turmoil. "I haven't cried since I was eight years old. Not even when old pop died. You've made a mess of me. Why did you come down here?"

"I was invited."

He wiped his face with his finger. "Why did you accept?"

"I had qualms, but Neill wanted me to take a break, get away from my bad dreams."

He looked out to sea. "I had friends killed in the war. It takes a while."

"That's what everybody says but then they say, 'He's gone. Time to get over him.' Well, let me tell you something, Mr. Graham Henry, your two-timing ways are nothing compared to losing a faithful, honorable man who was more than a friend."

"I was never unfaithful to you."

"You didn't have time. What? We're talking about two nights. Fit me in between dalliances with Josie, a little diversion for the famous flyer."

"It's not like that, and you know it. Stop and listen to your heart."

She shook her head. "I didn't walk with you to talk about William or what's past between you and me."

He rubbed his forehead. "It's not over."

"Yes, it is. In a few days I'll be gone. Goodbye, so long, farewell."

He turned in a circle and looked up the beach. "Shall we walk back? Teddy gets antsy with a sailboat in view." She stared at the small figures of Neill and Teddy moving around the picnic site and fell in step with Graham as they headed back.

He said, "I just wondered if … if Neill talked you in to coming here to … to meet me."

"Wonderful you?"

"I didn't mean it like that. Let me start over. I wanted to meet you. I saw your photograph at the Connolly castle. Neill talked about you a lot. He's quite fond of you, and I thought maybe he's got a crush on his cousin." He glanced at her. "Cousins often marry, you know."

"What? How dare you."

"Please, once I determined Neill had other interests, I wanted to meet you."

"Lucky me."

"Cleo, please. He said he needed to get you out of Philadelphia. He was afraid you were – how did he put it? – dying by inches. Under the circumstances, we didn't think meeting you in Philadelphia would give me much of a chance."

"We?"

"I."

"A chance at what?"

"Whatever might come of … Criminy Cleo." His voice sounded like he was going over a cliff. "I fell madly for your photograph." He flipped hair from his forehead. "Sounds stupid, so go ahead and laugh."

She let moments pass to keep her voice from trembling with anger and, yes, from the yearning that had crept into her, unbidden. "You say that now."

"I should have written it down and put it in a time bottle."

"Was this before or after the girl you were engaged to?"

He stared at her, his face draining color. "Who told you about her?"

"People on the island tell things."

"Doc."

"No, Doc would never tattle on you. Believe it or not, he likes you."

"Does he know?"

"Know what?"

"The lighthouse."

"You think he'd tell me that he knew I was making out with a cad?"

"I'm not …" He dug his hands in his pockets. "I've always liked Doc."

There was something in his faint frown that troubled her. "But what?"

He blew out his breath long and slow. "You'll tell him, I'm sure, but Teddy got a telegram from the Pinkerton man. He's coming to the island."

"When?"

"He didn't say. He was in Atlanta when he sent it."

"I don't think that should trouble Doc."

"Murphy thinks Doc's his man."

"Doc told me …" She paused to think on Doc's exact words. "What?"

"He sounded like he squared himself with the sheriff." She had to admit Doc had been vague.

"Cleo, darling, the sheriff doesn't give a damn who Doc is. If we like him, the sheriff likes him."

"We've gotten a long way from Barnabas."

Fifty feet from them, Neill and Teddy had the picnic basket ready to go and were folding the mosquito netting.

"I'll find a way, Cleo. But I'm depending on you to help me."

"Like how?"

"Go with me."

"Are you joking?"

"No."

"Think up another way."

"Shall we let Teddy and Neill in on the scheme?"

"Absolutely not."

Teddy and Neill showed an unnatural lack of interest when they arrived at the picnic scene. Graham said, "Cleo knows her shorebirds. She spotted an American Oystercatcher. Imagine that."

Teddy said, "I'll lend you my primer on birds of North America, Cleo. You'll find it most interesting."

Cleo interpreted Teddy's jerky movements to mean she still smarted from having her trunk opened, so she didn't reply.

Onboard the *Monongahela*, Cleo stepped to the bow to get the feel of being in the V, to see the water parting and sluicing under the boat. She stood beside the anchor locker. It was open. The anchor in it was different. Shinier. She noticed, too, the windlass. The original anchor had been attached to a chain Teddy called a rode. Now the substitute anchor was tied with a *line* and a chain. Why had Fredik changed the anchor? Were there different anchors for different conditions, directions, depths? Cleo reminded herself that she was not a seafarer and to not let suspicion rule. Facts, she needed facts.

Teddy directed her and Neill to sit atop of the superstructure because Fredik was going to raise the spinnaker. "We'll be running with the wind," she said.

No one spoke most of the way home. She enjoyed listening to the skippering commands from Teddy: "Ready to come about?" "Hard alee." "Gybe oh."

Graham's work done, he climbed up and sat next to her with his hands wrapped around his knees looking glum. Neill went downstairs to read. After a while, saying she needed to stretch her legs, she climbed off the cabin top, waved at Teddy standing at the helm and walked down the companionway. Standing on the sole of the saloon, she watched Neill read for a few moments.

But where were the trunks and the anchor?

She slid onto the bench opposite Neill. "Did Graham tell you the Pinkerton man is coming to the island?"

He put a finger in the book to mark his place. "I was there when the telegram came."

"Doc is not the man Murphy's after."

"Murphy thinks so." His eyes fixed on the middle of her face like he was studying the details of her nose. "I haven't spent any time with the man, so I can't lend an opinion. I say, kiddo, I don't want to be a square, but really, you should spend more time with the Henrys."

"You mean Graham?"

"Him, too."

"You wanted me to meet Graham, didn't you? Maybe get a crush on the handsome war hero?"

"I thought, well sure, he's the bees knees. You deserve the best."

"I'm afraid the best is yet to come."

"Don't put much stock in what you hear."

"Even from you?"

"I shouldn't have beat my gums like that."

"But what you said is true."

"Graham's no cake eater."

"Cake eater? That's a new one."

"Lady's man."

"That's not what you said. I think you used the word cuddler."

"We're men, Bearcat. But Graham didn't futz around with Josie. Bet your jack on that."

She looked around the saloon. "Where's the trunks? The anchor?"

"What trunks?"

"There were three next to this table before we went on our picnic. Now there's none."

"So?"

"Just wondering? One had clothes in it."

"You raised the lid?"

"Inadvertently."

He canted his head and grinned. "Maybe they were moved and stowed in Teddy's cabin." He got up, stepped through a passageway and opened a door. "Two're in here." He looked into the two guest cabins and came back to the table shaking his head. "Probably in a hold for ballast."

"It would be heavy, wouldn't it?"

"Yep." He got that studying gaze at her again. "Jeepers creepers. What's up? The case of the missing trunk?"

"We've got a missing body, a missing trunk and a missing anchor, Neill." She rose. "Think about it."

She heard him gasp as she crossed the saloon sole and ran up the companionway.

CHAPTER SEVENTEEN

Graham handed her a gin rickey. "Shafer's coming to dinner."

"So?" Cleo said.

He eased next to her on the rose sofa. "We can sound him out about Barnabas?"

"Sound out how?"

"Ask him if Barnabas's said anything about – you know, that night, with Josie."

"Don't you think Shafer would have told us by now?"

"He's all balled up."

"Doesn't it make you wonder why he doesn't want the sheriff's help?"

"Too embarrassing. Can't keep his wife. You know by now – Josie's reputation."

Yours, too. "The only people who are known to have left are the Thompson's."

"Josie could have stowed"

"That's an idea. Trunks are great for stowing, aren't they?"

"Big enough, yeah."

"Think about this. Barnabas and Fredik are related."

"True. But wait, my girl, Barnabas wouldn't confide something to Fredik just because they're related. Hell, they start gossiping about their benefactors and …" He drew a finger across his throat. "It's curtains."

"How cozy was Josie with the Thompsons?"

"Flirted with the old fart, but she flirted with everything in pants, except Teddy." He looked at her trousers and grinned. "I ever tell you you look swanky in trousers."

She didn't so much as blink. "Here's a possibility. We'll exonerate you for the moment. There's a man involved. Has to be, if she was crying on the steps."

"C'mon Cleo, sweets. She'd bawl her eyes out every time she had too many gins just 'cause she got a runner in her stocking."

"Could Shafer have done something to her? And don't give a snappy no."

"Was he capable, you mean?"

"Yes."

Graham raised his chin to think about that. "Every man can hurt someone he loves." His voice squeaked on those last three words.

"Not meaning too." Those words, too, echoed like a mouse scrambling in a bucket.

"Say Shafer and Josie got in a ruckus," she said. "Josie goes outside to cool down. She's crying. Barnabas comes out to comfort her. She goes back inside, Shafer's still mad as a hornet. He strikes her. Doesn't mean to and kills her."

"It's possible, but Shafer, when he gets stinko, falls asleep. He's always been a lazy sort."

She bit her lip. "If not Shafer, who else?"

"At least you know it wasn't me."

She let her eyes shoot prickly arrows at him.

*****

Supper began with asparagus soufflé. "Tasty," Shafer said. He'd been warned not to talk about Josie in front of Linith and Eagan. So nobody talked, apparently to keep Shafer from blabbing without thinking.

Next came roast beef and potatoes anna. Cleo wasn't particularly hungry and was anxious to leave the table. No one went for the cherries jubilee, except the children, so the adults adjourned to the drawing room where Mitty passed around the brandy tray.

Graham fired the opening salvo. "Shay, how's you man, Barnabas, doing?"

"Doing?"

"He's getting on in years. Has he thought about retiring?"

"Be'er not, not while I'm still aroun'. But who the hell knows how long that's gonna be."

"You got a buyer for Bellflower?"

"Hell no."

Teddy raised her hand, and, apparently the silent rebuke got through to Shafer. "Sorry. My language."

"I was wondering about his eyesight," Graham said.

"Bad," Shafer said and tossed back half a snifter of brandy. "But hell, excuse me, he watches – hic – for me."

"He did the night Josie left, didn't he?"

"Always does."

Neill looked up from his book and placed his finger in the spine.

Graham leaned forward. "Barnabas could have talked to Josie after you went to sleep?"

Shafer made a circle with his head as if to clear the cobwebs. "Don't know. He was downstairs when I came down in the morning, and he handed me that damnable note."

"He found it first?"

"Guess so, on a buffet."

Cleo asked, "Could Josie have written it at a different time?"

Shafer looked at her like he just noticed she was in the room. "Why?" He waved his snifter. "What's this, the third degree?"

"You said you had a lot to drink," Cleo said, "and that Josie was crying."

"I say – I don' think I said that."

"Wasn't Josie crying?" Graham asked.

"Who says she was? Not me."

"Maybe it was Barnabas."

"Barnabas? Say Josie was crying? When, by God?"

"You should ask him."

"Why?"

"Do you want me to?" Graham asked.

"Why would he? What's going on, who says anything about anybody crying?"

Cleo sneaked a look at Teddy, whose eyes were slits, but she wasn't near butting in.

"Perhaps we should send Fredik for Barnabas," Graham said.

"Be damned," Shafer said and tried to stand. He sank back into the pillows. "Nobody questions my man. You're all nuts." He tried again and got to his feet.

When he stumbled from the room, Teddy's eyes shot barbs at her son. "What was that all about, Graham?"

Graham looked at Cleo. "We've discovered something."

"Who's we?" She looked at Cleo. "As if I have to ask."

That's when Cleo knew there would be no more new outfits. And she wouldn't be taking a few favorites to Philadelphia when she left. Which reminded her again, time was running short. She'd begun to realize she simply couldn't tear herself away without knowing what had happened to Josie. It had gotten to be an obsession.

Graham was saying to Teddy, "Someone, whom I won't name – but it's not anyone in this room – saw Josie sitting on the Bellflower verandah's steps crying late Tuesday night. Barnabas was with her."

"Who?" Teddy said, her voice as rough as an old curmudgeon doctor Cleo worked with at the hospital.

"Anonymous, for now," Graham said.

"This will not do, Graham. You have been extremely rude to your cousin."

"His wife left a note implicating me in a lie. The note might even be a forgery."

"Are you accusing your cousin of something?"

"Something happened to Josie, an accident maybe …" Graham paused, perhaps to consider his next words. "Shay's lame but he's always loved that little so-and-so. They could knock each other around pretty good when they got tight."

"How crude of you." Teddy said, and looked at Cleo, letting Cleo know where he might have picked up this crudeness.

"We should go to the cops," Graham said.

Neill cleared his throat. "She's back in New York, I'd bet on it."

"I believe you are right, Neill," Teddy said. "She couldn't take the future of being poor with someone she only married for his money, so she took off. Problem is, she hasn't realized her dancing days are over, too."

Graham got up. "I hope you're both right. I'll be happy to bow before the altar of apology. I might even give the poor sap cousin of mine something to do in the company, something plum where he doesn't have to get his hands dirty."

"You're impossible," Teddy said and jammed her glass on the table so hard, it shattered the crystal stem. She rose and left like a shore bird trying to fly.

Neill got up. "Little tired. Buffeted by the wind today. Goodnight all."

Graham looked at Cleo. "Boy's a dud about books. It's you and me, kid."

When it was just she and Graham, Cleo said, "I didn't picture you nailing Shafer like that."

"Why not? Barnabas's not going to spill the beans. You don't ask servants questions unless you can prove they're nicking the spoons."

Cleo rose. "Neill's got the right idea. Sailing is invigorating while you're doing it, but tiring afterward."

"Want to walk on the beach?"

Her heart sprouted wings. "Idiot."

CHAPTER EIGHTEEN

Floating between sleep channels, the nightmare wrapped itself around her consciousness, spreading out on waves of fluid to hit the core of her fear. William looked at her with ghostly eyes. The hole of his mouth said words that came from the depths of his earthy grave. His smile macabre, he beckoned with a finger that looked like a fat black snake. "*Joignez-moi dans la mort, ma cherie. Joignez-moi. Ne m'oubliez pas. Ne me trahissez pas.*"

Her eyes flashed open; she scrambled to sit like she was escaping from his grave. Her chest rose and fell rapidly, her heart near explosion, her arms stinging from fending off William. She buried her head in her hands and whimpered. *Oh my dear William. It's not you. Whoever you are, leave me alone.*

She heard a click and glanced around the room expecting to see the furnishings of her own bedroom. In those seconds, she didn't know where she was, but she heard words, words that froze in the icy haze of her terror.

"Miss?" Eurella peered at her.

Her fist went to her mouth.

"Miss? You doin' okay?"

She took a deep breath and shook her head. "Bad dream," she said, hearing the words as if they were pulled from ghostly soil.

Eurella sat and touched her leg. "You need yourself a dream catcher."

She wrapped hair behind her ears. "Dream catcher?"

"My old granny be part Indian. She wove dream catchers be hanging on our trundles. Good dreams be going through the circle in the center. Bad dreams be caught in the web."

Cleo threw off the covers and stood by the bed. "Show me the pattern. I need a dream catcher."

Eurella laid two fine lace and silk frocks on the dressing table and said, "I be bringing you a dream catcher, miss. You look so scared. You see the devil?"

"Worse."

"You didn't see no dead people, did you?"

"Just one."

"We be runnin' him off next."

"Bye William," she whispered and crossed her fingers.

Eurella leaned her head toward new dresses she'd brought in. "Will you be attending services? Miz Henry wants to know."

"I hadn't thought …" She paused to take in what Eurella wore – a flowered full dress covered with a solid red tunic. Her hat had a bow of the same flowered material.

"The family's got Chapel in the Green wing," Eurella said.

"Are they Catholic?"

"No, miss. Presbyterian. They calls it Chapel here to take in all God's chillen. Preacher from Port Maria comes at 'leven. I got time to dress you 'fore I leaves for services."

"Where are you going to church?"

"African Zion at the village."

She couldn't say why exactly, but she said, "May I come, too?"

Eurella grinned and put her hands on her hips. "You shore may." She scooped up the new dresses and hung them in the wardrobe. "Now what do we put on you?"

"My Dotted Swiss, I think. And my white straw cloche."

Eurella clapped her hands. Apparently, Teddy had been willing to forgive her transgressions and send new clothes if she went to Chapel. Apparently, too, Eurella had correctly read Teddy right and knew Cleo must wear her own clothing.

Teddy waited at the bottom of the staircase, her dress simplicity itself, although it must have cost a small fortune. She watched Cleo descend, and, with each step, frown lines deepened in Teddy's forehead. Her face said it all when Cleo asked if she could drive Eurella and herself in the Model T to the village and the African Zion Church.

Teddy sniffed. "Be prepared. Services there can last into the afternoon."

On the way to the garage, Eurella said, "She be right, miss. We keep the Lord in our hearts as long as we can of a Sunday."

*****

Just before Cleo reached the village, she noticed the smoky aroma of meat, neither pleasant nor unpleasant. "What is it?" she said.

"They's roasting a pig," Eurella said.

She wondered who *they's* was, but didn't ask. "Why?"

"After services we doin' dinner on the ground."

"Like a picnic?"

"You might say. Miz Henry's cook's sending up chocolate cakes and apple pies for Southerness's part."

"Everybody brings something?"

"Those that can. We get people across from Port Maria. Some bring a bunch of onions or turnips, but most don't. Comes for the pig and greens."

"Greens?"

"Collards. You don't got collards in the north?"

"Never heard of them."

"Make 'em with fatback and vinegar. The soul of food."

"Ummm."

She parked at the one-room school house. Beneath a tree, smoke rose from a concrete block pit. Two large men broke away from the crowd around the pit and walked toward the car. The two young men kissed Eurella's cheeks. "My boys, miss," she said.

Cleo smiled and nodded to men who looked mild-mannered "How many people belong," Cleo asked

"Don't rightly know, miss." She looked at one of her sons. "You know how many be sign up for church of a Sunday, Leon?"

"Preacher said fifty-six, but some don't always come. Lay out from drink or go hunt and crab trap"

"Heathens," Eurella said.

Cleo observed that some of those heathens were roasting pig, laughing it up and showing no signs of coming into the church. She followed Eurella up the four wooden steps and through doors painted a bright green. Inside, the floor boards of the one room sanctuary were dark and highly polished. The back and side walls were horizontal slats painted white, each wall having two windows that brought in light, but no sun, giving the place a gloomy cast. She slid into a rough-hewn pew between Eurella and her boys. Looking toward the front, she saw that an arched recess contained a small white table with a Bible lying open. Above it, a picture of Jesus hung on the wall. Floor candelabras were placed each side of the picture. A small upright piano had been placed next to a wall. Opposite it stood the pulpit.

Eurella drew her attention to the Aladdin kerosene lamps bracketed on the walls. "Miz Henry had them sent down from Pittsburgh."

"Mrs. Henry is very generous," Cleo said, shooing a horse fly. The open windows invited all worshippers.

"The piano comes from the inn," Eurella said. "They got a new player and gave us one used to be in the bar." She laughed. "The Lord don' mind they sang *Oh! By Jingo* to it fore it got dedicated to Jesus."

A tall colored man dressed in a white suit went to the Aladdin lamps and lit each one. When he'd finished, a large woman in a pink satin dress sat on the piano stool.

Cleo felt a familiar presence behind her. She glanced back to see the bulk of Fredik slide into a pew followed by Barnabas. She looked across the aisle to see the teacher and four pupils dressed in their Sunday best. She wondered if Doc came to service?

The church was filling, mostly women and children. A scattering of men – she counted nine – were among them, but they were elderly. It said a lot about Eurella that her two sons were in church.

It quickly grew hot. Cleo picked a fan from the hymnal slot. One side showed the picture of Jesus; the other side depicted several colored people being baptized in a river. By now, all the ladies waved fans while men wiped their brows with handkerchiefs. Her nose twitched at the smell of old wood and human sweat.

Everything got quiet and two adolescent boys walked up the aisle with candle lighters. They were followed by an elderly stiff-spined man whose gray hair sprouted like wire. The boys lit the floor candelabras, and the preacher took his place behind the pulpit. When he opened the large Bible, the worshipers cried "Hallelujah!"

The service got going when a man in the back began a resonant chant: "We gonna shine, shine, shine." Other voices opened up and then feet began to stomp to that line. "We gonna shine, shine, shine." A man in front rose and threw his hands in the air and began to clap. The chant changed to "Going to paradise, shine, shine. shine. Yeah, Lord, shine, shine, shine." One by one, the worshippers stood, clapping and chanting. Cleo found herself in a tunnel of emotional flesh undergoing a religious commotion. Awed, she sat listening to the power in their voices. The normally calm Eurella, sitting next to her, had her head thrown back. Her hands came apart and back together in a smack that would crush a skull.

The chorus echoed in the room for some time before the chanting and clapping faded to "Praise, the Lords." The worshippers sat and the preacher said, "Amen." The audience answered, "Amen! Preacher, brother!"

The preacher held his Bible open in one hand and told the story of the Exodus – an entertaining version of Moses's flight from Egypt, the plagues, the parting of the Red Sea.

As time passed, the smell of human closeness brought on a bout of nausea, and she thought she might faint. Teddy was right. The service was going on forever. The preacher closed the Bible and began his sermon. She didn't understand a word. His style was florid, his arms rose, his fists punched the air, his body swayed, he'd occasionally dip and bang his knee, then rise up again. Worshippers would cry, "Hallelujah!" and "Praise the Lord!" and "Praise be!" and "Amen!"

He pointed his finger in dire warning and said something about the Lord smiting thee down, then lifted his hands and cried, "Be saved. All those who are saved, come to the Lord." Bodies rose and moved as the singing and chanting started again. She, too, rose so she could breathe. She couldn't figure out if these worshippers were agonized or ecstatic. All she knew was she thought she might faint. The heat was incredible. Eurella was soaked from her hat band to her waist and still shouted incomprehensible phrases. Cleo realized she was speaking in tongues, something she'd heard about.

She felt a hand on her arm. Fredik was leaning behind Eurella. He offered his hand. She clasped it and slithered behind Eurella, who evidently didn't feel what was going in back of her.

Outside, she gulped air and her thanks as they walked away and stood by the Model T.

Fredik said, "What brings you to African Zion Church?"

She had to raise her chin to see him above the brim of her hat. His bowler was pulled low on his forehead, the round rim resting on his ears. For the first time their eyes met and fastened. He had a smirk on his face like he suspected her of something nefarious. Finally she answered his question. "I wanted to experience something I've only heard of."

"You looked like passing out."

"I was about to. Thank you."

"You know, also, it is hot where the infidels of God go."

She wondered what he meant by that. "It is a remarkable service."

"Not like Chapel?"

"You go to Chapel?"

"I am Orthodox."

"Why did you come here this morning?"

"I was wondering why you came here?"

"I asked you first."

"I am free to go where I please. And you?"

"Eurella invited me."

He scratched a cheek with his long finger. "If she did, it is the first time."

"For what?"

"To invite an unbeliever to her religion."

Was he calling her an infidel? The impertinence of him. "We're all Christians, aren't we?" The sounds from inside the church grew louder.

He grinned, showing his gold tooth, and crossed his meaty arms. "You think talking in tongues is closer to your Christianity than Chapel?"

Standing close to him, she realized how elfin she was, but she wasn't going to let this giant's cheek slide by. "Did I say that?"

He let his arms fall to his sides. He altered his smile to amusement. "I meant no uppityness as our brown brethen would say."

She flipped a hand at him, and he chuckled softly.

Hysteria now flew from the church windows. The piano rocked above the voices. She looked back to see Barnabas open the door and walk down the steps.

She raised her head to Fredik. "Does Barnabas go to Chapel?"

"When Shafer goes. He did not go this morning."

"Alcoholics need looking after in church or out."

"Man loses his wife, he drinks."

"He was a lush before losing Josie. They both were."

His eyes shifted and he shrugged.

"Got drunk and mean on Tuesday night," she said. "I know that."

"Weren't different than any other night."

Barnabas came toward them. She leaned a little toward Fredik. "What will happen to Barnabas when Shafer sells Bellflower?"

He grinned. "Go fishing."

"He won't have to stay up all night tending to a drunken man and a crying woman."

He stared for several seconds. "You have a particular meaning?"

"I thought you knew."

"What?"

Before she could answer, Barnabas came up to his nephew. He doffed his fedora. "Morning, miss."

"We've never been introduced, Mr. Barnabas. I'm Cleo."

He twisted the hat in his hands. "Pleased, I'm sure."

Barnabas was easy to size up. First, he bore no family resemblance to Fredik. Although old, he projected an aura of spiritual innocence. But there was something else about him. He looked beat from within, as if he had an awful secret weighing him down. Maybe it was her imagination. She said, "There's something I don't understand about Josie's disappearance."

Barnabas's brows came together. "What is that?"

"She left a note she was going off, but no one saw her leave."

"I can not say what was in her head," Barnabas said.

"Neither can I, but I wonder."

"Ferry's in!" a pig-roaster shouted. Fredik and Barnabas turned their heads and so did she. A straggling of people walked from the lane by the orange grove into the village – men, women, children in their Sunday best – hands holding baskets and tins. Among them were a few white families.

"Come for pig-roasting," Fredik said with a sneer. "Think they could roast their own pigs in Port Maria. They left here to live there."

"No money," Barnabas said. "They have field work over the Sound, but come back to their roots on a Sunday."

"For a free dinner," the cynical Fredik said.

She gave more thought to Barnabas. He was an honorable man, a religious man wanting to do right by people and the Lord.

All of a sudden, the doors to the little church burst open and people spilled down the steps. They were clapping and singing. Cleo's heart swelled and she grinned. The teacher, minus her students, drifted over to where she stood. Fredik and Barnabas eased away to follow Eurella's sons to the pig pit. The teacher held out her hand. "Good to see you again."

Cleo shook it. "You, too, Ruth."

"You were a hit with the children."

"Billy was the star."

"You joining us for dinner on the ground?"

"I've never tasted roasted pig."

"It's quite delicious. You wouldn't believe it's wild pig."

She put her palm to her chest. "One of those wild boars in the woods is there on that spit?"

"Several small ones – sucklings." Ruth said. "The meat will be tender. It roasts over oak and pecan. Gives it a tang, but a nice tang. Try it. Or there's shellfish stew, collards, beans, corn and biscuits"

"I haven't been invited."

"Everybody's invited until the food runs out and the singers go home."

"More singing and clapping?"

"Yep. Everybody fills their plate, eats, then one of Eurella's sons brings out his banjo and the other a mandolin, and away they go. Sometimes, when the preacher leaves, they have their way with the piano. Lasts at least till dark."

"Sounds wonderful, but exhausting."

Ruth looked at her like she was a fragile lily. Then Ruth's eyes strayed away, toward the grove. "Here's Sam."

Cleo glanced over to see Doc emerge from the grove. Behind him, his horse nipped at the grass. Ruth had called him Sam; she was in love with him, and Cleo could see why. He wore a wide farmer's hat and carried an armload of blankets and saddle bags over his shoulders. From every corner of the clearing, children streamed toward him, and, after he dispensed the blankets, the children scattered back to their parents, who spread the horse blankets on the ground under trees. He walked up. "Miss Cleo. Miss Ruth." He tipped his hat. "Glad to see you here this morning, Miss Cleo."

Miss Cleo. Was he keeping her at arm's length because of Ruth? Considering the lack of white women presently on the island, maybe so. It appeared everyone had been paired before she got here, but then, she hadn't come to match up with anyone. If only she could reverse time. She pulled her nervous hands apart and swallowed the acid building in her throat. "I went to the service," she said.

"How was it?" he asked, his hat shadowing his eyes so all she could see was the slant of his lips.

"Fine. Hot."

Ruth looked at Doc with moony eyes. "I about passed out. From now on, I'll wait until cooler weather to go back."

"You can always go to Chapel," Doc said.

Ruth made a face at him. Apparently, she had something against Chapel, or maybe the entire Henry family.

Wanting to get away from the easy familiarity between Doc and Ruth, she gazed over the gathering. "I'll go find, Eurella."

Ruth pointed at a tree with tables beneath it. "There she is. Setting that table. They're bringing the pigs out of the fire."

"You staying for the dinner?" Doc asked her.

She couldn't look into his eyes. "I … no. I better get back. You?"

"Wouldn't miss it," he said.

Ruth laughed. "Sam brings his squirrel jambalaya, don't you Sam?"

"I didn't this time." He patted the saddlebags over his shoulder. "Some roasted gulls Billy roughed up this morning."

Cleo took a step. "If you'll both excuse me, I'll be on my way."

"You need some help starting the car?" Doc asked.

"Not at all."

The vocal rhythms around her churned to the manic rhythm of her steps as she made a beeline to Eurella. She felt an arm. It was Fredik. "I will start the car for you."

"No, I can do it." She saw Doc talking to Ruth. Ruth laughing.

Fredik said, "It is difficult sometimes to start."

"Thank you." As she turned away, her eye caught Doc glancing her way. *Are all men such asses?*

Fredik said, "I shall see you at the stable."

"I don't know when."

He made a pass at a bow. "As you choose." *Another ass.*

Eurella was pulling meat from the carcass of a burnt pig. Cleo could identify the animal by the hoofs and head and thought she might throw up. She put her arm around Eurella's small waist and thanked her for inviting her to the service. Eurella drew a piece of meat from the greasy skin and pressed it into a biscuit. "Here, chile, you take and eat this. You need some meat on those bones."

Eurella was the only reason she had to smile this day, a day that threatened to crack her head wide open.

CHAPTER NINETEEN

Her headache gathered might with each stride to the car. She crammed herself in, slammed the door and pushed her foot against the starter. It didn't crank. She tried again. No luck. How bloody wonderful. She got out and located the choke under the radiator when she heard footsteps. She raised her head to see Doc smiling.

She felt like the dumbest person that ever lived.

"I should have let Fredik ..."

Doc held up a hand. "Fredik has outdone himself. I suspect foul play here."

"Can he have ... on purpose?"

"Sure. He's ornery enough. Let's get this Tin Lizzy going." He reached for the choke with his left hand and deftly cranked with his right. The engine whined.

"Thanks," she said.

"You okay?" he asked.

"Yep, dandy."

"How was sailing yesterday?"

"I'd like to talk to you, but I don't want to keep you. It's a fine day for a dinner on the ground."

"Cleo?"

She looked away.

"What is it?"

"Nothing." *What am I saying?* Doc was her only ally. She felt tears push against her eyes. She looked at the car's bonnet. "All right, something."

"Tell me."

She raised her hand to her hat brim, pulling it lower to block her eyes. "Go eat. I'll meet you in the morning."

"I'll be on the bluff late this afternoon."

"I'll try." She made for the car door. "Teddy wasn't happy about this morning, my coming here."

"Teddy likes to be boss."

She waved backwards at him. "Go."

She pressed the pedal, thinking she'd never felt anything like this before and hoped when the feeling went away, she never would again.

*****

Teddy played squash. Neill read – how surprising – and Graham was at Shafer's house. The rest of the day was hers. She put on bathing pajamas – this time, the double muslin in blood red with a red and white striped long-sleeved tunic. She placed the wide-brimmed hat on her head and tilted it over her left eyebrow. With a book and a blanket in one hand and a large beach umbrella in the other, she passed through the house without making a sound or being noticed, that she knew.

Down the verandah steps, she skipped through the garden and hurried to the boardwalk. She saw a wooden beach chair with its legs anchored in sand, went to pull it free and dragged it close to the sea. Placing the blanket over the slats, she opened the umbrella and propped it in the sand. Settled into the seat, she cracked the book, a Sherlock Holmes. *Now, read,* she ordered herself.

Order, be damned. She couldn't concentrate on the first sentence of the first chapter. Looking seaward, at the gray-blue water white-capping to beat the band, she stuck her finger to bookmark the page, as if it needed bookmarking. The sun shone from above and behind spreading pure dazzle across the water. The sands sung in the gentle wind and she was mesmerized without a thought in her mind but the comingled effects of sea and sand and sun. She lay back and closed her eyes.

Next thing she knew, her eyes were popping open to an unnatural sound.

Neill stood at her side. "Nice nap?"

She shaded her eyes. "Very."

He bent and sat on his heels. "Is everything okay with you, Bearcat?"

"Everything's jake."

"We're concerned … "

"Who's we?"

"Graham, Teddy, me."

"I'm fine. I had a great time at the colored church. Neill, it's breathtaking. You wouldn't believe."

"I've heard the hullabaloo from that church."

"They feel their religion, not like you and me."

"Eh?"

"You know, going through the motions, genuflecting, crossing ourselves, parroting the responses. They get their souls into it."

"Like the tent preachers at revivals, I expect."

"I've never been to a tent revival," she said.

"Today you did, only with a wooden tent."

"What brings you to water's edge?"

"Finished *Hamlet*. Came to stretch my legs." He made a show of rising and stretching.

"And that's exactly what I'm going to do." She stood and released the catch on the umbrella.

"Where?" he asked, and looked at his smart shoes.

"I try to walk at least two miles every day for my figure," she lied.

"Don't say? Not my thing."

Which she knew. "Let me be off. I want to get it in before cocktails."

"You'll be joining us then?"

"Of course."

"Sometimes, you know, you don't."

"So serious, my cousin. I haven't heard a slang word out of your mouth."

"We've not long until we leave. Graham asked me if you might want to sail home with him and Teddy next week."

"Of course not, silly." She didn't want to leave at all, but she had to. The hospital expected her back in a week, Monday next, for the morning shift. If she missed, they would punish her and move her to the night shift. She'd worked hard to get mornings. She sighed. "I hate it that we'll be leaving a lot unknown."

"I've gotten the willies, but you've settled in quite well."

"What's giving you the willies?"

"Never seen Graham and Teddy so nervy."

"Josie's missing. Were I them, I'd be nervy, too."

"Yeah, Graham being under suspicion and all."

"Do you suspect Graham in her disappearance?"

"Never seen him so antsy, but no reason to. He says he didn't go for the doll, and I believe him."

She folded the blanket and handed it and the book to him. "He needs to talk Shafer into going to the sheriff."

"Shafer's not capable. Besides, the cops will suspect him."

She piled the umbrella onto his outstretched arms. "They always suspect the husband or wife."

"And with reason," Neill said. "Although I can't say from experience, of course."

"Nor I." Something tickled the base of her brain, a thought trying to get through. "I'm walking. Want to change your mind?"

"Er, thank you, no. I've got to get these things to the house."

*****

Would Doc be at Petrel's Bluff? At the thought of him not being there, her mind steeled itself against feeling let down.

The wind hit her in the face and swirled her pajamas. The tunic flapped back like she rode a broomstick. To keep her hat on required both hands.

He was standing on the summit of the bluff, Billy on his arm. She stared up at him, her nerves crawling outside her skin. He waved and disappeared. She walked to the bottom of the path and saw him at the top. He descended and saluted with two fingers to his hatless forehead, his black hair blowing wild. Billy did his taloned two-step while scanning the sky, likely dreaming of swooping onto some unsuspecting petrel.

The look on Doc's face told her he was trying to gauge her mood. The wind tugging at her hat was distracting and she thought, what the heck, and pulled it off. In the next instant, black strands lashed her cheeks.

"Like the witch of Balmoral," he said.

She turned toward the sea. The sun hadn't a chance against the thick gray clouds. "Can Billy fly in this?"

"Not too good," he said, standing behind her. "In the face of the wind, he'll still – meaning he's no match for a nor'easter. But he looks ready, so let's give him a run." He stepped forward and released the leash and jesses. Billy took a step then leapt and swooped low. His wings flicked against the wind as he circled. "He's not going higher," Doc said. "He'll be looking for a meal on the ground." Billy glided, with an occasional flap of his wings, and then made a flat line descent toward a dune. Something fluttered into the periphery of her vision. Billy rose and made another pass. The second time, with talons stretched, he hit the sand.

She heard squeaks. "Not a rabbit."

Billy rose with a small animal in his talons. "Rat," Doc said. "Good riddance."

"Whew," she breathed out.

"I saw your face." He laughed. "You like those rabbits, don't you?"

She felt deliciously giddy. "Yes, and not in the pot."

Billy's meal landed on the beach and he ripped into its throat. Cleo turned away. Doc put his hand on her shoulder. "So what did you want to talk to me about?"

That snapped her back to apprehension. She blew out a breath. "Graham told me that Teddy got a telegram from Atlanta, from Pinkerton's. Murphy's coming to the island."

If he were guilty of something, or fearful, it didn't show. "When?"

"Graham didn't know." She tried not to look worried. "Maybe here already. Maybe tomorrow."

"I'll check at the Dolphin later."

"He's not after you, is he?"

"Don't know why he would be."

"Can you think of anyone on this island who could be his man?"

"Not a soul. Waste of his time and money."

"When Graham told me, he knew I would warn you."

He twitched his upper lip and let an amused gleam radiate from his eyes. "That's kind of Graham."

"Graham likes you. All the Henrys do."

"And I like them. For rich folks, they're okay."

"Maybe you understand them because you're rich."

"Rich in history and land, not so much cash money."

"You ever going to go back to Valdosta?"

"Maybe. Some day."

She heard Billy kek. There was a tiny bit of rodent bone and ripped-up fur on the sand. "Let me get Billy jessed-up and hooded." He looked at the madcap sea, the rushing atmosphere. "We're in for a squall."

With Billy on his arm, they walked to the cliff path. "Thanks for telling me, but I'm not the man he's after."

They climbed the path, she in front of him. She decided to blunder into his private place, and hope it didn't anger him. Looking over her shoulder, she said, "I wanted to ask you, are you and Ruth …?"

He gazed at her like he'd fallen into a trance. "Your assumption has merit. But no, we're friends. Comrades in hiding, of sorts."

"Hiding from what?"

"I said that wrong. I'm not hiding from anyone. But Ruth is."

"Who?"

"Husband."

"Oh."

"Bastard's broken most of her ribs. He finds her, comes around here, his old ribs will one day pop up in the marsh tide "

It was unlike him to speak with such passion. Maybe he and Doc Holliday shared more than a name. She would go to the library and learn more about the legend and his family.

They reached the bluff and stood looking out to sea. The wind sailed down the beach, threatening a gale. "Let's get inside the truck," he said. "I'll drive you to Southerness. Won't make it before the rains."

Doc secured Billy in his traveling cage in the cargo box. He cranked the truck, got in, and got the truck rolling.

She listened to the wind beat on the metal and glass. Seconds later, they were hit with a wall of water.

Doc asked, "You say all you wanted to say?"

"No."

"You want to talk about sailing yesterday?"

"Yeah."

"You and Graham get along?" He wasn't much more subtle than she'd been when she asked about Ruth.

"Some ways, yes. Other ways, no. He says he'll think about approaching Barnabas, but he won't. He tried to grill Shafer, but Shafer was too drunk."

"That's when Shafer's at his cagiest. He doesn't realize he's drunk and tries very hard to be clever, which ends in a muddle of confusion."

"I talked to Barnabas briefly at the church. He seems a nice man. I think I'll go to him myself."

He turned on Oystercatcher, tires splashing in the sand potholes. She leaned closer to him because there was nothing covering her window. He said, "You'll find Barnabas is not talkative."

"Maybe not," she said and shrugged. "There was some funny business on the sailboat."

"I'm interested."

"There were three traveling trunks in the saloon. Two were locked, one unlocked. The unlocked trunk held Teddy's clothes. Unfortunately, she caught me red-handed."

"Ouch." He turned to grin at her. In the shadowy light of the squall, his casual sensuality, as she'd observed before, created an easy intimacy.

"I still can't look her in the eye."

"She'd do the same if she wanted to know what was in a trunk. She won't hold it against you."

"Also there was an anchor next to the trunks."

"Okay, so?" He hit a mud hole and the truck slid sideways. He got it righted and the rain came down through a crowd of ghosts.

"We had a picnic on the beach."

"The Henrys love a good picnic."

"Yes, well, when we got back, two trunks were in different places, but Neill and I couldn't find the third trunk, nor the anchor."

She watched his eyes blink slowly, as if his brain was trying to make sense of this. "Well, we'll have to see where they went."

"How?"

"Tonight, I'll go see."

"In this weather?"

"It won't rain all night. This is just a typical nor'easter. Line's are thin this time of year."

"You'll go over to the boat in the dark?"

In the ticking silence, she heard his labored breathing. He glanced at her. "Are you afraid for me?"

"Yes." She wasn't sure if the word had made it out of her mouth.

He reached over and slid his fingers between those of her left hand. "I'll be fine."

His hand of friendship had something enjoyably light fluttering along her chest wall. They didn't speak again until he pulled the truck up to the steps of Southerness. He gently pumped her hand. "Tomorrow morning? My lodge?"

She grabbed the door handle with her right hand. "Yes. Tomorrow morning."

*****

After dinner – but for the chattering children, a disquieting affair – the Henrys prepared for Swinny's visit. Tonight was to be a reading from Shakespeare's *As You Like It*.

When Swinny walked into the library, Cleo could swear he had on the exact outfit he'd worn to the dance – the ascot, the hacking jacket. His waxed moustache hadn't been touched by either wind or rain.

"Swinny," Teddy said, bussing his cheek. "You made it through the storm, I see."

"Thank Jehovah for slickers and rubbers. Mitty, your man, relieved me of mine." Looking at the drinks' cart, he wrung his hands. "Is that Kentucky bourbon I see warming a glass for me?"

"Right you are," Teddy said, taking a cocktail glass off the tray. "Bourbon for a blustery night."

Holding up his glass, Swinny beamed at Cleo. "My dear girl, I haven't seen you since you danced so divinely with our boy, Graham. Where have you been keeping yourself?"

"Enjoying the island's treasures," she answered.

"What in particular, if I may be so bold?"

"The groves, the village, the docks. This island even provided a mystery."

She heard Teddy clear her throat.

"Yes?" Swinny asked.

"Josie going missing."

"Ah, the show girl," he said, taking a swig from his glass. He wiped his mouth with his jacket sleeve. "New York, that's where to look, by calamity. Shafer's hit the bricks, so it's am-scram for Miss Long Legs." He raised his glass for another swallow.

"Now, Swinny," Teddy said. "We simple don't know."

Cleo shrugged. "For all we know, she might be dead in the marsh."

Swinny spewed bourbon from his throat. "I say, excuse me." Teddy fetched a bar towel and Swinny wiped his ascot. "Bad form."

Cleo didn't know if he meant her statement or his spewing the bourbon.

"Quite all right," Teddy said.

"I almost forgot," Swinny said, "I got a telegram from the Thompsons. It's at the lodge. Said – I'm not quoting verbatim now – something like: "Home finally. Re: Josie gossip. Henry runabout seen on Sound dead of night Tues. Looks Josie flew coup. Tommy."

"See," Teddy said, flashing her eyes at Cleo. "We shouldn't speak – or act – before we have facts."

"The gal's a loose screw," Swinny said. "Cat with nine lives. She'll be all right." He waved his newly filled glass. "Don't worry about that gal."

"Somebody had to have helped her. Who took her to a drop-off point and brought the boat back?" Cleo asked.

"She made friends on the island," Graham said. "Some poor sod taking a payoff to keep quiet."

"Wouldn't people around the docks have heard it?" she asked.

"Sure," he said, "but people mind their own business when it comes to we outsiders. They're happy for us to solve our own problems."

"Hear, hear," Swinny said, his glass raised.

"They'd whisper amongst themselves," Cleo insisted.

"My dear," Teddy interrupted, "are you going to join us tonight in reading The Bard – something light, away from all this drama? We'll all take turns reading different parts."

Hating to be abruptly rude, she put on a melodramatic face. "I think not. I've caught a chill from the rain."

"Tsk," Swinny said. "A good glass of whiskey will cure that."

Cleo went over and kissed him on the cheek. She whispered, "You can have mine."

He raised his glass. "Here, here."

"I'll have Eurella bring a water bottle and a toddy," Teddy said, sounding too sweet for Teddy.

"Night all."

She felt Graham's eyes on her as she left the room.

CHAPTER TWENTY

When sleep threatened to overcome her, the nightmares came rushing back. She feared closing her eyes, afraid of what she'd see rising from some ghastly miasma. Instead, she focused on what little time she had left. Two full days until Wednesday morning. Did he go to the boat tonight? What did he find? Was the Pinkerton's Murphy on the island? But sometime in the blackness before dawn, she succumbed, and, when she woke, she knew she'd had a bizarre dream but thanked all that was holy she couldn't recall it.

Standing at the window, she saw the vague, red blotch of dawn. She turned away thinking *red sky at morning, sailor take warning.* Was Doc already up?

Desperate to get out of the room and outside, she pulled the bell for Eurella and started ripping under garments from the chifforobe. Eurella arrived in time to give an extra tug to her lacings. She'd noticed that Eurella's black arms were empty of new clothes. The gospel church must have been the last straw for Teddy.

"I'll wear the sailing outfit, Eurella. It's comfortable, and I'm not sure what I'll be doing today."

"Miss," Eurella said, and hesitated.

"Yes?"

"I be sorry I made trouble for you."

"What trouble?"

She said to the floor, "The Lord's house, yesterday."

"I made my decision. Who's saying you made trouble for me?"

"I be saying too much already, miss."

"Teddy?"

"I cain't say, miss."

"You and I know the truth."

"For sure, amen."

"Tell you what, I'm going to wear my own mauve plaited one-piece."

"Miss, the clothes be made jes for you. I'm to pack them up when you go for home."

"No. Give them to the women in your village."

She shook her head with vigor. "Wouldn't be right."

"You mean Teddy would have your hide?"

"No one be wearing them for if to give offense."

Cleo flipped her hand. "I'm sure at some time Graham will have a guest that can wear them."

Eurella shook her head, pity in her eyes. But for whom?

*****

Not a creature stirred downstairs, allowing her a clear path out the back door, down the verandah steps, into the topiary garden. Rounding a large boxwood elephant, she heard the verandah door open and someone step onto the marble. Male steps, or Teddy in heavy shoes? She ducked behind the sculpture and listened to the footsteps pound downward. They didn't turn her way, and she ran lightly down a second set of steps and dashed away. Who was out so early? A servant, Teddy or Graham? Not Neill, that was sure.

She kept to the woods until she got to Oystercatcher, then ran to the other side of the trail into a pine and palmetto forest. She stepped lightly, her eyes to the ground. Reaching the path to the stable and the lodge, her ears picked up the truck's motor behind her. They were looking for her. When it passed, she laughed. Doc. She called to him and the truck stopped. Billy was in the back. She had missed his show.

Doc got out of the truck. He wasn't smiling. His eyes darted, not settling on her. He took her elbow with unaccustomed urgency. "C'mon, let's get Billy to the mews."

"Something the matter? Is Pinkerton's here?"

"I don't know."

"What's got you so heated?"

"Shhh." He almost pushed her into the cab.

When he was behind the wheel, she said, "Doc?"

He pressed the gas and the truck lunged forward. If he didn't speak up, she was going to start yelling, and soon. At the mews, he took Billy and the furniture out of the truck. Not long, he was back, getting in and driving the truck to the side of his lodge.

Inside the lodge, she placed her hands at her hips. "I'm about to have a nervous breakdown, Doc."

He touched the kettle on the dry sink. "Still warm." He poured two cups, his movements herky-jerky.

"Tell me now or I'm leaving."

As if he didn't hear, he placed the cups on the table and pulled out a chair for her.

She stared at him while he drank away half the coffee and wiped his mouth with the back of his hand. "Josie's body turned up."

Her vision blurred like she was staring into murky space, across time. She'd been expecting the news, but the reality drove her mind onto an unwanted path.

He said, "You don't look shocked."

"No." But what if they suspected Graham killed Josie? "The trunks?"

"Last night I found all three trunks on board, the anchors and more."

"More what?"

"Trunks. Full of white whiskey the locals make here. In the holds."

"Huh?"

"Gin runners. Your hosts are running home-made hooch up the coast to wherever."

"They have the stuff here. They're taking it home."

"No. They have fine whiskies for their use here, and I'd bet at home. This is to sell. My money says Fredik is involved."

Her thoughts shifted and she smiled slightly. "So Fredik wasn't suspicious of me because of Josie, but because he thought my snooping might reveal his illegal activities."

"He's trouble."

"I sensed it. What about Barnabas? He in on it?"

"I'd be surprised."

"Let's talk about Josie. Could you tell what happened?"

"Too much aquatic damage. Maybe the coroner can find something."

"Where was she?"

"In the Sago River. Up by where we flew Billy with the school children. Crabbers out this morning found the body."

She winced. "Did you see her?"

"It was Josie, although …"

"Although what?"

His pressed his eyes with his right hand as if to compress the sight from them. "Her face wasn't recognizable, but her clothes and shoes were. Her hair."

"Where has she been?"

"The tide brought her in."

"From the sea?"

"From Sago Sound. Some refer to the Sound as Sago River, too. It runs through the marsh to the sea."

"She wasn't dumped in the river?"

"Couldn't have been. She was taken out into the Sound by boat and dumped. She went to the bottom until decomposition gases brought her up. The winds and tidal currents brought her into the river's flow through the Great Marsh. If she had surfaced at a different time, she could have washed out to sea without anyone knowing what happened to her."

"Don't bodies wash up on the beach?"

"Not here. Her bones would wash up on Amelia Island in Florida."

"Where is she now?"

"In an unused shed. Damn fools wanted to take her to the ice house."

"The ice house?"

"Preservation."

She thought about Graham, about him being accused, and searched for another explanation. "Maybe, Doc, maybe she fell from the wharf into the Sound?"

"She'd wash right back onto the sound's rocky beaches quarter of a mile down from the wharf. It's shallow there. No. She was in Sago's main stream."

"You don't think she could have fallen into the Sago River near where she was found, got tangled up and just now surfaced?"

"The place is four miles from Bellflower. Josie would never go to the marsh. It's nasty, for women especially, with snakes and gators. Josie would know gators hunt at night."

"She went with someone."

He laughed like he'd eaten an unripe persimmon. "She sure did. Dead or alive."

"Do you have an idea who?"

He took a deep breath. "My ideas are my own."

"C'mon, Doc." He shook his head in a very determined way. "What happens next?"

"The Henrys must know by now. I sent the crabbers on a launch to Port Maria to summon the sheriff and coroner. The Henrys won't like it, but it had to be done by those who discovered the body."

"They'll suspect Shafer."

"Or someone else close to her."

He meant Graham. But Graham didn't kill anyone, he was with her. She was finding it hard to keep her shoulders from slumping. She finally murmured, "My God."

Doc gave a low sound of sympathy. "Time will come when everyone must tell what they know."

"Even you?" she asked.

"And you," he said.

She moved her mouth, although no words came out. "I can't."

He rose and stood behind her chair. Rising, she faced him. He reached slowly and drew her to him. His hand slipped to the back of her waist, and she rested her head on his chest. While she savored the sweetness of his concern and the musk of his maleness, he held her and whispered words that didn't penetrate the chaos of her thoughts. His kissed the top of her head, then placed his finger beneath her chin and turned her face up. His eyes filled with passion and curiosity. She looked away, but didn't care draw away for hurting his feelings. He spoke carefully, "Our time is short. Things will change in a matter of hours. I want you to know, I care very much."

For his unstated understanding, she had the urge to kiss him, but that would be a mistake. "I know."

"What happens next is up to you."

While she watched him speak, she thought about that first day they met. "You remember when we first saw each other? You on your horse?"

"That image of you stays in my mind."

"I have a confession," she said, touching his collarbone with a finger and then backing away. "That day I went walking where you found me – the day of the snake – I was looking for you."

"I think I saw you first, coming down Plover Lane. I tried to stake myself out where you might wander."

She grinned. "You and that snake set me up."

"I still come across him, coiled and pining for your touch."

Her eyes stared into his, and she knew his wit had a deeper meaning. "Oh Doc. What's going to happen?"

"You'll do fine."

"It's … I've …"

"I know." He bent like a courtier and kissed the back of her hand. "It's time to face the Henrys."

*****

At the garages, Fredik told them the Henrys had gone to Sago River.

On arriving there, she spotted a small crowd of villagers hanging back from the reeds on the bank. The Henrys, Neill and Shafer were at the edge.

Doc pulled up, parked and walked ahead of her. Shafer stood looking into the water where a scarf was tangled in the marsh grass. Holding a beer bottle that shook in his hand, he wept. Graham smoked and paced like a lion. Teddy kept pushing at her hair. Surrounded by tragedy, Neill looked out of place, jangling change in his pocket and looking at the sky. She thought again how untouched by grief he'd always been.

When Shafer turned and saw Doc, he said, "Who found her?"

Doc answered, "Crabbers."

"Where are they?"

"Gone for the sheriff."

"God, the sheriff. Why? She drowned."

Teddy said, "It was presumptuous of you, Doc, to send them to Port Maria before discussing the situation with us."

"It's an unexplained death, Mrs. Henry. The coroner has to come in."

Teddy looked like she could crack walnuts between her teeth, and Shafer protested like an angry crow. "The coroner! This is ridiculous. You've overstepped your bounds, Mister."

"No, sir," Doc said. "It's the law."

"We're the law here," Shafer hissed.

Graham said, "Take it easy, Shay. It'll be all right."

"You idiot! It won't be all right. You did this."

Doc went to Shafer and took the bottle away from him. "Man, you got to be calm now. Don't go throwing around harsh words."

"Damn him. Damn you." Shafer's eyes darted insanely from one of them to the other. "Damn all of you."

"People can hear you," Teddy said.

"Everybody the hell knows."

"Nothing's known," Graham said.

"Sure is. My Josie's been crab food for a week."

Cleo shivered and looked to the east where a pale defiant sun rose from the red horizon.

Teddy snorted. "Don't talk like that."

Shafer reeled away. "Got to see Josie, my baby girl."

Doc held out a hand. "No, man, you don't want to see her."

One of the Southerness trucks pulled up. Barnabas got out of the passenger side, Fredik from the driver's side. Fredik said, "Just came from the wharf. The ferry boat is in. The captain said the launch went the short way. Captain saw men dodging shoals, going fast."

Teddy emitted an oily laugh. "No need to hurry."

Fredik said, "There were two strangers on board the ferry."

"Murphy and a sidekick," Graham said, looking at Doc.

Doc said, "I'll be at the stable, anyone needs me."

Cleo walked with him to the truck. "Are you really going to the stable?"

His eyebrows raised into dark curved lines. "Yes." With curious serenity, he touched her lightly on the elbow. "Remember what I said."

"I will. At the bluff this afternoon?"

"You know where to find me."

"I'll come to the lodge."

He looked at her, nodded and walked away. She thought of William, how his eyes clouded on the last glance before he boarded the train for the war. When Doc drove away, a dull pain began in her breast.

Footsteps brought her back from sadness. "Cleo?"

She faced him. "Graham."

He took a deep drag on his cigarette. "This is a damnable thing."

She saw a touch of fever in his pupils. "We have to find out who did this."

"Likely an accident."

"Don't be an idiot."

"Cleo, don't."

"Josie wouldn't go near the marsh by herself."

"Then she was with someone."

"Dead or alive," she said, quoting Doc.

He swept his hair back with the hand that held the cigarette. "Extraordinary thing, this."

"Are you really surprised, Graham?"

He shook his head like he'd only thought of death as a concept. "I wish we could go back to last week when you came, and start over."

"Knowing what we know now, would we do something more clever than we did?"

"Would our instincts let us?"

She flicked a glance at him.

Teddy came up. "I, for one, am not staying here. We have no way of knowing when the sheriff will get here." She took a step toward the Depot Hack. "Who's riding with me?"

Graham's eyes swept over the scene, then he asked Cleo, "You riding with us?"

She looked back at river's edge. Her other choice was with Fredik. "Yes."

Graham put his hand on her arm to lead her to the Depot Hack. Teddy drove and Graham sat on the center bench beside Cleo. Neill and Shafer took the back bench. No one spoke on the trip; neither was much said in the breakfast room where a sumptuous meal had been prepared before the family got the terrible news. Now the food was warmed over and no one had an appetite, except Teddy. Shafer pushed his plate away and knocked back his tumbler full of whiskey. "How can anybody eat when Josie's been crab food for a week?"

Cleo had seen such injuries in the hospital, and she'd been nearby when doctors spoke with the police. When animals got at the body, you couldn't tell if someone had been stabbed, shot or strangled. Would that be the case with Josie?

Teddy looked at her empty plate. "At a time like this, food is comforting."

When they'd gathered in the morning room, Shafer collapsed in a chair, Graham threw himself onto the paisley sofa, and Neill stood at the window looking out. Cleo planned to exit as soon as possible. Teddy said, "I'm not sitting here. I'll do my mourning in the swimming pool. Anyone joining me?"

"I don't think I care for the water just now, Mother," Graham said.

Shafer was roused from his stupor. "Wasn't in the pool. Don' think you'll be bathing either, huh, swell?"

Neill turned from the window. "Bushwa, gents. Stop batting the gums." He looked at Teddy. "I'm going upstairs to read *The Sign of the Four.*"

Teddy's eyelids went into small rapid tics as if she expected no less from Neill. She looked at Cleo. "And you, my dear?"

"To the beach for me."

"You were up early," Teddy remarked. Cleo nodded and prepared for the barb, and Teddy threw it. "You could have driven a car to the stable. I came after you to tell you that, but you'd run away."

So it was Teddy who came down the steps right after she did. Defiant, she said, "I like to walk."

"Were you going for a horseback ride?"

"I thought Doc might be flying Billy."

"You enjoy Billy, don't you?"

"Very much."

"He's a wonder," Teddy said, and started to cross the room.

Graham rose from his chair. "One wonders if our Cleo doesn't think Doc's a wonder, too."

Cleo raised her chin. "I think anyone who can train an animal like he did is a wonder."

Teddy had stopped in the middle of the room and turned to Graham. "Rudeness doesn't become you."

Graham rubbed his forehead. "I've a devil of a hangover. I apologize."

At that moment, Shafer began to snore. Teddy said, "Get Barnabas here to get that drunk home and cleaned up."

Her eyes met Graham's. *Barnabas.*

CHAPTER TWENTY-ONE

Neill had taken himself off, and Teddy had come down in her bathing dress and left for the swimming pool. That left her and Graham and the sleeping Shafer in the room.

She moved to the sofa to sit by Graham, not too close, just enough to talk without waking Shafer. "Now's our chance to speak to Barnabas about what happened that night," she said.

His eyes showed too much white. "I hardly think ..."

"Hardly think what?"

"Now's not the time to draw a bead on him."

"The sheriff is coming. He'll want to talk to Barnabas. We'll prep him."

He reached out to touch her knee. "That might work, my girl. Just might."

Barnabas crept into the room, a towel over his arm and carrying a porcelain basin in both hands. He prepared to soak the towel in the bowl of water. "Mr. Shafer smells bad," he noted.

"Sure does," Graham said. "Gets blotto by ten in the morning. Drinks all night."

Cleo got up from the sofa. "Barnabas, is it because of Josie going missing, or does he drink like this all the time?"

Barnabas was a man who didn't speak off the top of his head. After thinking, he said, "Worse, lately, miss. The liquor business being taken away."

Graham stood and put his hands in his pants' pockets. "What happened that night?"

"Happen, sir?" Barnabas said, squeezing water from the towel.

"With Shafer and Josie?"

"Wouldn't know, sir." He began to bathe Shafer's face.

"You were there, man."

Barnabas shook his head and dabbed Shafer's slack cheeks.

"You were seen consoling Josie on the verandah steps."

Barnabas straightened. If a man with the complexion of a gypsy could pale, he did. "Seen when, sir?"

"Last Tuesday night, sitting on the steps with Josie when she was crying."

"Who saw me?"

"I don't think I should say, but look here, you'll have to tell the sheriff when he gets here."

"I am in Mr. Shafer's confidence, sir."

"You can't lie, Barnabas. Not to the gendarmerie."

His glance moved from Graham to her. "I do not lie."

"You were seen," she said.

"Tell me who, miss."

"Doc."

"Sam, the doctor?"

"That's right."

A sly smile appeared on Barnabas's thick lips. "He could not see me unless I saw him."

Since Cleo wasn't familiar with the layout at Bellflower, she couldn't contradict him, but she believed Nora. She looked over at Graham. He looked like they'd fallen into a trap. She said to Barnabas, "You have shrubs …"

"Verandah's closed in, miss."

Graham waved a loser's hand. "Clee, it's not like ours, wide open, surrounded by gardens. Bellflower sits closer to the sea. It has no back garden, so the walled verandah steps leads directly onto the boardwalk and down to the beach. No hiding places."

Barnabas held up his chin, but his eyes gave him away. He'd been there, but wasn't going to admit it. "Mr. Sam would need to be crawling on his belly for me to not see him, miss."

Just as the little girl must have done. Drat. She couldn't compromise Nora. Who knew what she'd suffer? "Barnabas, Doc says Josie was crying and you were comforting her. What's wrong with that?"

"If that happened, nothing," he said, toweling the water off Shafer's forehead.

"Shafer says you took him upstairs and put him to bed and stayed up all night while he slept. Is that true?"

"That is between Mr. Shafer and myself, miss."

Graham was growing ever impatient. "The sheriff is coming. We'll all be questioned."

Barnabas shook his head.

Graham took a deep breath. "I did not plan on marrying Josie, and you know it. That note is a fake."

Barnabas shook his head. "I know Miss Josie's handwriting, sir."

Cleo walked closer to Barnabas. "I think the note is genuine, it just wasn't written on the night Josie disappeared." Barnabas's mouth tightened. "Was Josie in the habit of writing Shafer notes?"

Shafer stirred, his eyelids fluttered and he made a move to rise. It was too much effort and he flopped back in the chair, breathing in and out in a whispered snore.

Barnabas said, "Ask Mr. Shafer, miss."

"I will, Barnabas."

Graham said, "Shafer will have to talk to the sheriff, so get him up and ready."

"I shall do that, sir."

Graham said, "Barnabas, you know how Josie and I were. You got eyes in your head. You got brains. When the sheriff asks you about that night, are you going to tell him about the note?"

"That would be up to Mr. Shafer, but I suspect we should."

"But neither of you know when that note was written."

Barnabas looked like a man harassed beyond his responsibility. "It was laying on the buffet the next morning. That is what I will report to the law."

"Did you see her write it?"

"No, Mr. Graham, and I will tell that to the law if they ask me."

"How often did Josie write notes to Shafer?"

"I cannot say."

"Will not, more like it," Graham said. "What about last week when Josie had to apologize to Shafer for staying all night in Port Maria?" He looked at Cleo. "Not with me, I swear it on Mother's brow." Graham reached a hand to his forehead and brushed his hair back, then said to Barnabas, "I bet you know why Josie was crying, and why she was in the marsh."

"I must get Mr. Shafer home to change his clothing."

Graham ran his hand through his hair again. "Sorry. Barnabas. I just think – you got to believe me – you must know more than you say. You've been on this island long enough now to be an islander. I consider myself as much an islander as you do. I was born on this island."

"I was not born here, sir. I am not an islander."

Cleo thought good for Barnabas. He wasn't supposed to back talk, but he had. And good for Graham, he hadn't yet gone berserk over it. But he still looked like he could jump out of his skin. He said to Barnabas, "I appreciate your confidentiality and support of your master, but hell's bell's man, I'm in a pickle, here. I'll be suspected, all because of that friggin' note."

Barnabas poked two stiff fingers at Shafer's shoulder, saying, "Sir."

Shafer's eyes popped open. "What?" It was painful to watch him drag himself to sitting. He hiccupped several times. "You talking, Barnabas?"

"No, sir."

"Talking about what?" Graham asked.

"Nothing, old buddy, old schport." He tried to get to his feet. "Old cake-eater fly boy."

"You're fried to the hat, Shay."

Barnabas took Shafer's arm and urged him up. "Know why?" Shafer's body wavered as he tried to stare at Graham. "'Cause you and Josie got a wiggle on and she's dead – crab food."

"That's a lie. You're too sozzled to know what's what."

"I alwaysh know what's what."

Barnabas broke in. "Sir, we must get ready for the authorities."

Shafer wagged an unsteady finger. "Don' got nothing to say to bulls. They won't get no goods on me. Better put away your bootleg booze, cuddler cousin of mine."

"Are you threatening me?" Graham asked.

Shafer saluted so hard, if Barnabas wasn't there, he would have fallen backward into the chair.

*****

"Now, I'm really in the soup," Graham said when Barnabas got Shafer walking out the door.

Cleo folded her arms. "We'll have to find a way so you won't get scalded."

"So you believe me."

"If I wasn't there, and knowing what I know now about you, I wouldn't believe you at all."

Teddy rushed in, wearing a long beach dress over her wet bathing dress. She finger-combed her long hair back. She had the oddest shoes on her feet. They looked like rubbers cut off at the ankle. "A filly is loose," she said. "Graham, go get Doc. The filly's on Plover. I don't want it going into the woods."

Snakes, Cleo thought.

"On my way," Graham said. "Want to come, Cleo?"

Although she wanted to speak to Doc in the worse way, she was in no mood to be with both men at the same time. "I'm going to the beach for a rest."

"Wind's picking up," Teddy said. "Another squall coming, I fear."

Graham looked back at Teddy. "Let's hope the sheriff gets here before it gets too choppy on the sound. I want that body gone from here. Shay's getting worse."

"The sheriff should be here by now," Teddy said.

"It's a big county," Graham said.

"Get going," Teddy said, making shooing motions with both hands. He left.

Teddy said in that syrupy, teasing voice that accompanied a demand, "Cleo, dear, please let us know where you'll be today. Can't be looking for you when the sheriff comes calling. No sneaking off with Doc. Promise?"

"I'm going upstairs to change into beach pajamas. I couldn't find Eurella earlier."

"She's gone to the village. She cleans the church on Mondays from ten until two. Hard to believe it takes four hours to clean that small building."

Upstairs, on impulse, Cleo knocked on Neill's door.

"Enter," he called out.

His pipe lay in the ash tray. His glasses were perched on his nose and he'd lowered the book to his lap. "What's up, cous?"

"Gotta smoke?"

"For the Bearcat, anything." He rose, tapped a cigarette out of the pack and handed it to her. Lighting it, he asked, "Barnabas getting Shay cleaned out?"

"No small task, that," she said, blowing smoke. Going for an easy chair, she sat and asked, "How well did you know Shafer and Josie?"

He took his time. "When Graham and I were in school, Shafer wasn't married. When we got home from Limeyland, Graham and Shafer went to New York. Shafer hooked up with this dumb Dora. I shouldn't disparage the dead, but she was a showgirl. He shouldn't have married her, but he loved her. Love. Huh! What's it get a chap?"

"You ever been in love, Neill?"

Neill flashed his white smile. "Twice. Should have learned my lesson the first time."

"You're good looking."

"There's girls that don't like red hair and freckles."

"But there's girls who do."

"Never been keen on looking like a goof."

"Who was your first love?"

"Radcliffe girl. Came down with Graham's sheba. We made a few rounds. That's when I cottoned I'm no smoothie."

Graham's sheba. She got up, pressed her cigarette into an ash tray, and kissed her cousin on the forehead. "I'm off to the beach."

"Toodles," Neill said, waving his fingers and picking up his book.

*****

She'd no sooner settled in the beach chair and laid back to nap, when she heard footsteps on the boardwalk. She turned to see Graham pounding toward her. *What now? The sheriff?*

She rose to face him. He hurried across the dune, and stopped, nearly out of breath. "Do you know where Doc is?"

She tried to keep the apprehension out of her voice. "Doc? No."

"Can't find the fella. His truck is gone. He tell you where he was going when he left you off at the marsh?"

He studied her mouth as if she would bleat something aloud. "Just what you heard," she said. "The stable." *Please don't be gone. You promised.*

"Billy's gone, too, and Doc's not in Billy's flying places."

"Billy flies early in the morning or late in the afternoon."

"I know, that's why I'm surprised."

"Once he took Billy to the village to show the kids."

"Where in the village?"

"Great Marsh. By where we found Josie." An ugly picture formed in her head and she made a round O with her lips.

Graham shook his head. "Raptors eat living things that they kill."

Doc had told her that. "Have you been all over the island?"

"Over the roads," he said. "I'm off to the village now."

"I'll come, too."

He looked at her beach clothes.

She said, "I'll stay in the car."

He laughed. "You don't have to. You're covered from neck to ankle with – how many layers does that thing have?"

"Enough so you don't get ideas."

"I always got ideas, Cleo. I …"

She picked up her book. The blanket and umbrella could stay. "Let's go."

On the boardwalk, she kept up with his long stride. He said, "Don't take Shafer's rambling seriously."

"What do you mean?"

"The names he called me. It's man talk, same with Neill. Doesn't mean anything."

"You doth protest too damn much." *You and your Shebas.*

"I don't think I can protest enough for you. It'll take a lifetime."

Suddenly she was swamped by a curious wave of nostalgia like she'd been transported to a time ten years from now and speaking about what happened just days ago.

When they got to the village, she spied Eurella sweeping the wooden steps of the church. Graham parked the car. She opened the car door. "I need to speak to Eurella."

He gestured with his shoulders as if to say, go ahead. "I'm going to ask around if anybody's seen Doc. You ask Eurella, okay?"

She hurried across the open space.

Eurella's eyes were as wide as her smile. "Chile, you be a long way from the beach."

She looked down at her Aladdin-like trousers. "Someone told me this covers me more than a dress."

"That be for sure, Miss Cleo."

"Have you seen Doc?"

"He was leaving the village just as I got here."

"Going which way?"

"Only way, on the road."

"In his truck?"

"Yes, miss."

"He have his falcon?"

"Didn' see. He wave and go on his own. What's the matter?"

"A horse got loose."

"They's all over the place."

"There's something else I want to ask."

"Surely."

"I want to talk to Josie's maid."

Eurella's forehead wrinkled. "Ain't possible lessen you look north."

"She's gone?"

"Come inside the church, chile. Folks're staring at you."

She looked over her shoulder to see two young men avert their eyes.

"I don't know about going into church in ..." She spread the balloon of her trousers.

"Lord don't care what you wear, Miss Cleo. You could be buck nekkid."

She laughed and followed Eurella. She would her miss her greatly, and with a start that almost caused her to trip, she knew she would be homesick for this place. For Doc. For Billy. For thorny Teddy. She wouldn't consider Graham. Except that Graham now saw himself as a whipping boy.

"Sit yourself," Eurella said.

She remained standing. Standing in beach pajamas was one thing. Sitting, making herself comfortable in a church seemed – well, unseemly. "Where is Josie's maid?"

"Elsie lef three days now."

"Where to?"

"Folks of hers up north somewheres."

"Had she planned on leaving Josie?"

"She tole folks since Josie run off, she don' have no job and be goin' up north for work. You know, miss, them Drakes loss all their money."

"Prohibition."

"Tis a mighty good thing, but brings bad for folks like Mr. Shafer."

"When I get back home, I'm joining those who work for repeal. It didn't stop drinking from what I can see."

"Sure didn't. Half the men here makes their own."

"Did Elsie talk about Josie?"

Eurella gave her a knowing look. "Now, miss, what we been talkin' 'bout?"

"Confidentiality?"

"I'm not sposed to spread talk I hear from other folks' help."

"With Josie dead, the sheriff will ask questions of you, too."

Eurella put her hand on her breast. "What in the world for?"

"What you observed, or what you heard, like did Shafer ever hit Josie?"

"Why would I be knowing? I don' lives in that house."

"Elsie talks, doesn't she?"

"Reglar chatterbox."

"Did she say if Shafer hit Josie?"

"Don' tell Miss Teddy I tole you, but he did when in drink. But that Miss Josie, she could hit back."

"Barnabas would protect Shafer, wouldn't he?"

"He wants keep working, he will. He'll go north, too, when Bellflower gets away from Mr. Shafer."

The door opened and Graham stuck his head in. "You seen Doc, Eurella?"

"Tole Miss Cleo. He was leaving as I come from your place."

He nodded his thanks, and looked at Cleo. "I'll wait outside."

She turned to Eurella. "Anything else you can tell me?"

"No, miss."

"Are you sure?"

"Let me think on it."

In the car, she told Graham what Eurella said.

"Josie never told me Shafer hit her," Graham said.

"If she hit back she probably felt it made even-steven."

"It's a real sap who'd hit a woman."

"The question is, did he hit her that night?"

"If Barnabas knows, you're not going to get him to tell you that."

"She was crying, we know that."

"The sheriff doesn't need to know," he said. She felt his eyes on her profile. "He doesn't need to know everything."

She kept her eyes trained on the road. "I understand the consequences to you, Graham."

He looked over and reached for her left hand. His was warm and soft. "It's all right, Cleo. I'm your man. You can count on me."

His expression, the taut lines around his blue eyes, sought to appease her perceptible tension. She knew then that Graham would never tell about her being in the lighthouse with him, even if it meant a smear on his character, or worse. She turned her face from his and looked out the window, at the tumult building in the sky, at the mismatched shadows of the old oaks and the leaves skipping from the forest to play in the road and nearly gagged on the sob.

Whispering   193

He waited while she changed from the beach pajamas into her purple and white silk day dress with the pleated bodice.

Neither spoke as they rode on Oystercatcher to the south end of the island and the boat docks. What would the coroner find? What if he found a bullet in Josie's head? A knife blade in her chest? Would they ask Graham questions about where he'd been, and if he could prove his alibi? He could prove it, and so could she, but therein lay the quandary. She couldn't bear the thought of Neill, who worshipped her, knowing she'd been – it wasn't thinkable. But could she let Graham go to jail? Jail – the word was harsh. The reality was harsh. But would they lock Graham up? He, a war hero?

"S'all right, my girl," Graham said. She glanced at him, seeing his worry in the golden light and was reminded how sun rays could shine through an oncoming storm.

CHAPTER TWENTY-TWO

The wharf buzzed with wonder. Two motor boats were missing.

"Junkers," Graham explained to her. "They are runabouts islanders use to conduct business across the sound." They walked across the dock planks. "One was used by the crabbers to alert the sheriff and coroner, but who took out the other?"

"Do you have a sign-out system?" she asked.

"Not hard and fast, but it's proper to tell the Dolphin's proprietor you're taking a boat out. He writes the name and time down, and when it comes back."

"What if it's late into the night?"

"The record log is on a table. The honor system, but sometimes it's abused. Doesn't usually matter, though."

She followed Graham into the Dolphin Inn. The innkeeper, who had spoken so freely about Graham's romantic life a few days ago, looked a little dog-faced as he led them to a table in the lounge.

"Can I get your something to drink Mr. Graham? Miss Cleo?"

"Root beer," Graham said.

"Me, too," she said.

"Fine," he said, and left.

Holding out a chair, Graham said, "Fella looks a little dodgy today."

"I want to tell you something, but I don't want you to act on it."

"What, my girl?"

"Your proprietor tells tales."

Graham sat. "What tales?"

"Josie. You."

"Damn him." His fist hit the table lightly. "He's lying if he ever ..."

"Lila."

"He's out of line. Our business stays with us."

"Wouldn't we all like it to be that way?" She saw tension spring into his jaw. "He told me you and Lila were engaged."

"It was a misunderstanding on her part."

"Lots of misunderstandings with the women in your life." He shook his head, his eyes cast downward. "When a girl's mother travels to meet the parents of her lover, over hundreds of miles of land and sea, usually it means ..."

He rubbed his forehead. This was a man not used to explaining himself. "With Lila, it was a case of both mothers pushing and shoving, mine and hers. Teddy and her mother are tennis partners. Teddy wants me to marry and settle down to the business. Lila's mother wants her to marry a rich man. She *is* marrying a rich man. Teddy's going to the wedding."

The innkeeper brought their sodas in glasses with straws, and a plate of short bread. "The missus baked it this morning," he said.

"Fine, man," Graham said. "She makes the best shortbread on the island."

The man smiled warily. "She'll be pleased you said that."

"Have you seen Doc?"

"When?"

"In the last couple of hours?"

"No. Hardly comes in here except if my dogs get sick."

"He didn't check out a runabout?"

"No, Mr. Graham."

"Two are gone. One went to summon the authorities. What about the other?"

He scratched his chin. "Don't know about the other. I'll check the log," he said, going away.

The door opened and two strangers came into the lounge. They sat on the opposite wall, near the dead fireplace. The innkeeper came back and told Graham that the second boat was unaccounted and walked over to wait on the strangers.

Cleo said quietly, "Thanks for not jumping down his throat for gossiping."

"What good would it do? Look Cleo …"

She interrupted. "The innkeeper said Josie stayed at the inn a couple of times, visibly upset."

"Not upset with me."

"How do you know that? She was upset last Tuesday on the dance floor. Teddy looked like she could smack her."

"It's not your fault, but it was because of you," he said, grasping her arm, his eyes trying to peel through her defensive posture.

She looked at his hand on her arm. "Josie has no right to expect you wouldn't dance with another girl."

His hand tightened, quickening her pulse. He said, "I don't think it's personal to you, or even me. She likes … Josie liked to be the gayest, prettiest thing in the room … on the whole island … in the whole universe."

She couldn't resist saying, "Just the sort a war hero goes crazy over."

His face took on the look of a starved warrior trying not to give up. "Cleo, you're torturing me."

His couldn't have been worse than the torture she'd endured, was enduring.

The innkeeper started toward them, and Graham took his hand off her arm. Stopping at their table, the innkeeper canted his head toward the strangers. "Those two men came on the ferry. I asked if they saw any small craft out on the sound. One of the fellas said the ferry was pulling away from Port Maria when one of the runabouts was docking. That was the crabbers arriving in Port Maria, I reckon. When the ferry docked this side of the sound, another boat went out from our docks with a single man in it."

"So Doc went to the mainland," Graham said.

"He always checks in with me," the innkeeper said. "Sets an example, I'll say. Some young bucks could follow when they're down here in winter, taking out what's not theirs, using the gasoline, bringing the boat back empty."

"Thanks, man," Graham said, nodding.

The innkeeper walked away. Graham said, "We got the Pinkerton man coming from Atlanta. You tell Doc that?"

"I did." He studied her with candid eyes. She added, "You knew I would."

"Thing is, he didn't bolt immediately."

"Why would he bolt now?"

"Sheriff's coming."

"Doc made sure the crabbers went to get him."

"Inevitable."

She dug in. "Teddy reprimanded him for it."

"Teddy is the matriarch, the queen. He should have asked her first."

"She's not the law."

"Don't tell her that."

"What usually happens when somebody dies on this island?"

"We take care of things ourselves. We notify the coroner. Tell him what happened. He writes up a piece of paper."

"He examine the body?"

"Not if we tell him some colored man fell off a roof and broke his neck. Everybody knows what a broken neck looks like."

"Where do you bury the dead?"

"The colored cemetery's smack in the middle of the island, on the high ground, behind the ruins of the old Spanish mission."

"What if something happens to people like you?"

He paused to stare at her. "You seem to imply that we're a different species than you. People like me are people like you, only with more money."

"But you wouldn't be caught dead in the colored cemetery."

The muscles of his face squeezed together like he wondered if she were serious or joking. "If you'd get to know me better, you'd learn that I wouldn't give a damn."

"Answer my question."

"White families here have their own cemetery sites on their land. My father preferred to be buried in one of our Pittsburgh plots." He looked at the two strangers across the room, sitting, drinking. He frowned. "Wonder if they're from Pinkerton's?"

"Me, too. Let's ask the innkeeper."

Graham rose. She got up, too. The men paid no attention to them. The innkeeper was at his desk in the foyer. Graham asked, "What business do those men have on the island?"

"They signed the register as agents of Tontine Assurance, Ltd. You know the company?"

"Yes, damn them."

"Sounds very fancy," Cleo said. "What's it mean?"

"A fancy title for an old scheme. They go from house to house and sell insurance for a dime to poor folks." He asked the innkeeper, "How long are they staying?"

"Open check-out."

"Thank you."

Outside, he said, "Teddy will need to know about this. Don't want insurance peddlers coming here every month collecting dimes from people who don't have a lot of them."

"Is it legal?"

"If it goes to a life insurance policy, sure, but most of those fellas are cheats."

*****

They got into the Model T, and she adjusted her headband against the wind.

"Squall coming," Graham said.

"But the sheriff isn't," Cleo said.

"Man might be out of town. Our sheriff isn't like city cops. They pretty much like the folks to take care of their own messes."

"Like the wild west."

"Maybe."

"Like Doc's ancestor."

"Don't go thinking Doc was telling the truth."

"I don't believe he's the man Murphy's looking for."

"Cleo?" There was something skittish sounding in his voice.

"Yes?"

"What … I mean … what's with you and Doc?"

She lingered over her answer, thinking mostly about Billy. "Do you think Doc took Billy with him?"

"If he did, the man's a thief."

"Sounds like you got your mind made up. Why is taking Billy thieving? He found him."

"He belongs on this island, to the island."

"That's not true. Billy's a wild bird. He could fly away any time."

"Peregrines are territorial."

"He'd go where the food is, where he could find a mate if he got the notion."

"Doc boning you up on the mating habits of falcons?"

"What's it to you?"

"Look, Cleo, I don't care. Doc can have Billy."

"How big of you."

The wind rattled against the car. "Don't be like that?"

"Like what? Sensible."

"You didn't answer my question."

"What question?"

Large raindrops splatted the wind screen. "What's Doc to you."

She gave him a long, evaluating stare. "I don't think I'll answer that."

"I won't give up, you know."

She ignored the humming along her nerves. "We have other things to think about."

The rain came hard. A clap of thunder had Graham gripping the wheel tighter. A bolt of lightning splintered a tree behind them. "Doesn't look like we'll have much help from the sheriff."

"As you said, he's not much of an investigator."

"We'll have to do it, then."

And I'll see to it we do it right.

Graham pulled into the garage, cut the engine, got out and went to a far corner. He rummaged through a stand and brought out an umbrella. Beneath it, they dashed to the house.

*****

"Get the shotgun," Teddy said.

Graham held out a hand. "They haven't committed a crime yet."

"And they're not about to," Teddy said.

Cleo stood beside Graham. She needed to go to her rooms and get the wet band off her head, brush her dress dry and change her stockings. But she didn't want to miss a word.

"They won't be out peddling in this weather," Graham said. "Let's handle them in the morning."

"First light," Teddy said. She lit a cigarette. "So, our Doc's run for it."

"Appears," Graham said, glancing at Cleo.

"Damn, the man." Teddy said. "Well, if he's the guilty party, I wish him Godspeed. Didn't like Murphy. And his client sounds like a gambler and a dumb ass."

Cleo couldn't help smiling at Teddy's profanity. Graham, too, laughed. "Can't be both. Gamblers who are dumb asses don't gamble for long."

"So it goes," Teddy said. "I wish Doc would have told me. I'd have stood up for him. Nobody comes on this island and takes people off for no good reason."

Mitty was half way across the drawing room floor before anyone noticed him. Teddy said, "There you are, Mitty. Bring some glasses and the gin bottle."

"Excuse me, madam. It's the crabbers come back from across the sound."

Teddy doused the live ash in a tray and crossed to the door. Graham grabbed Cleo's hand and followed.

Teddy said, "I'll speak to the crabbers myself."

"They're at the stable, madam."

"Then let's get to the stable."

"It's mighty wet," Mitty said.

"I won't melt."

The rain had let up, but the clouds were still black as coal smoke. She followed Graham and Teddy, splashing through mud puddles until they reached the Depot Hack. Teddy got in the driver's door. Graham sat next to Cleo, taking one of her hands from her lap and folding it into his, making her heart ricochet around the walls of her chest.

The crabbers sat on a bench in the stable's long middle aisle.

"Good men," Teddy said.

Graham whispered, "Just like a good chatelaine, she knows everyone on the island – names, personalities, foibles."

"Glad I don't live here," she said, causing Graham to grin.

The crabbers stood and removed their hats. Teddy reached a hand out and each, in turn, shook it. "Now, tell me, what's going on with the sheriff?"

"He weren't aroun'," the first crabber said. "We wait till the win' pick up. Had to ride on back. Sound was gettin' bad."

"What about the coroner?"

"Up Woodbine way. House burn down. Whol' family gone."

The second crabber chimed in, "We lef word we need dem bof."

"You see Doc in Port Maria?"

"No um," the first crabber said.

"You see one of our runabouts?"

"Shore did," he answered. "Hooked at da dock."

"Fine, I'll pay for your lost catch." Both nodded, turning their hat brims in their hands. "Go on home. Get warm."

They put their hats on and walked out. Watching them, Teddy said. "I swear they walk like crabs."

Outside the stable, Teddy didn't go for the Depot Hack. Instead she walked toward Doc's lodge. She said, "Josie's body being in the shed gives me willies. I don't want Shafer going there. He's been threatening the whole time you've been gone. If he takes a notion, Barnabas can't keep him from going."

"Man's off his onion," Graham said.

"Can you blame him?"

Teddy banged on the lodge door. No answer. She hesitated ten seconds then gripped the knob and pushed. The door swung in. Cleo entered behind Teddy, Graham on her heels. She expected the lodge would be stripped, but it was exactly like she'd last been in it.

"At least Doc didn't steal anything," Graham said.

Cleo turned on Graham. "Why would he?"

"Whoa, my girl," he took a step back and held up his hands. "Everything in here belongs to Southerness."

Opening a drawer, Teddy said, "Son, you should know better by now. Cleo has good instincts. She trusts Doc and so do I."

Graham touched Cleo's shoulder. "I honestly didn't think Doc would run off with the tables and chairs."

"Didn't steal the spoons, either," Teddy said. She opened two more drawers. "Wonder if he intends to come back."

"Why?" Cleo asked, going to the chest where Teddy had drawn out an album.

"Photographs," Teddy said, flipping through the black pages. "Not ours."

Cleo held out her hand, aware that Graham was looking over her shoulder. There were old photographs of people in rigid poses. She always wondered why people never smiled back then. She came to one. "I've seen this one in the newspapers." The man in the photograph had a wide forehead, grayish eyes and full lips. He wore his light brown hair parted on one side and puffed in a pompadour on the other. On the back of the photo, it read, "Dental School, 1872." She turned the photo over again. The man's full lips made her smile.

"What amuses you?" Graham said.

"It's Doc Holliday. The gunfighter and gambler. Our Doc's ancestor."

"Let me see," Graham said, taking the album.

"Hmmm. Resemblance, I guess. Skinny guy, like Doc. Doc's darker, though."

"He had a mother," Teddy said, taking the album. "Wide forehead, just like Doc's here." She turned the page. "Family trait. Look at this picture. The men here all have big ears and wide foreheads. And the way their hair lies on their heads." She shut the album. "Okay, so he's related to the gunfighter. Why'd he leave the album here?"

Graham shrugged. "Maybe he's coming back. After the coppers get off his tail."

"Maybe," Cleo said, "his leaving has nothing to do with coppers on his tail."

Graham shrugged again. "Have it your way, my girl. I hope you'll always think the best of me."

She gave him a look.

Teddy finished her inspection. "Took everything belonging to him, except a clean handkerchief and a nail clipper, and this album."

"If he doesn't come back soon, we'll need to find another animal man," Graham said.

If he didn't come back, she wondered, what would they do with Doc's belongings? Throw them away? She'd have to make it clear that she'd like to have these small things as mementoes.

Teddy put the album, handkerchief and clipper in a drawer and closed it. "We'll leave it here. I hope he comes back. I miss him. I miss Billy."

Cleo cast a short, keen glance at Teddy, then turned away. Teddy was smitten with Doc, Just like Ruth. Just like she'd found herself.

CHAPTER TWENTY-THREE

The cocktail hour had come and was never to be missed, Cleo concluded. Her liver would soon be expanding she feared like the surgeons at City Hospital often warned drunkards. She'd never seen a human liver because women were considered too delicate to handle the bloody insides of a human body. However, three young women at her hospital were challenging that. They were going to medical school, which had the male docs trembling, aghast. *First the vote, now the professions!*

Mitty announced that Shafer was passed out in the drawing room, so they went into the study, a large room filled with leather and wood and desks and ledgers. Crystal glasses shone on a leather inset table. Gin bottles stood like soldiers at the ready and limes were cut into twists and squeezes. Neill sat at a small round table, his book in front of him, drink at one hand, cigarettes and an ashtray at the other. Cleo looked closely at him. His tie was askew, his slick hair slightly mussed. It was the first time she'd seen him disheveled.

"Who let Shafer in?" Graham asked Neill.

"Fella came in the verandah door, tripped in I should say, out of his gourd." Neill tried in vain to keep from slurring.

Teddy grinned at Neill, apparently appreciating his drunken state. "You gentlemen seemed to have drowned your sorrows early."

Neill waved a hand. "Barnabas told us the sheriff wouldn't be coming before tomorrow."

"Let's hope it's tomorrow, soonest," Teddy said, pouring gin over ice.

"Damn goose … wanted to take Josie to the ice house." Neill said. "I refused to help – hic – him."

Graham pushed strands of hair off his forehead. "We better keep an eye on him and the shed. He might pick her up and take her himself."

Cleo watched Neill's eyes roll away. He said, "It's a terrible thing … nature ravaging something as beautiful as Josie."

Cleo narrowed her eyes at the look on Neill's face. He'd cared for Josie. It never occurred to her that Neill… What a donkey she'd been, never recognizing that Neill could have been a target of Josie's peccadilloes … or the other way around. Neill came here often to visit. Neill was rich, and, for that reason alone, Neill would interest

Josie. Neill and Josie. What had Graham said? *Once I realized Neill wasn't attractive to his cousin because he had other interests ...*

She heard Graham say, "Dust to dust. But before we're dust, we're pretty messy."

"The war," Neill said, his voice coming from far away. "You see the dead. At first it's unbelievable, then you get used to it. Don't think I'll get used to seeing Josie ..."

The shock of his admission raised the silky hairs on her arms. Neill had gone to the shed to see Josie. The room filled with silence, veritably sizzled in it. Neill slouched in his chair, his eyes glazed with sorrow and memory. She remembered back sadly when William's mother called to tell her William was missing in action, presumed dead. She cried her eyes out, and when her mother came home, they cried together, then they had their cordial before dinner and wine with dinner. She drank the wine and skipped dinner despite her mother's admonition that she needed to eat to keep up her strength. It never occurred to her to drink more wine – which was legal then – to drown her sorrows. In retrospect, she'd given William his full due, the stark recognition that the man she loved was dead, never to brush a curl off her forehead or press his lips to hers.

Ice tonged into a glass. She glanced up, not having realized that she'd been looking at her hands. Graham was staring at her. "Care for another?"

"No, thanks."

"Takes the edge off," he said.

"I'll second that," Teddy said, rising for a refill. "God were it tomorrow. The sooner we get this over with, the sooner we can go back to normal."

"Not for old Shay," Graham said.

"He'll be better off in Pittsburgh," Teddy said. "He can go back with me on *Hela* next week."

"He'll want to go with Josie," Graham said.

Teddy appeared appalled. "No dead bodies on ships. Bad luck."

"He'll take the train with her is my bet," Graham said.

"One departs day after tomorrow, if we can get things cleared up by then."

"Depends on what we tell the sheriff and the coroner," Graham said.

Teddy pinched her lips with her thumb and first finger. "We don't know what happened. No one on this island does. When that occurs, they usually write something like, 'Death by Misadventure.'"

Graham said, "A lot of people know about that note Barnabas and Shafer found. I don't think Shafer, once he sobers up, will let it go DbM."

"We'll convince him."

"And the islanders? The innkeeper at the Dolphin? The bartender at King's Inn? Even Murphy – we asked him about Josie."

"What are you getting at?"

"We knew she was missing and we were looking for her."

"And?"

"Barnabas might not pass information onto strangers about his master and mistress, but you can bet your bottom dollar he talked to his kin."

"That may be, but no one knows for sure how Josie met her end."

"The coroner might figure it out."

"You read too much Sherlock Holmes."

Neill raised his head. Neill, devotee of the Arthur Conan Doyle canon, stammered. "We need us a Sherlock – figure out who done this to Josie."

Graham said quietly, "Neill has gone off his nut."

Teddy said, "I don't pretend to be Sherlock, but it's evident Josie went to the river that night, drunk and angry, and fell in and drowned."

"At midnight?" Graham said.

"Didn't have to be midnight. Could have been the next morning early."

"She would have been seen by shrimpers and gill-netters, Mother. What would she have been doing in the morning in her dancing dress?"

Cleo felt the heat rise in her cheeks.

Teddy flicked her eyes away from Cleo. "Graham, don't you want to get this ghastliness behind us? You realize, of course, the longer it takes …"

"I realize I'm implicated, but the note's a lie."

"Then the note shouldn't come into it."

"Tell Barnabas and Shafer."

"Shafer is family. We can also deal with Barnabas."

"Blackmail, mother?" Graham grinned, but Teddy's glared. Graham went on, "Add that to bootlegging. Where shall we set up Barnabas and his family? South Hills? He can caddy at the new country club. His daughters can scrub cutlery."

"Don't be absurd. I'm not in the mood for mockery."

Cleo thought about what Doc had said, about where the body would have been placed in the water. Out in the sound, he'd said. She said, "How thorough is the sheriff?"

Teddy frowned as if Cleo hadn't been invited into the conversation. "Why?"

"Wondering, because of something Doc said."

"What did Doc say?" Graham asked.

"That given the time it took for Josie's body to turn up where it was, she would have been put into the sound by boat, then washed from there into the river."

"I see where you're going," Graham said. "Since her body wasn't – uh – fresh, she wouldn't have been where she was found for very long, because that's a favorite place for fishermen out early. She was passing through, so to speak."

Cleo said, "Doc said in a matter of hours she'd have washed into the sea from the river." *Where are you, Doc?*

Teddy said, "Passing through at high tide. Everyone on this island knows about tides and the way the marsh river flows. The sheriff and coroner won't miss that."

"Not only that …" Cleo stopped speaking because she'd lost her thought, thinking about Doc.

"Not only that, what?" Graham asked.

"The boat. Whoever took the body out would need a sturdy boat. The day we went sailing, I remember how the launch rocked back and forth and how we had to balance our weight."

"Someone strong," Teddy said.

"Agile and athletic," Graham said.

"Maybe two people?" Teddy suggested.

"Better," Cleo said.

"Have you any ideas?" Teddy asked.

Cleo looked from Graham to Teddy. "Would the village people talk if they saw something? If we asked?"

Graham said. "If the guilty party is one of us, they wouldn't tell us. If it's one of them, they sure as hell wouldn't tell us."

"A sturdy boat, on the choppy sound, in the middle of the night," Cleo mused.

"Or, think about this," Teddy said, brightening. "Josie is so mad, and, filled with gin, she took a boat out on her own and went overboard."

"How'd she get to the docks?" Graham asked. "Shafer said all his cars were accounted for."

"Let's start with who could have killed her," Cleo said. "Who made her cry? Shafer's the obvious suspect. There's Graham, of course, with the note."

"Stop right there," Graham demanded.

She shrugged him off. "There's Teddy, who was sore at her. There's Doc, the mystery man. Then Thompsons and Swinny. Everyone else is north for the summer."

Cleo didn't look at Neill, but she saw Graham's and Teddy's eyes flash toward him.

Teddy said, "We've come full circle, it seems." She sat, crossed her legs and looked at Graham. "Is it possible someone saw you at the lighthouse that night?"

Graham shrugged. Cleo's eyes shifted to the wall, to a painting of blue flowers in a pitcher. Matisse? Graham said, "Someone might have been walking on the beach and saw the light. But that would have been in passing. I swear this. No one saw me carry a body to the boat and dump it over the side into the sound."

"It won't come to that," Teddy said. "Still, I don't want the shadow of suspicion on you."

"Then we must, as Cleo has said, find out what happened." He caught her eye. "Right, Clee?"

She looked from Graham to Teddy and thought about Renoir as she did that first day, the day she arrived and felt the butterflies in her stomach when she first laid eyes on Graham. She shook the image and said, "Shafer could not have put Josie in the sound."

"Okay, we'll concentrate on Shafer. Why not?"

"He's a small man, not athletic," Cleo said.

"Josie was thin, even though she was tall," Teddy said.

"Shafer was drunk as a lord."

"So was Josie."

"Hear me out," Cleo said resolutely. "You and Graham said he's not good with boats."

Graham shook his head. "Doesn't know which end of the oar is which."

Cleo said, "Therefore, if Shafer did something to Josie he had help."

"Barnabas? You think Barnabas?"

"I'm not thinking old Barnabas. Fredik."

Teddy hummed a second. "Fredik would help Barnabas, if he asked."

"Trouble is," Graham said, "we can't get Shafer to admit it. Asking Fredik would be like asking a stone."

"Shafer could have been drunk and doesn't remember," Teddy said. "Even so, what good does it do us to presume it happened that way when we're not going to give Shafer over to the law?"

Graham gave Cleo a long measuring look. "You wouldn't want us to, would you?"

What could she say? "It would be hard, I know ..."

"Shafer's a drunk. He lost his business and now his wife, and we don't know for a fact he had anything to do with whatever happened to her."

Teddy toyed with a ring on her finger. "It started in our ballroom, on the dance floor. You know, of course, Josie always wants to be the star of the show, but our beautiful guest stole it from her."

Cleo could barely breathe at the suggestion of culpability.

Graham said, "Cut it out, Mother. Cleo had nothing to do with Josie's anger."

Teddy looked at her like she'd discovered the secret of the Pharaohs. "What I meant was Cleo was a catalyst."

What the hell was Teddy talking about?

"For what? For whom?" Graham asked.

Teddy said, "We've been hypothesizing between ourselves, so let's keep it that way. We'll tell the sheriff the facts that can be verified. We won't speculate. Is that all right with everyone?" She looked from Graham to Cleo, where her gaze remained.

"Sure," Graham said.

"Of course," Cleo breathed out.

Mitty must have been listening at the door for a proper moment to intrude because he announced that dinner was ready to be served. He looked at Neill, slumped in the chair, and asked, "Will the gentlemen be awakened for dinner?"

Cleo stared at her cousin, head sideways resting on the open pages of his book, snoring lightly.

Rising, Teddy said, "I think dinner will be more pleasant without Shafer and Neill. If they want a tray later, they may be served."

Graham came to stand by Cleo. "Teddy insists on having a proper dinner."

In the dining room, the children stood behind their chairs. Teddy turned and whispered, "No talking at the table with the kiddies."

Graham said, "Maybe they saw something. They're always sneaking around."

"We will not discuss Josie at the dinner table."

"Amen and out," Graham said.

*****

When the knock came, Cleo thought about ignoring it, but that wouldn't keep Teddy from badgering her tomorrow. She fastened her finest lace dressing gown, one her mother gave her on her engagement to William in case she ran off with him before he went to war. There were times she wished she had; life would have been so different. But would she have been happier? Coming to this island, experiencing the full flower of love, the power of sexuality, and the pit of deceit, had changed her emotional perspective. Would she have ever been wildly in love with William? She feared not, but she wouldn't have experienced deceit, just boredom. *Oh devious brain, how can you think such things?*

Teddy swirled in wearing a satin robe and velvet slippers. She lit a cigarette and offered one to Cleo. "Just us girls," she said, shaking the match until the flame died and going to the white chaise. She sat and crossed her legs.

Cleo sat on the pink boudoir chair, back braced for questioning, holding the cigarette at a jaunty angle.

"First," Teddy said, "I want you to understand, I shall never judge you or another human being."

"Hmmm." She blew cigarette smoke from the bottom of her lip into the air.

"I've always considered myself a student of human nature."

Cleo let her eyebrows rise. *Who doesn't?*

Teddy flicked ashes into a crystal ashtray and took another drag. "Human nature is changing, for the better I would say." She stared through the fog of her cigarette. "The war was an awful thing, but it catapulted us into a new era. The way we women performed during the crisis proved we could be more than a wife, mother and homemaker." Cleo felt like laughing because homemaker was never a role of Teddy's. Teddy went on, "Prohibition, the grand experiment, is grotesque, but attitudes are lightening up. We don't stuff our flesh into those god-awful corsets anymore. We cut our hair. You young women don't have to be chaperoned when you're around men. We've entered an era of liberation. We can vote. We're becoming equal with men. Society is admitting women have libidos, which is another word for sex drive."

Knowing where this was leading, Cleo cringed. "The Victorian secret."

"You understand then."

"My mother wouldn't."

"I don't know your mother, but she must see women have become liberated." She crushed her cigarette in the crystal.

"She closes her eyes to liberation."

"Did you kiss William when she was looking?"

"A quick cheek smooch."

"You perform duties in a hospital."

Perform duties sounded better than work. "In the women's ward, yes."

"What did you do during the war?"

"Roll bandages, clean instruments."

"Ever bathe a man?"

"It is considered inappropriate for unmarried women to do that. Older married women did."

"It wasn't considered proper for a young *virgin*."

Flames shot into her cheeks. She brought her cigarette to her mouth and saw her hand shake.

Teddy waved, dismissive of her embarrassment. "The last time Neill was here, he brought a picture of you."

She nodded. "I remember when he asked for the latest portrait of me."

"You are as lovely in person as in the picture. Graham couldn't take his eyes off it, and Neill left it with him."

Cleo suddenly stubbed out her cigarette. "My cousin, the matchmaker."

"He did a good job, don't you think?"

"Do you?"

"Yes." Teddy lit another cigarette. "Now to our trouble at hand." She shook the match flame into smoke. "Remember, when we talked before, I said if anyone could prove Graham spent the night in his aerie, the lighthouse, he would be exonerated?"

Cleo thought about Teddy's exact words, which were stuck in her head: *If Graham was with someone that evening ... that would make a difference.* She said, "I suppose he would be exonerated if he was with someone the entire evening."

"I've asked Graham outright if he was with anyone."

Teddy paused and stared at Cleo through the haze of smoke. Cleo cocked her head and tried on a questioning expression. Teddy said, "It says a lot about a man who won't squeal when his reputation, even his life, is on the line, don't you think?"

"I would agree."

"What would you do if you were me and you knew someone was with Graham that night?"

"Let Graham work it out."

"Do you think that person would accept a bribe?"

Somehow she knew it would come down to this. "Not if that person is as honorable as Graham."

"I think that person is, which is why I'm counting on that person to come forward – to me."

"What would you do?"

"Frame my words carefully to exonerate Graham and protect the person who confided in me. The authorities will be objective about who the person is, as long as the person isn't dishonorable in other ways."

"What other ways?"

"Graham wouldn't have a guest in his personal and private quarters if that person wasn't honorable." Teddy rose and stubbed out her cigarette. "I'll say goodnight then. You've helped me through this." At the door, she turned, "I love my son and all my children. I would do anything for them and for those they love, especially those they love. I hope you know what I'm saying."

Cleo stood. "Good night, Teddy."

Once the door closed, she thought: *the nerve.* And then she began to laugh.

CHAPTER TWENTY-FOUR

She dressed for the beach, not caring if it was proper or not to show up in the breakfast room in beach pajamas. Neill sat reading his book with his cigarettes by one hand and a saucer and cup of coffee by the other. He looked up when she walked in. "Morning."

"Morning," she said, staring into his red-rimmed eyes. "Good night?"

"Beastly hangover. Got splifficated yesterday." His hand shook a little as he took his time lighting a cigarette.

She went to the buffet and helped herself to eggs, bacon, and a tomato. "Never saw you looking so rummy before."

"Been plenty of times. During the war, nothing to do but sauce up."

"You and Shafer put on quite a show at cocktails. Snoring and what not."

"Forgive me?"

She turned and bent to kiss him on the cheek, then went to sit across from him, face-to-face. "Nothing to forgive."

"One more day," he said, taking a long drag on the cigarette.

"For tomorrow we drive."

"What would you like to do today?" he asked. "Plans?"

"I think the sheriff will determine that."

"If he ever gets here."

"Where's Graham and Teddy?"

"Went to the Dolphin early to run those insurance torpedos off."

"Isn't this island a public place?"

"About twenty percent of it. Henry families own the rest."

"They don't own the village, do they?"

"No, but they don't want some bohunks coming in cheating the natives."

"It's nice Graham and Teddy look out for them."

"It's their fiefdom; it's what fief lords do."

What if the natives didn't want fief lords looking out for them?
She said, "Barnabas is going to be out of a job soon."

Neill stubbed his cigarette. "He'll be taken care of."

"I know, it's what fief lords do. When Shafer goes to Pittsburgh for the … for Josie's funeral, will he come back?"

"He says not. He's fed up. Between me and Graham, we'll help him get a new life."

"Department store life might be more suitable to him than open hearth steel furnaces."

"Got to dry him out first."

"Did you go with Shafer to the shed?"

Neill's gaze dropped to his coffee cup. "I tried to stop him."

Cutting the tomato, she said, "Shafer wasn't in the war, was he?"

He lit another cigarette. "Bad legs."

"He's never seen death like that, has he?"

Neill sucked on the cigarette and blew out as he talked. "He sees fresh death when islanders die."

She chewed the tomato slowly. "He wasn't prepared for what he saw, was he?"

"No, poor bloke." Neill's Englishism failed to amuse this time.

"You've seen it, though?"

His gaze finally skimmed her face. "War."

She swallowed. "How did you feel about Josie?"

The cup drew his interest again. "Nice enough. Bit of a twit sometimes."

The cup or Josie? "Her death shocked you, didn't it?"

He shrugged and flicked ash into the saucer, something she abhorred. "Sure," he said, "anybody you know, well, it shocks you."

"Did Josie ever make a play for you?"

His chin came up. "What?"

She cut her eggs with a knife and fork. "I wondered how well you knew her. She certainly had a thing for men."

"Not me. Graham."

"Graham wasn't her only conquest."

"Ha. Conquest." There was something physical in his bitterness.

She reached out her arm. Her hand couldn't touch his across the table, but she laid her palm flat in the middle. "Neill, I'd understand if you fell for her. I've come to learn falling for someone isn't something you can help, no matter what you want, or don't want to happen."

He shook his head, his eyes riveted onto his book. "She ... it's just that I'm rich."

"I've always known you to be inhibited around girls."

He laughed at his cigarette pack.

She said, "Josie's a predator."

His glimpse at her said it all. "She's dead, Bearcat." He rubbed his finger beneath an eye.

"I'm not speaking ill for the sake of it. I'm stating fact."

He sat back and raised his arms in surrender. "I fell. Okay."

"Why was she mad at Graham that night we danced?"

"Let's go outside."

She tossed her napkin on the table. "Sure, I'd like a walk on the beach."

She strolled next to Neill feeling the compression of sadness. Neill, her favorite cousin – the war hero with a soft heart, a man back from hell who didn't quite know what the future should bring for him – had his hands in his pockets, leaning forward, pressing his lips against an inevitable future. Neill who came to this island to visit his buddy from the war, to escape the deadly dull pace at Connolly's Department Store. No thrills there after his sky antics over France. Poor Neill, would he ever let go of the drama of war for the realities of peace? She looked at his bowed head. *Oh Neill, what are we going to do?*

They stepped off the boardwalk, onto the dune, and she took off her shoes.

"Why was she mad at Graham that night," Cleo asked again.

Neill glanced at her, a man resigned to say what he must. "She wasn't mad at Graham." His eyes flashed to the sea, the stare in them seeking infinity. Finally, he said, "You remember when she and Shafer came into the ball room?"

She thought back and knew her recollection hadn't been what it should be, because Graham was at her side, ever on her mind. Already she'd fallen in love with him. She understood the meaning of having eyes only for the one you love … and ears and all the other sensibilities. "No," she said, and bent to pick up a broken sand dollar.

"She always carried on with Graham," Neill said, "so no one thought anything about her flirting. But I did." He looked at her. "While you danced so divinely with Graham, she danced with Shafer until his two left feet got to her. When they swung by me, she flipped her finger for me to cut in."

"I sort of remember."

"I still remember how entranced you and Graham were."

She tossed the shell at a gull flying overhead. "Don't cause me to blush."

"I think it's swell."

She smiled at him. "Do you really?"

He smiled back. "Honest Injun. Graham's a fine man. I shouldn't have said those things that morning."

She looked at the broken shells strewn at her feet. "You've said."

"What happens between us fellas should stay between us fellas."

"I would agree, but when the truth comes out, it can't be put back in."

He bobbed his head. "That morning, when Josie was gone, I was just …" He halted.

"What did Josie say while you were dancing?"

It took a few moments, but he got it out. "Snippy comments about you and Graham. I said to her, 'What difference does it make, you're my sweetheart now?' She made a cutting remark, like she always does, saying crazy things." He kicked at the sand. "Crazy things. Crazy Josie. We were going to be together." He raised his head and his upper lip twitched into a grimace. "Shock you?"

"Not after I thought about it. Once Shafer was down to his last red cent, she'd leave him."

"She needed nice things."

"She needed a kick in the pants. When were you two supposed to get together?"

He kicked at a crab crawling from its hole. "That night, as we danced, she kept insisting we 'fish or cut bait.'"

"What did she mean by that?"

"Get a quickie divorce and marry."

"And you said?"

"I said next year, after Shafer gets settled, when you've gotten a proper divorce, and I'm not named as the cad in it."

"How'd she take it?"

"She marched off, leaving me right there on the dance floor."

"After that, she snagged Graham," Cleo said. "I was dancing with Mr. Clodhopper."

"She wanted to get my dander up."

"She did, didn't she?"

"Graham's my best friend. I was used to being second fiddle. We'd go into the pubs, all the girls …" He grunted. "There I go again."

"It's all right. I've grown up a little, I think."

"You don't want to learn the ways of men. We're a no good lot."

"Neill, you're not no-good. Neither is Graham. Girls go for the good ones."

"For Graham."

"C'mon, you had a few."

"Sure, but I wanted a girl to love me, for me, not for my money."

"Did you think Josie loved you for you?"

"I didn't kid myself. But that didn't stop me loving her. I was sap for her, just like Shay."

"What happened after Josie danced with Graham?"

"Graham went outside with you."

"It wasn't long before Teddy came out to tell us the party was breaking up."

He breathed in. "Josie's fault."

"What did she do?"

"She announced she was having try-outs for her second husband."

"What?" Of all she'd heard, she found this truly shocking.

"I swear, I couldn't believe my ears. She came up and kissed me. Said I might do, if I'd open my mouth like Graham does." Neill's eyes flashed at her. "Sorry, I'm a mutt."

"Yes, you are. Did Shafer hear that?"

"He was dancing, I think with Mrs. Thompson, but Teddy heard."

"What happened?"

"Teddy told Josie if she said another word, she'd slap her."

"Good for Teddy."

"Josie started to cry and said she was kidding, that Graham never kissed her."

"Did you believe it?"

"Absolutely. Graham said once he ducked her mouth so many times, it was like eluding a sky full of Huns."

They turned back the way they'd come, walking in welcoming silence until they reached the boardwalk. "Have you seen Josie's note?"

"I heard about it that morning. Shafer told me about the contents," he said, brushing back his hair, a certain reluctance in his voice and step. He looked at her. "Yeah, I lied. I hate myself for that. Mostly, because I betrayed Graham. An officer and gentleman doesn't lie about his comrades, his best buddy especially."

"Why did you?"

"I didn't want anyone to know, to suspect who the flyboy was. I came up with that because …"

"Because?"

"I wasn't thinking clearly; I didn't know which way to turn. She'd gone off …"

"Neill, what are you trying to say?"

"I met Josie later that night, after the dancing."

"Where?"

"In my rooms." A squeak involuntarily pushed from her throat. "She knows a way in from the other wings."

"Seems everyone does. She came to your room. Was it the first time?"

"No."

"I don't need to hear any more."

"I love her." His voice cracked. "I loved her."

"What happened?"

"She wanted to go away. She had two suitcases. She wanted … God, can you believe the woman? She wanted to go away then and there."

"That night?"

"That minute."

"She had a lot to drink."

"Sozzled. I tried to reason with her."

"And then?"

"She left, cussing and bawling her eyes out."

"That must have been when Barnabas saw her coming up the verandah steps and sat with her."

"How do you know that?"

"A little birdie told me."

Neill's face drained of color, like dead people's the minute they die. "Doc?"

"A villager."

He breathed easier. "They don't talk."

"One did – to me. What happened after she left you?"

"She'd left her suitcases. I went after her with them."

"And then?"

He swallowed. "She was in Bellflower's garden, sitting with Barnabas, crying. The garden's overgrown. Poor sap Shafer, can't keep the garden up. I was behind a cedar. They didn't see me. I couldn't make out most words, but I was glad I didn't hear my name. Suddenly, I heard a door bang and Shafer yelling. He must have come outside. Josie and Barnabas ran up the steps. I got clear of the cedar. She was cussing a blue streak. I saw Barnabas push Shafer back inside. I sat the suitcases on the bottom steps. Josie turned around and saw me. She came running down the steps assuming I'd changed my tune. When I told her I was just returning her suitcases, she started calling me names, among them son-of-a-bitch. Nobody calls my mother that, nor me a bastard. But I calmed myself, and I turned to leave. Next thing I knew, she comes flying at me. Tried to claw my face. Barnabas came outside and called out, 'What's wrong down there?' Then I think Shafer came out, too. Anyway, Josie was trying to scratch my damn eyes out. Her fingernails are red claws. I …" Neill looked like a man about to go under for the last time. "I didn't mean to – I didn't mean – she went down …"

"You hit her?"

"I struck out to keep her from scratching my face. I wanted to stop the claws and the gutter words."

"You hit her?"

"I didn't mean to." His eyes suddenly gushed tears.

"So what then?"

"She went down." He rubbed his face. "I heard footsteps coming down the steps. I did a damnable thing."

"You ran."

"Yeah. I've never been yellow, but I ran."

"Was she dead?"

"No. Not even hurt. Just raving mad."

"Was she moving?"

"I don't know, but crying."

"Maybe not," she said. She'd heard the noise of the dying. Air accumulated in the throat came out sounding like a cry or a moan. "Did it sound like she was choking?"

He wiped tears with his fingers. "Yeah, maybe. I don't know, just bawling like a brat."

"The next morning must have been shocking for you."

"I was balled up because of the note. Then … then I did another damnable thing. But she could have meant Graham. I mean …"

"She didn't mean Graham in the note. She meant you."

"Damn me."

She gave Neill a wondering stare. "Shafer had to know about you and Josie."

Neill shook his head, still wiping his eyes. "She never said, and I didn't ask. He seemed okay toward me." They'd reached the gardens. He avoided her by looking up at Southerness. "I went back to my rooms after I … I don't know what happened to her after that. I swear to God on all that's holy, I didn't put Josie in the marsh."

"Fredik put her in the sound."

"How do you know that?"

"Had to be. Barnabas came down, saw Josie dead, and couldn't do anything himself because he's too old and so he called Fredik."

Neill shook his head. "Why would he do that?"

"Get rid of the body."

"I didn't kill her. I know I didn't."

She took his arm. "What did you think the next morning when she couldn't be found?"

"I didn't think she was dead, that's certain. I thought she ran off and hid to make me jealous. I decided to wash my hands of her. She scared the crap out of me."

After five or six steps, she asked, "What are you going to do, Neill?"

"Do?"

"When the sheriff comes."

"I don't understand what you mean. I told you …"

"You told me you might have caused Josie's death."

He hesitated, and she knew he was lost. "I can't admit that to a bull."

"It was an accident."

"Bearcat, you're on my side, aren't you?"

"Yes I am, but you must tell the truth."

"Look, I spilled to you. We're family. We stick it out. We don't rat on each other."

"I've no intention of ratting on you, but Graham is not taking the fall."

"He won't. This is Sago Island. They own the damned place. They *are* the law."

"That's what Fredik thought when he chucked Josie overboard."

Past the path lined with Oleanders, they came to the tabby steps leading to the balustrades of Southerness. She looked up to see Graham standing, looking down, his hands draped over a rampart. She said to Neill, "What are you going to say to your good buddy?"

"Bearcat, leave this to me. It's my business."

Graham shot down the steps like a sleek bullet. When he came to a halt beside her, she could barely concentrate for the fluttering of her heart. Graham said, "There you two are, bathing by the sea when the law comes calling."

"Shit," Neill said under his breath.

"Amen, old sport. But we'll get this over with."

"We leave tomorrow," Neill said. "Can't hang around. Bearcat's got to get back."

"We'll send the bulls packing before you know it."
*****

The sheriff and the coroner sat on the left side of a long table in the library. Teddy and Graham sat at the head and foot. Shafer, with his head hanging like a man condemned, took a seat at Graham's right. Cleo and Neill also aligned across from the authorities. The sheriff was a young man, around Graham's age. The coroner had to be in his sixties, a Mark Twain lookalike. Neither looked stupid. The coroner said, "Before I look at the corpse, give me some facts. Where was it found?"

Cleo winced at the ugly word. "The corpse, it has a name. Josie Drake."

No one spoke for several seconds, then Teddy said, "Mrs. Drake was discovered by two crabbers who alerted our veterinarian, Doc – Sam Holliday."

"The crabbers reported it," the sheriff said. "We'll go to the scene directly."

"I know Sam," the coroner said. "Where is he?"

"He went to Port Maria," Graham said. "Don't know when he'll return."

"When was Mrs. Drake last seen?"

That was the start of at least a hundred questions. Teddy and Graham answered them, some forthright, yet skillfully evading most. Whenever drunken Shafer tried to answer, Graham would lay his hand on his cousin and take the words out of his mouth.

When the sheriff asked, "Any idea where she was going?"

Graham answered, "We don't." He repeated that Shafer and Josie had a lot to drink and that Shafer went up to bed leaving Josie in the drawing room. What Graham said was true, but she, Cleo, knew where Josie went after that. She looked sideways at Neill. He pressed his lips with the obstinacy of one who wasn't about to squeal on himself.

The coroner rose. "Let's take a look."

Teddy had asked Fredik to stand by to take the men to the shed.

When they'd gone, Teddy breathed out. "Not so bad."

"Omissions," Shafer slurred. His head came up wobbling, and he fixed his eyes on Graham. "The note, the one you wouldn't let me say a word about …"

Teddy got up and stood beside him. "Shafer, the note is family business, like I told you. No one knows where she was going or when she passed on."

"Passed on, ha. Crab food."

"One day you'll sober up and understand what I'm saying. In the meantime, keep your mouth shut."

"Aw right," Shafer said. "I gotcha." He looked at Graham. "Futzing with my Josie."

Cleo stood. "He was not."

Shafer stared up at her, eyes looking out from dark purple rings like a lobotomized raccoon. "Wha …?"

Graham jumped up. "That's okay, Cleo. Stop right there."

She said, "He …"

Graham held up his hand. "Don't."

"What?" Shafer demanded. "What's going on?"

"Nothing," Graham said. "Cleo believes in me."

Shafer's head swung back to her. "That right?"

"Yes."

"He futzing around with you, too?"

She wheeled back, but not from embarrassment, but from a stoic firmness of spirit, of purpose.

Graham grabbed Shafer's arm. "Mind your tongue, you drunken ass."

Shafer raised his head to the ceiling and beat the table with the flat of his hand. "Har, har, har."

"Call Barnabas," Teddy said.

Mitty came in, as always, with impeccable timing. "Mr. Barnabas is in the pantry. I've summoned him."

Barnabas came in like he had something urgent on his mind and determined to do something about it. He stood by Shafer's chair and formally addressed them. "I will continue to look after Mr. Shafer. If he dismisses me, I will go to relatives in New Jersey. I must tell the truth about when Miss Josie disappeared so that innocent men are not blamed."

Cleo thought she was hearing things. There were certainly gasps around her, and maybe one came from her own impulsive throat. Neill turned to face her, his mouth open and working like a goldfish.

"What the hell?" Shafer said and wavered to his feet.

Barnabas gently pushed him into his chair.

"We're listening, "Teddy said.

"That night, Mr. Shafer was not himself with drink."

Shafer hit his fist on the table. "Here, that's damn cheeky ..."

Barnabas paid no attention. "Miss Josie was in a state of hysteria outside. I took Mr. Shafer up stairs. I came down and heard an argument in the garden. I found Miss Josie on the ground. She wouldn't get up. I went to fetch my nephew to carry her up the steps. I was with Mr. Shafer when Fredik came to me and said she was dead."

Cleo interrupted, "When you saw Josie on the ground, was she alive?"

"Yes, miss. She was crying."

"Did you talk to her?"

"She wouldn't listen. She wouldn't let me help her."

Neill's face showed unrestrained relief.

Graham asked, "What happened then?"

"I fetched Fredik. He came upstairs without her. He said she was dead."

"Did you look at her to see what happened?"

"I did not go down the steps, nor did I ask how she died."

Cleo thought Barnabas may have departed from the truth here. Teddy asked, "What about the note?"

"It was on the buffet. That is where Miss Josie put her notes to Mr. Shafer."

Shafer thrust his arm up in a victory salute. "She sure did. Always."

Teddy's eyelids blinked rapidly. "She wrote the note meaning to leave, but she didn't. She died, instead."

Cleo flashed her eyes at Graham. He was staring at her. She breathed deeply to relieve the tension scampering through her deep muscles. She asked, "Before the situation where she was on the ground, did Josie leave the house for any length of time?"

Barnabas nodded. "Miss Josie was gone from the house for a while and when she came back she was upset."

"Did you see suitcases?"

"Suitcases were near the steps when I found her weeping in the grass."

"Did Fredik …" Graham started to say, but was interrupted by Mitty standing in the door frame.

"The authorities have returned."

Teddy said, "Show them in."

Although Cleo had seen death and smelled it, she shrank back from the men. Their clothes reeked. Teddy pinched her nose. Graham seemed to be holding his breath.

The coroner said, "I have made a cursory examination of the cor … body of the late Mrs. Josephine Drake. I will offer my report in writing. It is my duty in this instance to further examine the body."

Shafer scooted his chair back and tried to get to his feet. Graham grabbed hold of his arm, but Shafer shook off his hand. "Tell me, goddamnit."

"Mr. Drake …" the coroner began.

"Tell me medical man, how … what happened to my Josie." He flopped back in the chair.

Teddy said, "Yes, please do tell. We have a right to know."

"I can only report what I've found without a more careful examination.'

"Then report to us what you know now."

"Mrs. Drake had three distinct skull fractures."

"Three?"

Cleo glanced at Neill, who had gone white.

"Means what?" Shafer asked.

The coroner continued, "The cranium was battered."

"Beat to death?" Graham asked.

Neill gasped. Teddy's mouth hung open.

The coroner answered, "In the absence of a fall, that looks the case, sir."

"Must a been a h'accident," Shafer said. "Down the ol' steps."

"There are no other injuries that I can see on her body, but I shall know more when she's in my mortuary suite," the coroner said. "If you'll excuse me, I'll see that the body is made ready to move to Port Maria."

"Going, too," Shafer said.

The coroner sighed. "I can't restrain you. Be at the dock."

The sheriff said, "I'll need to ask you questions."

Shafer got out of the chair and leaned across the table as if to spit in the sheriff's face. "No, you don't. You need put that sonna-bitch in handcuffs." His hand waffled left, at Graham.

The sheriff said, "What are you talking about, Mr. Drake?"

"I saw the sonna-bitch – my garden."

Cleo jumped up. "You did not." Shafer's glassy eyes met hers as he fell back into his chair. "Graham was not in your garden."

"You don't know."

"He was with me. I was with him."

The quiet that fell across the room screeched loud enough to register shock on everyone's face. Teddy stood.

The sheriff said, "I don't think we need to take this up here and now. I'll talk to each of you individually."

Shafer pointed a trembling finger at Cleo. "Take up for the cuckold; should be shamed."

Teddy said, "Shut your mouth, Shafer."

Shafer turned to Graham. "I saw you. I 'member. My Josie on the ground. I look down from my dressing room and saw damn you."

Cleo looked at Neill. How very much alike Neill and Graham were, except for the hair. At night, from above, in the moonlight, they could be mistaken. And now Neill's face was opaque with doggedness. He wasn't about to confess. She glared at him and announced, "Graham and I were in the lighthouse." She turned toward Shafer. "He wasn't in your garden."

Graham moved fast, toward Cleo, and knocked into the back of Shafer's chair. He reached for Cleo and said, "Stop now. This isn't necessary."

She looked at him, defiant and unashamed. "Yes it is."

"Nice going chump," Shafer said, forcing a laugh. "Steal a man's wife an' go futzing a fool girl."

It took all her self-control to keep from pounding Shafer on top of his head. "He didn't steal your wife. You lost her. I'm not the fool here, you are." She looked at the sheriff. "Where's Fredik?"

The sheriff looked around the long room, and, seeing no Fredik, said, "Why, he showed us back here."

Teddy said, "Graham get Mitty to find him."

Barnabas, who had been leaning against a wall, cleared his throat. "I believe you will not."

"Why not?" Teddy demanded.

"I told him I was going to tell what I knew."

"What do you know, Mr. Barnabas?" asked the sheriff

"I did not see who hit Miss Josie in the head, but my nephew put her in the sound."

"Why?" asked the coroner.

"Fredik said it would look like she ran away up north and would never be found to prove otherwise."

"He doesn't know these waters then," the coroner said. "The tides and currents. She'd wash up somewhere."

"Fredik is recent to this country," Barnabas said.

"Could Fredik have knocked her in the head?"

"He was in his bed when I went to fetch him."

"It's your word," the sheriff said. "Why would he want her to disappear?"

"To save my position with Mr. Shafer."

Graham said, "Your position was tenuous since Shafer was going broke."

Barnabas said, "Mr. Shafer will always need someone, Mr. Graham."

Shafer, who, on hearing his name, shook himself and got to his feet. Cleo turned to him, but he couldn't or wouldn't look at her. He put his hands in his pants' pockets and listed forward, his chin nearly touching his chest.

"You killed her," she said.

Shafer shook his head.

"She finally got to you, and you killed her." Shafer listed to the left. "You've lost yourself in the bottle, but it hasn't helped you forget what you've done."

He put a hand on the table to steady himself. "My Josie …"

Cleo said, "Barnabas told us what he saw and did that night. But he didn't see everything. He went to get Fredik to pick Josie off the ground since he couldn't do it himself. In the time it took him to fetch Fredik, you, Shafer, came downstairs and found her suitcases on the steps and her crying over another man. You found something to bash her head in …"

"Stop," Shafer said, whimpering, shaking his head. "It's not…" He leaned back and lost his balance. On the floor, he rolled on his side, crying in great gulps. Cleo looked at the ashen faces around her and wondered if she'd come into this family and destroyed it. *How bold of me to think that. Didn't it all start before I got here?* She glanced at Neill, who sat with his hands together, watching his thumbs roll over one another.

Time seemed to stop and no one moved or spoke. When Shafer had sobbed himself to sniveling, he struggled to his knees. He looked up at Cleo and tried to raise his arms in appeal. "Accident. Didn't mean … I had to stop her … leaving." He coughed and rubbed his eyes. "Leaving. She was leaving me…" He leaned over, elbows on the floor, his head bowed.

Cleo looked at Teddy. "I'm sorry. I had to."

Teddy walked to Cleo and reached out to hug her. "I know." Patting her shoulder, she said, "We'll see to Shafer. He's going to be all right."

The sheriff said, "Mrs. Henry, I'll let his man get him ready. We'll be at the docks."

"We'll be there, too," Teddy said.

CHAPTER TWENTY-FIVE

Her head swam with the hoopla of sending Shafer off to Port Maria. You'd think he was a war hero riding in an open car down Market Street, past Strawbridge's.

She turned to Graham, sitting beside her in the Depot Hack, noticing how his straw fedora tilted at a slight angle. She motioned her head toward Shafer, beside Teddy in the front seat, waving to onlookers. "Quite amazing when you think about it."

"Old Shay's not a bad sort, really," Graham said.

Shafer looked content and seemed sober enough. Ice had diminished the puffiness around his eyes and dissolved the purple beneath the skin above his cheeks. His suit was an impeccable brown gabardine, pressed knife-sharp. His white shirt was so starched it could have stood on its own. Barnabas had done for his man.

"Shay won't go to the big house," Graham said.

"He doesn't look afraid," Cleo said.

Graham put a hand on her shoulder. "I wanted to say, don't know if this is the right place, but it's in my mind. What you did … said … was beyond brave."

"Ditto for what you didn't say. Old Shay was trying to send you to the big house."

Graham shook his head. "Lashing out, that's all."

"Convince me."

"Did you always think Shafer did something to her?"

"Like killed her?" Graham nodded. "I thought it possible. I think Doc knew that he did."

"Why wouldn't he tell us?"

"I can only guess that he saw justice in Shafer's actions."

"Hmmm. Maybe avoiding the law, too?"

"I don't believe Doc cheated at cards or shot anyone."

"Okay, I'll go along with you on that. I always liked the fellow, but thank God Barnabas has a conscience."

"I saw it that day at church."

He grinned. "Bet you worked him a little, didn't you?"

"Maybe."

"So maybe, he, like Shafer, was forced to tell what they knew by a smart little bearcat."

"Once Neill told me his story …"

"What story was that?"

"Oh, I forgot. You don't know."

"You mean that he was getting a little nookie from Josie?"

Eons ago, she would have been embarrassed. "You knew. Why didn't you tell me?"

"Officers and gentlemen don't tell on each other. Why do you think he came down here so often? Because I'm the gnat's whistle?"

"Haven't heard that one."

"You' haven't been in gnat-land long enough."

"Neill was an officer and a gentleman, too, yet he double-crossed you by letting everyone think you were the flyboy she wrote about."

"He didn't mean to make me look bad."

"Yes he did."

"To deflect from himself. Hell's bells and cockleshells, I knew locking himself in his reading room was to mourn the loss of his gold digger."

"He knew what she was and still planned to marry her."

"What?"

"She wanted him to run away with her the very night she was killed. Thus the suitcases Shafer saw."

"Holy cow. I had no idea he had it that bad."

She laughed and Shafer turned in his seat to look back. His grin was wry as if he knew what they talked about. Maybe he had heard despite the wind and the noisy engine.

Cleo said more softly, "Neill may have had it bad, but not bad enough to get out of his dressing gown and pack a bag that night. She came to his rooms ready to elope."

"She was married."

"Run off with him."

"Bugger dug in his heels, did he?"

"I wish he would have gone off with her," she said.

Graham appeared to give that some thought. "Me, too. Of course then we'd have a scandal of a different matter."

"She'd be alive."

"We wouldn't be privileged to know that she'd be dead if he didn't."

"Cat chasing its tail."

"Do cats chase their tails?"

"Neill wasn't the smoothie you are."

"We come down to that again."

"Even though he was stubborn, he was awkward with women."

"Great baboons, Bearcat. You didn't know your cousin. He had dames coming out his kazoo."

"Graham …"

Teddy had stopped the truck alongside the docks.

"No kidding," Graham said, opening the car door. "He was a daddy to the dolls. Rich as Croesus, bathing in war hero glory."

"You two must have cut a swath over in Limeyland."

"For crying out loud, Cleo." He held her elbow while she stepped down. After glancing around the wharf where fishermen were coming in with their catch, he leaned closer to her ear. "I'd get on my knees here and now to beg you to believe me, but it's a little public."

She savored the warmth spreading through her and the grin on his lips. "Believe what?"

"I goofed. I'm sorry. I shouldn't have rushed you. I should have taken my time and convinced you that, whatever my past, you are the one for me."

Her entire body felt like an air ship, ready to rise off the ground. "I am?"

"My God, what do I have to say … to do?"

She was thinking of a snappy retort when she saw Teddy steaming away from them, toward the boardwalk where the ferry waited. "We'd better follow her."

They fell in step to catch Teddy. Graham asked, "Where do we go from here?"

"I go to Philadelphia."

"Don't …"

"Graham …"

The sheriff met Teddy midstride. When Cleo and Graham caught up to them, the sheriff said, "Captain's ready to cast off. You ready to board, Graham?"

Graham had a quizzical look on his face. Teddy said, "You need to go with your cousin, then bring back the runabout Doc left at the wharf."

"Of course," he said. He touched Cleo's arm. "Come along?"

To watch him leave the dock, to part from him, was unimaginable. "I'd like one more boat ride, yes."

"You shall have all you want."

*****

Aboard the ferry, his cuffed hands on his lap, Shafer sat on a bench looking down at the water chopping the hull. Cleo walked up and sat beside him. "I'm sorry."

"Don't be," he said, moving his head up and down as if his world had just brightened.

"You don't seem worried."

"I'm not. Not at all."

"I'd be a mess."

"I was a mess."

"Two hours ago you were slobbering drunk."

He sucked in air and exhaled with deliberation as if giving himself time to put his thoughts into words. He canted his head at her. "You know, Cleo, I don't think I was ever drunk, try as I might." He sat straighter and looked over the sound. "I'm the sort that can hold a lot of booze and keep my head. Even when I was drunk, or just pretending, I knew what I'd done, but I didn't want to face it. I didn't want what I did staring at me all day and all night. Living in the bottom of the bottle, I tried not to see the mess I'd made of my wife." He looked at his hands. "In all of this, I loved her. I still do."

"You can't help who you fall in love with, and stay in love with, no matter how hard you fight it."

"I'm getting what I deserve."

"Did you deliberately murder Josie?"

His steady eyes met hers. "You know … I think I did." He seemed to expect a reaction, and she nodded because she knew he had. "You don't mind sitting next to a murderer?"

The wind changed directions and almost blew her cloche from her head. She reached to pull it down. "I'm sitting next to a human being who was goaded into murder."

He reached out with handcuffed hands. "No, sweet Cleo. Don't think that. I goaded myself into marrying a girl my mother said was beneath me."

"By social standards, maybe she was, but she was a human being."

"That was my answer to Mother's diatribes. In the end, Mother was right. It wasn't just money, or society, or her being a dancing girl, or anything like that. She was a damn nympho." His laugh was corrosive. "Said she was born that way and would never change. Hell, she admitted she was palling with someone who could keep up with her."

Cleo flushed as Neill's face flashed in her head "Did you know who?"

"Graham."

She shook her head and watched drops of rain pelting the waters of the sound. "It wasn't Graham."

"Good girl like you, believing in him, makes him a good man."

"He doesn't need me believing."

He snorted good-naturedly and sat back. "I've let Josie's ways affect my feeling for Graham. I'd always trusted him. I remember when we were kids. He's four years younger than me, but when he was eight, and I was twelve, in our fancy-pants prep school, he looked out for me. Kids have always been cruel. Graham wouldn't let anyone pick on me. Made the soccer ballers pick me first, instead of last. Or else."

She smiled slightly. "Or else what?"

"He wouldn't do anything mean. They just wouldn't have the pleasure of his company."

She could believe Graham had that kind of magnetism at the age of eight. "It wasn't Graham who betrayed your trust."

He tried to raise a hand, maybe to push hair off his face, but the handcuffs stopped him. He faced the wind and his hair blew back. "I get it now. Everyone but Graham did. Hell, Doc, probably. I don't care. Fredik? If he wore pants, she wanted in." He leaned forward. "I'll be all right."

"The Henrys won't let you go to jail?"

He looked out over the sound. "The Henrys won't have a damn thing to say about whether I go to jail or not."

"If you're convicted …"

He faced her. "Of course, I'll be convicted. I've confessed. They'll measure me for a striped suit and I'll get me a cell with a crapper. I'll get three meals a day. More than I can guarantee myself when the rest of the roof caves in."

"Graham would get you a job."

"In a steel mill?"

"In an office in a steel mill."

"Same thing. I'm a salesman, Cleo." He looked proud. "Mouth jobs is my living."

"Don't sound so happy."

"I told you, I'm getting what I deserve."

The sheriff came up. "Excuse me, miss … We're about to disembark."

She rose and looked down at Shafer. "I'll come and see you."

He shook his head. "Don't bother. I'm going to where I belong. In a zoo with all the other animals, but I don't want to be looked at from outside of bars."

She said, "If that's your wish."

Shafer rose, and the sheriff took him by the elbow. They walked toward the ramp, and she followed. By the rails, Shafer stopped in front of Graham. "Sorry, Graham. No harm intended. I wouldn't have let you down, you know that."

"I know," Graham said and hugged him.

"Got crazy," Shafer said, walking out into the gentle rain. He raised his cuffed hands. "See you." A deputy took hold of his arm. The coroner followed down the plank.

Graham asked the sheriff. "Can we come along with him?"

"Best not. You'd just be waiting in a smelly old building. We'll hold him for the magistrate in the morning."

"What time?"

"Docket's ten o'clock."

"See you then."

"You go on," the sheriff said, "take that boat on home. Oh, I forgot." He reached into his jacket pocket and pulled out a yellow paper, a telegram. "This came in as I was boarding the ferry over to Sago. Telegram office asked me to hand this to Teddy. Sorry in all this, I forgot."

"Is it bad news?" Graham asked.

"I shouldn't say, but I expect it's saying the same as the telegram I got."

"Which is?"

Cleo held her breath. Doc had been captured.

Graham ripped the envelope. He scanned the print and laughed out loud. "From Murphy, the Pinkerton skunk. Says here, 'Holliday not my man. Got him in Birmingham. Regards.' Regards my butt. Hounding a man to run …" He turned to Cleo and the sheriff with a perplexed expression. "So why did Doc run?"

Cleo looked up at the sky, at the sea birds, and felt the rain on her face. Doc hadn't run from Murphy. He'd run from her. *What an absurd idea. What conceit.*

The sheriff said, "I told the Pinkerton fella Doc wasn't his man. Pinkertons. Bah. Their high-handed tactics'll put them out of business before long." He walked off, then turned back. "Forgot something else." He put his hand in his pocket and held out a key. "To the runabout. Doc dropped it off at the harbormaster's."

"Any idea where he went?"

"Doc never said much. Hails from Valdosta, though, and somewhere up near Atlanta."

"Thanks," Graham said. He took her arm and walked down the gangplank. The rain had become mist. The sky glowed eerily, the clouds a string of peaches and plums in a silver bowl. He looked at Cleo. "It's just us."

Just then rays of sun shot through the nervous sky, highlighting his hair, his face, his sapphire eyes.

"Us," she said so quietly she didn't hear her own voice.

*****

The drive over Oystercatcher Trail with the ticking silence stretched her one last nerve.

"Don't go home tomorrow," Graham said.

The last thing in the world she wanted to do was go home tomorrow. "I …" But she couldn't say it.

He turned his head to grin. "See you don't want to."

She bit her bottom lip. "Graham …"

He pulled the car off the road into an orchard. He looked at her and spoke solemnly. "I love you. I've loved you from the moment I saw you."

Her lower lip quivered.

He got out of the car and came around to open her door. She slid out. His hands grasped her forearms and pulled her to him. "Tell me not to make love to you, and I won't."

So much emotion came at her now, she couldn't think. "Here? Now?"

He grinned. "Why not?" He lifted her chin. "My darling girl, why not?"

She took his hand and squeezed. "Because there are snakes and chiggers and all kinds of things, and there are more romantic places to …"

"Where would that be?"

"I'm … uh …"

"Can I guess?"

"If you don't embarrass me."

"I won't, my darling girl. It's our place."

All reticence fled, overcome by the euphoria that had taken over her mind and body. "Our place. Yes."

CHAPTER TWENTY-SIX

Day gently lowered itself into the live oaks, they with their ogre beards and clinging, whispering branches. On the beach, the first smudge of dusk darkened the sea. She held Graham's hand feeling like a sand castle overcome by frothing waves. A gull screamed. Graham picked up a spent starfish and tossed it upward. The bird zipped away squealing. He caught the starfish and gave it to her. "Make a wish upon this star." She saw in the particulars of his face what he must have looked like as a little boy. She wanted to know all about the little boy who became the man she adored, all the way back from the time he made Shafer's playmates pick him, or else.

He ran ahead and turned around to skip backwards as he looked at her. "You're beautiful. I love you." He looked like a kid at a party who'd pinned the ribbon smack on the donkey's tail.

"I love you, too," she said. The sound of her voice saying that made her feel like she'd stepped on a magic carpet.

She ran to him. He grasped her waist and turned her to face the sea. He kissed the back of her head and laid his hands on her carefully, maybe not wanting to be so bold as before. He leaned into her and nuzzled his lips against her throat. She heard herself moan and turned as he wrapped his arms around her and bent to kiss her lips with gentle fierceness. She closed her eyes as he pushed hard against her, feeling her own desire blossom like a sun-kissed rose.

He broke free and pushed an arm under her knees and lifted her.

"Graham Henry, you'll hurt yourself."

"Light as a feather," he said, his voice hoarse.

He only stumbled once as he hurried over the dunes to the lighthouse.

He managed to turn the knob and knee the door open, but before he carried her over the threshhold he set her on her feet. "I'm going to do a silly thing."

"You're going to leave me standing here longing for you?"

"While you're longing," he said, rubbing her cheek, "I'm going to ask you something."

"I may not answer."

He dropped to a knee.

"Graham, you're not …" She started giggling, bending at the waist to keep her tummy from churning. "Graham …"

He looked up and grinned. "I said it was silly."

She eased downward, to her knees and faced him. "Oh, darling, you look so silly and wonderful."

"Will you marry me?"

She caught her breath as if surprised. "Now you've done it."

"What?"

"Just as I was ready to make love with you, you go and ask me to marry you."

An eyebrow shot up. "What's wrong with that?"

"Now I'll have to wait until we get married so we can have a proper honeymoon."

"Wait?"

"No cart before the horse, forgetting, of course, the first time, which doesn't count."

"Doesn't count?"

"We didn't know each other."

"I get it." He jumped up. "Okay, then," he said, grabbing her arms, lifting her. "We'll get married now." He pulled her down the steps. He skipped over the dunes, gently tugging her along.

It was all her feet could do to keep up with him. "Now?"

His voice was loud against the wind. "As soon as we can take the preacher away from his supper."

"What preacher?"

"Your speaker in tongues."

"He didn't speak in tongues, everyone else did."

"C'mon, Bearcat. Let's go round up witnesses."

*****

"I thought I was going to have to drink alone," Teddy said when Graham led her into the drawing room. Teddy waved a lit cigar and lifted the cocktail glass off the lamp table.

"Where's Neill?" Graham asked.

"Upstairs mooning over himself. Damn man should have gone off with Josie."

"He tell you the whole story?" Cleo asked.

"Once I told him I knew, I couldn't shut his cake hole."

Graham grinned. "Teddy's adopting RAF jargon."

"You brought it home with you," Teddy said.

"So I did, Mother dear. And, guess what else I brought home with me?"

Without moving her head, Teddy's marble blue eyes glanced up and stuck on Cleo's face. "What or who?"

"My fiancé."

She raised her eyebrows. "Well, well."

"Surprised?" Cleo asked.

"By no means. Just, I thought you two might wait another day at least."

"No time, Teddy," Graham said. "Get the Neill, let's get to the church."

"Huh?"

"We're off to the African Zion Church."

Teddy laid her palm on her breast. "What?"

"But first we have to roust the preacher. Be at his meal, probably."

"No, Graham ..."

"Yes, Mother."

"Your father would be mortified."

"He of the multiple mistresses? But you aren't. Come on, let's get a move on."

Trying to hide a confused smile, Teddy rose, and Cleo saw excitement in her shoulders and hands. Teddy hurried to the study door and looked into the hall. "Mitty, where are you?"

Mitty apparently had been hanging out at the door and appeared instantly. "Yes, Mrs. Henry."

"Get Neill. Tell him his damn idiot buddy's getting married to his beautiful cousin."

Mitty's wide eyes rolled and blinked. He seemed stuck to the floor.

"Get a move on. You come, too. We need an audience."

"Marvel," Mitty said, going away.

"Tell Neill not to tarry. This isn't formal," Teddy called after him.

She faced Cleo. "I knew this day would come. Never a dull moment with my unorthodox son." She turned to leave, but stopped. "We'll have a shebang-up in Pittsburgh as soon as I can make arrangements."

"No, Teddy." Graham looked at Cleo. "Unless Cleo ..."

"Of course I want a formal wedding," Cleo said, "so I can invite ten thousand of my best friends."

Teddy grinned. "I've got to change. You, too, Cleo. That dress has handprints all over it."

*****

It took fifteen minutes for Eurella to squeeze Cleo into the pale mauve chemise and tunic she'd brought from Philadelphia. She wanted to wear her own clothes to her wedding. *My wedding.*

She said aloud, "What will Mother say?"

Buttoning the back of the dress, Eurella said, "She be happy, you gaining weight like this, and she be lovin' Mr. Graham, just like she be lovin' you."

Wait until her mother met Teddy. The pants-wearing, cigar-smoking suffragette meets the Victorian Gibson girl.

No surprise, Teddy insisted on being the chauffeur.

She pulled up to the preacher's cottage. Graham got out and so did Cleo. "Don't be offended when we haggle over the price," he said. "It's expected."

The preacher came to the door. Graham said without stuttering, "We want you to marry us."

The preacher put a finger to his ear as if he hadn't heard right.

"Right now," Graham said.

The preacher closed his gaping mouth and glanced at Cleo's waistline.

"In the church," Graham said.

"In the church," the preacher repeated, clearly dazed.

"You don't have to dress up in your Sunday best, Preacher, and I'll make a handsome contribution to the church."

The preacher looked past Graham's shoulder, toward the car where Teddy waited, her arm resting on the sill. "You got yourself a license?"

"No, we'll take care of that tomorrow."

He hemmed for a few seconds, rubbing his mouth. "I guess the Lord won't mind. Adam and Eve didn't have no marriage license. You wait right here 'til I get my coat and preaching scarf."

He left them standing in the doorway, and Graham said, "We'll build him a new church with the money we save on a high church wedding."

She looked across the open sandy place to the little white church. "I bet he doesn't want a new church. He could use some hymnals, though. And more fans."

A few minutes later, the preacher came out wearing a white linen coat and a white silk stole. "My wedding garments," he said. He turned to Cleo. "We'll do this right. Mr. Graham comes with me. You stay in this house until you get the call to the church."

She looked at Graham, who smiled, and said, "We're going to do this right."

She heard car doors slamming and turned to see Neill, Eurella and Mitty stepping from the Depot Hack. Neill and Mitty joined Teddy, Graham and the preacher as they chatted near the cars. Eurella came to the cottage. The cottage was clean and comely and smelled of boiled seafood and vegetables. The preacher's wife seemed in a mighty hurry, leaving her and Eurella standing in the parlor.

Cleo watched from the doorway as the preacher began the procession to the church. His sons followed him carrying torches. Next came Graham, then Teddy, Neill and Mitty, all straight-lining to the church. The preacher opened the doors and turned to his sons. They fumbled with matches and got the torches lit then followed their father inside. At the church door, Mitty stood straight and tall.

She heard muffled sounds and, suddenly, doors were opening and people were spilling out of surrounding cottages dressed in church-going clothes. "How did they find out so fast?" she asked Eurella.

Eurella grinned. "Preacher's wife snuck out the back door to announce a weddin'."

She pictured the preacher's wife as Paul Revere, passing the word from house to house. Cleo whispered, "Listen my children and you shall hear … of the wedding of Graham, our landowner and peer … Ready to wed his Cleo, his dear … for this gathering of folk to witness, to hear …" She laughed. "Apologies to Longfellow."

"Amen." Eurella said.

The pews in the church must have filled because people milled around outside. Mitty came out of the crowd, making for the preacher's cottage. She met him at the door. With great dignity, he announced, "It is time for the ceremony."

"Oh my God," Cleo cried and clutched Eurella's waist. "I haven't had time to be properly nervous."

"No need to be scared. Mr. Graham be a gentleman."

Eurella was thinking of the wedding night. Of that Cleo was not afraid.

Neill stood at the door, his arm cocked to be taken. She smiled at him and squeezed.

The piano player started the bridal hymn.

"You ready?" he asked in a whisper.

"Can't wait."

"My brave little bearcat. It took courage to exonerate Graham."

"No it didn't."

"Like you, I shall be brave. In the morning, I'll go to the sheriff."

"No need, Shafer's confessed."

"It's a matter of honor."

She smiled at her cousin and looked at Graham standing by the preacher at the altar.

Butterflies fluttered through her midsection.

Neill felt her shudder. "Nerves, Bearcat?"

More like nausea than nerves.

Suddenly, panicked squeals shocked the air. With one foot across the church door threshold, she paused to look back, toward the sea, knowing what caused the sea birds to shriek out a symphony of terror.

Billy.